A PLAGUE OF
BOGLES

A PLAGUE OF BOGLES

CATHERINE JINKS

ILLUSTRATED BY

SARAH WATTS

HOUGHTON MIFFLIN HARCOURT

Boston New York

www.hmhco.com

Design by Christine Kettner
The text of this book is set in 12/19 Carre Noir Std Light
Fortunaschwein typeface by Anke Art

The Library of Congress has cataloged the hardcover edition as follows:
Jinks, Catherine.
A plague of bogles / Catherine Jinks.
p. cm.
Sequel to: How to catch a bogle.
Summary: Jem Barbary becomes a bogler's apprentice in 1870s London and
gets the fright of his life in a city where science clashes with superstition and
monsters lurk in every alley.
[1. Monsters—Fiction. 2. Apprentices—Fiction. 3. Orphans—Fiction. 4. London
(England)—History—19th century—Fiction. 5. Great Britain—History—Victo-
ria, 1837–1901—Fiction.] I. Title.
PZ7.J5754Pl 2014
[Fic]—dc23
2013042823

ISBN: 978-0-544-08747-7 hardcover
ISBN: 978-0-544-54067-5 paperback

Manufactured in U.S.A.
DOC 10 9 8 7 6 5 4 3 2 1
4500563533

To Erica Wagner

LONDON, ENGLAND, C. 1870

A Chance Meeting

The man stationed at the door was small and stout. He had a red face, blue eyes, and wispy gray curls. His satin-breasted coat was trimmed with silver lace. His top hat was the color of mulberries.

"Walk in! Walk in! Now exhibiting!" he boomed. "The best show in London, ladies and gentlemen! A menagerie of mythical beasts! Living, breathing monsters for only one penny!"

The narrow shop front behind him was plastered with brightly colored advertisements. One of them showed a picture of a very young girl cracking a whip at something that looked like a giant toad.

"See our griffin! See our mermaid! See our erlking!" cried the man in the purple hat, tapping at the picture with his bamboo cane. "See Birdie McAdam, the Go-Devil Girl, tame a fierce bogle and a dainty unicorn!"

Across the road, Jem stopped short. He stood goggle-eyed as the crowds surged past him. In one hand he carried a cheap broom. On his feet he wore nothing but a thick layer of mud.

For a moment he stared at the man in the purple hat. Then he darted forward, dodging a pile of horse manure and the rattling wheels of a carriage.

"See the world's greatest novelties, ladies and gentle-men! Marvel at the legendary two-headed snake of Libya! Touch a genuine dragon's egg for only one penny!" The red-faced showman raised his voice a little, drowning the chant of a nearby coster selling nuts and whelks. "Now exhibiting! Satisfaction guaranteed! The world's greatest wonders, here in Whitechapel Road!"

He was perched high on a wooden box, with a good view of all the bobbing umbrellas that filled the street. But he didn't see Jem until the boy tugged at his coat.

"Sir? Hi! Sir?"

Glancing down, the man saw only a filthy little cross-ing sweeper in a ragged blue shirt and striped canvas trousers, torn off at the knee. A cap like a cowpat cast the boy's gleaming brown eyes into shadow. It also concealed most of his thick, black, glossy hair—which was his best feature, though it made his head look too big for his body.

"Hook it," the man growled. "Go on."

"Please, sir, I'm a friend o' Birdie McAdam. Will you let me in? She'll want to say hello."

"Get out of it, I said!"

Jem flushed. "I ain't gammoning you, sir! Jem Barbary's the name. Why, Birdie and me—we used to knock around Bethnal Green together when she were just a bogler's girl. Ask *her* if we didn't!"

The only reply was a quick swipe with the bamboo cane, which left a red welt on Jem's knuckles. He jumped back, grimacing. Then he retreated a few steps to take stock of the exhibition venue. It was a small, two story building wedged tightly between a pastry shop and a public house. Over the door was a faded sign, but Jem couldn't read it. Nor could he see any side alleys piercing the impenetrable wall of shop fronts breasting the street.

But the public house was on a corner, and would probably have a rear yard of some kind. Jem's gaze moved up a drainpipe, along a brick ledge, and across a roof that bristled with chimneys. He'd burgled many a house in the past, and this one was no strongbox. He thought that he could probably find another way in—without paying a penny for the privilege.

"Begging your pardon, lad, but is it true?" a soft voice suddenly asked. "Do you really know Birdie McAdam?"

Startled, Jem spun around. He found himself staring up at a pretty young woman in a velveteen mantle. She had rosy cheeks, gray eyes, and lots of rich brown hair piled up under a hat that was barely big enough to support all the feathers, flowers, veils, and ribbons sewn onto it.

She was sheltering from the rain under a pink silk parasol.

"What's it to you?" he said, wondering why a decent-looking female would approach him in the street like a common beggar. The young woman glanced around nervously before leaning down to address him.

"I'm Mabel Lillimere," she murmured. "I'm a barmaid at the Viaduct Tavern, on the corner o' Newgate Street. If you *are* a friend o' Birdie's, and can persuade her to talk to me, I'll stump up your fee so as you and I both can get in." Eyeing his grubby face with a touch of suspicion, she added fiercely, "But if you're lying—why, I'll box your ears so hard, you'll have your left ear on the right side o' your head and your right ear on the left!"

This threat didn't worry Jem. He'd suffered worse. "Why not talk to her yerself?" he wanted to know.

"Because she'll not see me! Or so *he* says." Mabel gestured at the man in the purple topper, who was now reminding all the damp pedestrians scurrying past him that Birdie McAdam was "well known to the public" owing to "newspaper reports of her bogle-baiting prowess." "Mr. Lubbock, he calls himself," Mabel continued. "Claims he's in charge. Says Birdie's not inclined to speak to the public. Says she's too shy, and needs to rest her voice."

Jem snorted. "Well, *that's* a flam," he declared. "Birdie's as forward as they come. Did you offer him extra?"

"Tuppence."

"Then he's a-humming you." His suspicions confirmed, Jem scowled at Mr. Lubbock. "I'll wager Birdie ain't here. Last time I saw her, she were living with a fine lady near Great Russell Street, eating plum cakes every day and wearing lace on her petticoats. Why would she want to come back to the East End and work in a penny gaff like this'un, when there's fine folk as think she's too good for the life?"

Mabel's face fell. Her troubled gaze slid toward Mr. Lubbock. "You think that there feller is lying, then?"

"Why not?" Jem shrugged. "He's a slang cove. Lying's what they do best." Studying the barmaid with frank curiosity, he added, "Why d'you want to speak to Birdie? You can't be kin — she ain't got a soul to call her own."

Mabel hesitated. At last she said, "I read about Birdie in the newspapers last summer, and never thought of her again till I passed this here gaff. Then I saw her name and recollected how she killed them monsters that you find in privies and coal holes and chimneys and such." Seeing Jem shake his head, Mabel frowned. "Didn't she?"

"Birdie *helped* kill 'em," Jem corrected. "She were bait for the bogles. Alfred Bunce did all the killing."

"Alfred Bunce?"

"The bogler. Didn't you read about him, too? He were in the papers, same as Birdie."

Mabel bit her lip. "I daresay," she mumbled. "But the little girl is what stuck in my head. There was a picture, as I recall. Such a pretty thing, with all them golden curls . . ."

"And Mr. Bunce ain't pretty, which is why there wasn't no pictures of *him*." By now Jem was feeling confident. He knew that he was onto something, so he fixed the barmaid with a shrewd and penetrating look. "You got a bogle problem, miss?"

The barmaid sighed. "I think so."

"Why?"

"On account o' poor Florry." Edging farther beneath the jutting first-floor window of the pastry shop, Mabel suddenly blurted out, "Florry used to be our scullery maid. She went down into the cellar last month and never did come out. And not a trace of her was left, though Mr. Watkins and me looked high and low—"

"Who's Mr. Watkins?" Jem interrupted.

"The landlord. He keeps the place. And would never have took it on, had he known."

"Known what?"

"About the *beer cellar*." Mabel shuddered, as if someone had walked over her grave. "The tavern's fresh built, but the cellar's old. There used to be a prison on that very spot, for debtors and the like, and our cellar was where they put 'em. I never go down if I can help it. Not without Mr. Watkins. Even before Florry vanished, I misliked the air. It felt . . ." She paused for a moment, frowning. "It felt *bad*," she said at last. "Unwholesome. As if someone had died there."

Jem thought back to the previous summer. He thought about Alfred and Birdie. He thought about the two bogles that still haunted his dreams; the one he'd glimpsed at a gentleman's house near Regent's Park, and the one he'd helped to kill some four months later, in a cutting on the London and North Western Railway.

"How old was Florry?" he inquired.

"That I can't tell you. Twelve, perhaps? But she was very small."

"Then it could have bin a bogle as took her." Jem tried to inject a note of authority into his voice. "You should talk to Alfred Bunce. Mr. Bunce will know what to do. He's a Go-Devil Man. He kills bogles with the same spear Finn MacCool used to kill fire-breathing dragons in times past."

"But how can I talk to Mr. Bunce if I don't know where he is?" Mabel objected. Then she narrowed her eyes at Jem, who grinned when he saw her skeptical, measuring look. "I suppose *you* do," she said wryly. "Is that your lurk? Are you touting for this cove?"

"I'll take you straight to him for tuppence ha'penny," Jem offered. And as she rolled her eyes in disgust, he argued his case. "Mr. Bunce don't care to go bogling no more. He changed lodgings a while back on account of it. Where he is now, there's no one knows what he used to do, and no one to plague him as a consequence. But he'll listen to *you*, I'll be bound."

"Why?" asked Mabel. "Why am I so different?"

"You ain't," said Jem. "You got a kid gone, same as all the others. That's why he'll listen." Seeing her confusion, he tried to explain. "Bogles eat children. Mr. Bunce don't like that. He don't like using kids as bait, neither, which is why he stopped bogling. There's a boy lodging with him now—a mudlark called Ned—who'd be a deal happier bogling than scavenging on the riverbank. Mr. Bunce won't oblige him, though. Thinks bogling's too dangerous." Jem paused, then took a deep breath. "But what if someone should come along, a-weeping and a-wailing, asking for help?" he concluded. "Mr. Bunce ain't got it in him to turn 'em down. *That's* why he changed his lodgings."

Mabel nodded slowly. She seemed to understand. "Where does he live now?"

"Near enough," Jem replied, "if we take a bus there."

Mabel's lip curled. She raised one finely plucked eyebrow. "Oh ho!" she exclaimed. "So it's the omnibus fare you're after now, is it?"

Again Jem shrugged. "Unless you want to *walk* to the Strand," he said.

"Mr. Bunce lives near the Strand?"

"Off Drury Lane. But that's all I'll tell you." Gazing up at Mabel from beneath his cap, Jem held out one dirty palm. "Tuppence ha'penny," he repeated. "You'll be needing me there to soften him up, like."

Mabel sniffed. Then she grunted. Then she glanced up at the sky, which was low and gray and as wet as a sponge.

"We'll take a bus," she remarked, before turning to Jem with a crooked smile. "By the by, how old are you?"

"Eleven."

"And already you're bargaining like a Billingsgate fishmonger!" There was a touch of admiration in Mabel's tone. "I'll give you a ha'penny up front," she said. "The rest you'll get when we reach his crib."

"Done."

"And if this here is a caper, my lad, I'll give you *such* a hiding—never mind what I tell the police when I'm done!"

She scowled at Jem, who beamed back. But then something else occurred to him, and his smile faded.

"You ain't acquainted with Sarah Pickles, by any chance?" he asked, fixing her with a quizzical look.

"Sarah Pickles?" Mabel sounded perplexed. "Who's she?"

"It don't signify." Sarah Pickles was a private matter, which Jem didn't want to discuss. Not in the street with a perfect stranger. So he flapped his hand, turned on his heel, and made for the bus stop.

2

FLYPAPER

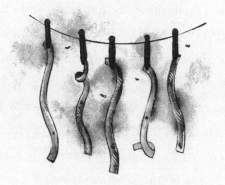

Alfred Bunce lived in a narrow lane cluttered with costers' barrows and piles of rubbish. Mussel shells and squashed cabbage leaves were scattered everywhere. People filled every window and doorway, smoking or chatting or darning socks. There was a strong smell of rotten fruit.

To reach Alfred's lodgings, Jem had to lead Mabel up half a dozen flights of stairs in a rickety old house that leaned to one side like a drunkard. On the way, he passed a clutch of dirty, barefoot children who taunted him for carrying a broom. "Did you come here to sweep the mud from our chimneys?" they cried. He ignored them, having better things to do than exchange insults with a pack of idle scroungers.

Alfred's room was high up under the eaves. When he answered Jem's knock, a wave of heat seemed to roll out of the doorway into the stairwell—along with a strong smell of turpentine. Though the day was dank and chilly, Alfred wore his shirtsleeves rolled up to the elbow. A dusting of red powder covered his knobbly hands, his drooping mustache, and his thick, graying hair.

He raised his bushy eyebrows when he saw Jem.

"Well, now," he said gruffly. "*You* bin quite a stranger."

"This here is Miss Mabel Lillimere," Jem replied, getting straight to the point. "She needs help."

The barmaid offered up an uncertain smile as Alfred studied her, his dark gaze unreadable. Jem pushed past him without waiting for an invitation. The room beyond Alfred was as hot as an oven, thanks to the fire blazing in the hearth. Dozens of paper strips, each as red as blood, dangled from lines strung overhead. Walls, floor, and furniture were smeared with the same reddish powder that clung to Alfred.

"Why, what's all this?" asked Jem in astonishment.

"Flypapers," said Alfred, ushering Mabel across the threshold.

"You make *flypapers* now?" Jem was appalled. "That ain't no job for a bogler!"

"Flies is vermin, same as bogles," Alfred rejoined. Then he invited Mabel to sit down, though not before quickly dusting off one of the two available stools with his shirt cuff. "This here is all red lead," he explained. "For coloring the papers."

"And what's this?" Jem demanded, wrinkling his nose in disgust. He was peering at the gooey stuff that bubbled in a large pot over the fire. "Not yer dinner, I hope?"

"That's what catches the flies," said Alfred. "I lay it on with a brush."

"Smells like linseed oil," Jem observed.

"There's linseed in it." Alfred turned back to the barmaid, who had seated herself gingerly. "What can I do for you, miss?"

As Mabel explained her plight, Jem inspected Alfred's room—which he hadn't seen for some time. The old table was still there, along with Alfred's bed and tea chest. There was a new washstand. Alfred's brass scissors were also new, as was the framed photograph on the windowsill. It showed a pretty little girl with fair curls and a glazed stare. She was dressed in shiny clothes trimmed with lace.

On his way to examine the picture more closely, Jem passed Ned Roach's straw paillasse.

"Is Ned down by the river?" Jem queried, once Mabel had finished.

Alfred looked at him.

"Ned ain't scavenging no more. He's a coster's boy now, selling fruit from a barrow." Alfred coughed suddenly, then spat on the floor. "Brings home a steady wage. And helps with the flypapers, too," he finished.

Jem felt a pang of envy, which he attempted to disguise by snidely remarking, "Must be hard for Ned, since he don't talk overmuch. How does he cry his wares?"

"He's learning," Alfred replied, before resuming his conversation with the barmaid. "This tavern o' yours— where is it?"

"Giltspur Street," said Mabel.

"Giltspur?" Alfred frowned. "Ain't that off Newgate?"

Mabel gave a nod.

"There's a generosity o' dangerous folk as lurk around Newgate Prison," Alfred pointed out. He produced from his trouser pocket a clay pipe and a tobacco pouch. "Might yer maid not have fallen foul o' one?"

"She went down to fetch the sherry, sir, and now she's gone." Mabel was dabbing at her flushed face with a handkerchief. Beads of sweat were forming on her upper lip. "Could we not open the door, Mr. Bunce? Else I'll faint from the heat."

Obediently Alfred lifted the door latch. Jem tried to push the window open a little farther but found it too stiff. Then Alfred said, in his low, rumbling voice, "I don't bogle no more. Did Jem not tell you? I've no 'prentice, see."

"*I* could be your 'prentice," Jem quickly cut in. And when Alfred fixed him with a morose look, he added, "I'm quick on me feet, ain't I? Quicker'n Birdie, for all that I can't sing like her. Why, I spent the day dodging hansom cabs on Commercial Road and never once took a tumble. I'd make a prize bogler's boy!"

Alfred's gaze shifted to the broomstick in Jem's hand. "I doubt Mr. Leach would agree with you," he growled. And Jem flushed.

"I ain't working for that grocer no more."

"Oh, aye?" Alfred seemed to be waiting for an explanation. And though Jem didn't want to give one—not with Mabel in the room, listening to every word he said—there was something about Alfred's weighty silence that forced him to speak.

"I ate some cheese off the shop floor, and when Mrs. Leach beat me for it, I called her an old cat," he admitted. "That's why Mr. Leach let me go—on account of his wife. She never did like me. 'Once a thief, allus a thief' is what she used to say. But I never prigged a thing, save for that morsel o' cheese. And it were picked off the floor like kitchen scraps!"

Alfred sighed as Jem scowled. The barmaid watched them both curiously, still patting her face with her handkerchief. A cross draft was now blowing through the room, making Alfred's strips of paper dance and spin.

"I'd as soon have you beg as sweep a crossing," Alfred said at last, still glumly eyeing the broom. "Where do you lodge now? You ain't on the street?"

"No," said Jem. To change the subject, he quickly added, "Miss Mabel didn't tell you, but there's a cove as runs a penny gaff on Whitechapel Road, and he claims he has Birdie inside, taming bogles and such."

Alfred's jaw dropped. He sat down suddenly.

"I took one look and thought, 'Well, *that* ain't true,'" Jem went on, pleased to see the impact he'd made. "I'll wager Birdie can't stray as far as her own front door nowadays, let alone set foot in Whitechapel Road."

"But—but Birdie ain't singing in no penny gaff!" Alfred spluttered. "Birdie's being schooled in Bloomsbury! Miss Eames says she could sing opera one day!"

"I thought as much." Jem flashed a smug look at the barmaid. "Lubbock's a dirty liar. Didn't I tell you?"

"Miss Eames ain't going to like this," said Alfred, shaking his head in consternation. "She'll not like this at *all* . . ."

He trailed off, biting his lip, his pipe in one hand and his tobacco pouch in the other. Mabel watched him for a moment. At last she cleared her throat and said, "Uh—Mr. Bunce?"

"No." Alfred spoke brusquely. "No, lass, I cannot. I told you, I ain't a bogler no more." He gestured vaguely at the strips of paper drying above him as if to prove his point. But Mabel wasn't impressed. Her dark brows snapped together.

"Mr. Bunce," she protested, "my employer is hiring a new potboy as we speak. Would you condemn the lad to a fate like Florry's?"

Alfred didn't answer. He was stuffing tobacco into his pipe, carefully avoiding her eye as he did so.

"I'm afraid for him—indeed I am. He's a big lad, but no more'n twelve years old. And I cannot *always* be chasing him about." Mabel had a very strong voice when she chose to raise it. Jem suspected that she had strengthened her lungs by shouting orders across a noisy taproom, and grinned to himself when he saw Alfred's face lengthen. "What about poor Florry?" the barmaid continued. "There ain't no one else to care what befell her—she hadn't a single relation to mourn her passing. And you say you'll not punish the beast that ate her up! For *shame*, sir!"

Alfred winced. "Miss Lillimere—" he began.

"How much do you charge for your services?" she demanded. "What is your fee, Mr. Bunce?"

Seeing Alfred hesitate, Jem answered for him. "Six shillings for each bogle, fivepence for the visit, and a penny for the salt."

"I'll pay you eight shillings." Mabel stood up suddenly,

startling Alfred, who blinked and dropped the match he'd just plucked from his pocket. "Eight shillings down and as much grog as you can drink."

Jem laughed. "Blimey," he crowed, "ain't *that* the plum in the pudding!" But a glare from Alfred quickly wiped the smile from his face.

"Well?" said Mabel. "Will you help, Mr. Bunce?"

"I told you before, I ain't got no 'prentice—"

"What's wrong with the boy?" Mabel interrupted, pointing at Jem. "He's spry enough."

"He's untrained," mumbled Alfred. "I need Birdie. I can't kill a bogle without Birdie."

"But she never comes here no more!" Jem was stung by Alfred's lack of confidence in him. "And even if she did, that Miss Eames wouldn't let her so much as soil her clothes, never mind dodge a bogle." Before Alfred could object, Jem exclaimed, "*I* can be your boy! It ain't so hard! Didn't I see it done on that navvy's job last summer? All I need is a looking glass and a bit o' nerve!"

"Please, Mr. Bunce," begged the barmaid. "I'd not ask if I weren't going mad with the strain of it. A bogle downstairs—why, it don't bear thinking on! How am I to work in such a place?"

Alfred sighed. He had retrieved his match and struck it against a wall; now he was drawing on his pipe as he lit it. *Puff-puff-puff.* For a moment his face was obscured by a cloud of smoke.

Finally he rose and flicked his burnt match into the fireplace.

"Aye, very well," he rasped. "You'll want me there now, I daresay?"

"As soon as ever you can," the barmaid replied happily. And Jem took advantage of her mood, edging up to her with his hand outstretched.

"Tuppence, miss?" he softly reminded her.

She flashed him a narrow, sideways look but paid up without protest. Alfred, meanwhile, was on his knees, fishing around under the bed. He soon produced an old brown sack, which Jem recognized with an inward shudder.

The sight of it brought back horrible memories.

"You'll do exactly as I say, lad. *Exactly*," Alfred insisted, turning his head to fix Jem with a grim look. "Is that clear?"

"Yessir."

"Don't you take yer eyes off me. Not for one instant. And when I move, you move. Or you'll pay the price, make no mistake."

Jem nodded. He had always favored the idea of being a bogler's boy, because bogling was such a flash occupation, like smuggling or highway robbery. People respected boglers. Unlike a grocer's boy or a crossing sweeper, a bogler's apprentice could walk down the street with a swagger in his step—not to mention a steady wage in his pocket.

Of course, a pickpocket could attract just as many admiring stares, if he was walking down the right street, in the right part of town. Jem knew how *that* felt. But he also knew he'd been fooled into thinking that all those respectful glances were a tribute to his own skills—when in fact Sarah Pickles, his employer, had been the important one.

"What's me own cut o' the fee, Mr. Bunce?" Jem asked, smothering a sudden pang of rage at the thought of Sarah Pickles. "How much did Birdie get for a job?"

"She got what she deserved," Alfred said shortly. "As you will."

Then he started to lay out his equipment, unwrapping his spear and testing the hinges on his dark lantern. Watching him, Jem felt slightly unnerved. Bogling could be dangerous. Jem understood that. He'd almost been eaten by a bogle once. And just because Alfred had saved him the last time didn't mean it would happen again.

For all he knew, he could be making the biggest mistake of his life . . .

3

A Cellar Bogle

The Viaduct Tavern was all gilt and glass and polished wood. Roaring voices filled the taproom. Gas jets flared in a haze of smoke, keeping the dismal afternoon at bay. The air smelled of sweat and cheap spirits.

Things were very different downstairs, though. Jem knew at once that the basement was much older than the house above. Slimy stains covered the walls. Iron bars were pitted with rust. There was black grime all over the vaulted brick ceiling.

Gloomily surveying all the kegs and barrels stacked near the bottom of the staircase, Alfred said, "This is bigger'n I expected."

"Half a dozen rooms, at least," Mabel confirmed, handing Jem her paraffin lamp. "You'll not be needing me, will you? I only ask as it's busy, and by rights I should be at the bar."

Alfred grunted. "D'you know where Florry might have gone?" he queried.

Mabel shook her head. Then she flapped her hand at one shadowy doorway. "She were sent to fetch sherry, which we keep in that room, with the port wine. But there's coal down here, and lye, and sand . . . Ain't no saying where she might have gone if prompted to."

"Mmph," said Alfred. Taking his nod as a kind of signal, the barmaid abruptly turned tail and hurried back upstairs. Alfred let her go without comment. He gazed around, sniffed the air, sighed, and told Jem, "Don't you wander off, now. Stay close to me."

"I'll do that," Jem assured him.

Together they began to explore the maze of cellars, which weren't as well stocked as they could have been. One room was full of coal. Another contained buckets of sand, bags of potatoes, and crates of glass bottles. But there was also a lot of empty space, dotted here and there with shelves, sinks, alcoves, iron-barred screens, and dark, mysterious holes.

"Looks just like a prison, don't it?" Jem remarked under his breath. When very young, he had once visited his uncle in a debtor's prison—before his mother's death had left him homeless—and he had never forgotten the clang of metal doors swinging shut. The memory made his heart sink. He'd spent years worrying that one day, when his past crimes caught up with him, he would end up locked in a dank, musty prison cell.

"You'd pay fourpence a night for a crib this dry down near the docks," he joked, in an effort to shake off a sudden overwhelming sense of gloom and dread. "Mebbe I should ask the landlord if he'd care to take in a lodger—cheap, like, on account o' the bogle . . ."

"Shhh!" Alfred had stopped on a threshold. Peering past him, Jem saw that the room beyond was small and low and murky. There was an assortment of junk stacked in one corner: a broken chair, a cracked coal scuttle, a bent poker, a length of pipe.

In the floor was an iron grate set over a drain.

Alfred hissed when he spotted this grate. He pulled Jem back from the door and hustled him in the opposite direction, growling, "That's the one."

"What?"

"She'll have met her end in there, poor lass." Having retired to a safe distance, Alfred dropped his sack and rummaged through it. "Bogles like drains," he said quietly.

"But that drain's so small," Jem protested. "And there

ain't nothing in the room — not to speak of. Why would she want to go in there?"

Alfred shrugged. "To drink a sly nip? Or eat a stolen crust?"

"But—"

"As to the size o' the drain, never think *any* hole is too small for a bogle. You never know where a drain might lead." Alfred's knees cracked as he rose again. He held a small leather bag in one hand and his spear in the other. "Can you sing?" he asked. "Whistling ain't no good."

"I can sing," Jem confessed, "but not like Birdie."

Alfred snorted. "No one can sing like Birdie. What *I* want is someone as can pipe away till the bogle comes. For hours, if need be."

"I can do that," Jem assured him.

"And not falter when you see it?"

"No."

Alfred eyed Jem with a skeptical look. Jem stared back defiantly, though his guts were already beginning to churn. At last Alfred gave a sigh and said, "Take off yer hat and leave it here, for you'll not be needing it. Wait nearby but don't move or speak. Step into the ring *only when I tell you*. Take care not to touch the salt."

Jem opened his mouth to point out that he wasn't stupid, then thought better of it.

"I'll signal when I want you to sing," Alfred continued. "Don't move till *I* move. And whatever you do, lad"—he leaned down until his beaky nose was almost touching Jem's snub one—"*do not* touch the salt on yer way out o' the ring. Is that clear?"

"Yes." Jem was annoyed to find that his voice sounded a little hoarse. So he coughed and said, "Where's me looking glass?"

Alfred straightened. He propped his spear against a wall and reached into the pocket of his long green coat, from which he produced a small mirror. "I'll be wanting that back," he warned as he surrendered it.

"Was it Birdie's?"

"Aye."

Jem felt pleased. He liked the notion of using Birdie's mirror, which was bound to have at least a trace of good luck attached to it.

"Any more questions, afore we start?" Alfred wanted to know.

Jem shook his head.

"Good," said Alfred. "Then I'll begin."

Jem had watched the bogler lay out his circle of salt once before, in a half-constructed railway tunnel. On that occasion there had been much more light and space. This time Alfred pottered about for a while after igniting his dark lantern, measuring distances and assessing vantage points until he finally chose his spot.

It was just outside the room with the drain.

Jem kept his mouth shut when he saw this, though he had some last-minute questions he wanted to ask. Would this bogle be smaller than the previous one? Should he run from the room once it had been trapped? Did the peculiar sense of despair creeping over him have anything to do with the bogle, or did it stem from his own lack of confidence?

At last Alfred traced his ring of salt on the flagstone floor. He placed a gap in the ring directly opposite the door from which the bogle would be emerging. Then he stationed himself to one side of this door, armed with his spear, his salt, and his dark lantern.

Finally he nodded at Jem, who took a deep breath and stepped into the center of the circle. It was a large circle — so large that it filled Jem with dread. How big did it have to be before the bogle was contained? With his back turned to the low, lightless doorway, Jem felt horribly vulnerable, like a rat in a baiting pit. But he positioned his mirror so that it gave him a clear view of Alfred *and* the door.

Then he began to sing.

"There is a nook in the boozing ken,
Where many a mug I fog,
And the smoke curls gently, while cousin Ben

Keeps filling the pots again and again,
If the coves have stumped their hog."

Jem's voice was naturally husky, but it didn't usually crack or wobble — not the way it was cracking and wobbling now. He was ashamed of himself. So he paused, cleared his throat, and tried again.

"The liquors around is diamond bright,
And the diddle is best of all;
But I never in liquors took much delight,
For liquors I think is all a bite.
So for heavy wet I call."

Framed in Jem's little hand mirror, Alfred stood against the wall — a hunched, motionless shape holding a spear. At the bogler's feet sat his dark lantern, which didn't do much to illuminate his face. The paraffin lamp had been left at the opposite end of the room, which was piled high with old kegs. There was a strong smell of ale, mildew, mouse droppings ... and something else. At first Jem thought it was sewage. Then, gradually, he began to change his mind.

What *was* that smell?

He tried not to let it distract him, even though it seemed to be getting stronger. Instead, he focused his attention on the miniature scene captured in his hand: the bogler standing by the doorway, bathed in a flickering light. Luckily, Jem knew "The Thieves' Chaunt" off by heart, so he didn't have to spare a thought for what he was singing. He just crowed away like a jackdaw while he watched Alfred like a hawk.

> "The heavy wet in a pewter quart
> As brown as a badger's hue,
> More than Bristol milk or gin,
> Brandy or rum I tipple in,
> With me darling blowen, Sue."

Suddenly Jem spied something stirring in the shadows behind the doorway. He knew at once that it was a bogle. What else could it have been, after all? His voice quavered and caught on a gasp; for one panic-stricken moment, he thought that he'd lost the use of his lungs altogether. But then he found his breath again.

As one of the denser, blacker shadows in the adjoining room detached itself from the others and began to slide toward him, he launched into the next verse.

> "Her duds, they're bob — she's a kinchin crack,
> And I hopes as how she'll never back;
> For she never lushes dog soup or lap,
> But she loves me cousin the bluffer's tap."

Jem's previous bogle had been a huge, hulking thing with horns and teeth and tentacles, like a cross between a goat, a bear, and an octopus. This bogle was different. It seemed to pour through the doorway like a wave of black treacle, or a giant ball of jelly. Then, as it swiftly gathered itself into a kind of crest — rearing up behind Jem — a huge, gaping hole opened up in its body.

Still, however, Alfred didn't move. So Jem had to keep singing, in a voice like a rat's squeak.

"She's wide awake, and her prating cheat,
For humming a cove was never beat;
But because she lately nimm'd some tin,
They have sent her to lodge at the King's Head —"

Jem suddenly noticed that the bogle was starting to encircle him. It had slid through the gap in the ring of salt, and now, on the floor at his feet, two viscous arms were flowing toward each other like channels of sludge, one from the left and one from the right. When they merged, he was left standing on a small, round, rapidly shrinking patch of flagstone in a sticky black puddle.

Glancing down at the slimy noose that was about to tighten around his ankles, he took his eyes off Alfred for half a second.

"JEM! NOW!" screamed the bogler.

Jem sprang into the air. He did it without thinking, as he would have dodged a blow or a cart wheel. The patch of floor beneath him disappeared—engulfed by a tide of goo—as he threw himself across the room and landed on both hands, then executed a clumsy backflip that left him sitting on his rear end, staring at a wall.

Somewhere along the way, he'd dropped his mirror.

There was a cry and a loud hissing noise. The air filled with foul-smelling steam. Jem jumped to his feet and spun round to face Alfred, who was barely visible through a cloud of grayish mist. Between them, on the floor, a large pool of fluid was rapidly drying out, like honey in the sun. A crust was forming around its edges.

Looking at it, Jem realized that Alfred must have speared the bogle.

4

OLD FRIENDS

Are you all right, lad?" Alfred's rough voice seemed to be coming from very far away. "Did you hurt yerself?"

"N-no . . ." Jem was still in shock. He staggered a little as Alfred hauled him to his feet.

"'Pon my soul, I ain't never seen tumbling like that there," Alfred went on. He was pouring sweat; Jem could see it shining on his hollow cheeks and dripping from his nose. "Where did you learn the trick of it?"

"Along the crossings," Jem mumbled. "When it's dry, there ain't no mud to sweep, so it takes a tumble or two afore you can tickle the pennies out of a gentleman's pocket."

He didn't mention the fences he'd climbed or the

policemen he'd dodged while working for Sarah Pickles. It didn't seem the right moment, somehow—not while Alfred was looking at him with frank admiration. At last the bogler grunted. He turned away to pack his bag while Jem retrieved his mirror, which was still intact. By the time they'd finished clearing up, the crusty slick on the floor had crumbled into dirty gray dust, only slightly darker than the line of salt surrounding it.

"We'll leave that here," said Alfred, "since no one stayed to watch." As he climbed back upstairs, he explained to Jem that some customers would balk at paying if they hadn't seen the bogle for themselves. "Ain't never much that remains of a bogle once it's dead. A stain or a smear or a puddle is all you'll see. People expecting a corpse is often disappointed and will refuse to stump up, thinking as how I'm a-slumming 'em."

But Mabel Lillimere didn't refuse to stump up. They found her upstairs, dispensing pots of ale. One glimpse of Alfred brought her straight to his end of the bar.

"Is it done?" she asked loudly, straining to be heard above the roar of voices. When Alfred nodded, her face brightened as if someone had turned up the gas behind it. "God bless you, Mr. Bunce, for avenging poor Florry. She'll rest easy now and not haunt this place." Reaching into the pocket of her apron, the barmaid pulled out a handful of coins, adding, "Mr. Watkins says as how he's much obliged, and would you care to take a drink for your trouble?"

Alfred hesitated. He was being jostled on all sides by loud men in dirty clothes, many of whom were so drunk that only the press of bodies kept them upright. Jem noticed at least two gaping pockets just asking to be picked—pockets belonging to men who would never know, by morning, whether they had spent their missing money or been fleeced of it.

But he restrained himself.

"I'd be grateful for a drop o' brandy and water," Alfred said at last, accepting his eight-shilling fee.

Mabel ducked her head. "Sixpenn'orth?" she inquired.

Again Alfred nodded. She immediately rushed away, returning seconds later with a small glass of brown liquid, which she set down on the zinc counter with a sharp rap. "That there is the real thing," she announced. Then a call for a half-pint of gin and peppermint drew her back down the bar, so that Alfred was left to swallow his brandy unobserved—except by Jem.

"I'd have favored a nip o' that," Jem remarked sulkily.

Alfred ignored him. After finishing his drink in two brisk mouthfuls, the bogler turned and began to push toward the nearest exit, nudging people out of his way. Jem followed. When they finally emerged onto the street, Alfred's hat was sitting crookedly on his head and Jem had been splashed with gin.

Outside, the light was beginning to fade. A steady drizzle had turned the road to slush. Standing on the corner of Newgate and Giltspur Streets, Jem was confronted by a scene of unrelenting grimness. To his right, the spire of Saint Sepulchre's Church pointed at the sky like a reproving finger. To his left loomed the dark stone walls of Newgate Prison, which Jem feared more than any other place on earth. He had often dreamed about the gallows at Newgate. He'd known several people who had been hanged there.

"We'll take a bus up Holborn," said Alfred. "I'd favor walking, but it's already late, and Miss Eames might not be wanting callers at suppertime."

"We're going to visit Miss Eames?" asked Jem.

"Aye." Alfred nodded. "I must tell her about the penny gaff."

He led Jem across the street, where they waited on the corner for an orange omnibus. The view from this spot was chiefly of the prison and the Old Bailey Courthouse, neither of which Jem particularly wanted to look at. So he busied himself watching traffic in and out of several nearby taverns—because that was how he'd always spent most of his time. Watching. Listening.

These days, however, he wasn't on the lookout for a

well-padded pocket. These days he was watching and listening for Sarah Pickles.

It was while enjoying a scuffle between two drunk navvies that Jem spied a familiar face in front of the George Tavern. He couldn't remember whose face it was, and it disappeared so quickly into the Newgate Street crowds that for a moment he thought he might have imagined it. But was he *likely* to have imagined a face that he couldn't put a name to? A woman's face, fat and colorless and pockmarked, with a red nose, a sulky mouth, and a walleye . . . ?

He was still racking his brain when the bus arrived, some ten minutes later.

Twopence gained Alfred a seat on the bus, but Jem had to sit on his knee—for even the benches up on the roof were packed with people. Wedged between a carpenter in a flannel jacket and a factory girl who kept coughing into her handkerchief, Jem sat with his feet dangling, clutching Alfred's sack and making funny faces at the little girl who was perched in the lap of the woman directly opposite. Jem enjoyed making this little girl wriggle and titter. He enjoyed the whole trip, though it was very slow. The horses seemed to be struggling, weighed down by the water on their coats or the mud on their fetlocks. The road was rough, so the vehicle rocked from side to side, making doors rattle and heads bang together. The passengers themselves, squeezed in flank to flank, were forced to breathe into one another's faces and tread on one another's toes.

But Jem so rarely had the pleasure of watching London roll past from the window of an omnibus that he savored every minute. Through the steamed-up glass, he caught glimpses of many theaters and music halls, all larger and finer than those in the East End. The shops were finer too; even the coal merchants' shops looked cleaner than the ones in Whitechapel. And some of the horses were a delight to behold.

At last the bus reached Bloomsbury Street, where Alfred and Jem alighted. From there it was just a short walk to their destination. They found themselves splashing through puddles as they hurried down streets full of tall, white terraces. Then Alfred stopped suddenly in front of a narrow brick house near Saint George's Church. He hesitated, as if wondering whether to climb a modest flight of stairs to the front door or descend another, longer flight to the stone-flagged area in front of the kitchen.

Jem was glad when he chose the front door.

"That's Birdie," said Alfred after he had rung the bell. "D'you hear? She's singing."

Jem heard. Somewhere inside, a pure, high voice was trilling away, repeating the same notes over and over again. "La-*la*-LA-*LA*-LA-*la*-la." It wasn't much of a tune, Jem thought.

All at once the door opened. A red-haired, freckle-faced maid peered out.

"Oh!" she said. "It's you, is it?" She didn't sound too pleased. And she grimaced when her gaze drifted down to Jem's bare, muddy feet. "What do *you* want?"

Alfred took off his hat. "Is Miss Eames in?" he asked.

"I'll see," the girl replied ungraciously, slamming the door in their faces. Jem scowled. He was about to stick out his tongue when the door was abruptly jerked open again — this time by Miss Edith Eames.

"Mr. Bunce!" she exclaimed. "Master Barbary! How *very* nice to see you!"

Jem had never known quite what to make of Miss Eames. She wasn't as pretty as Mabel Lillimere, who was plumper, with a rounder face and pinker cheeks. Miss Eames was skinny and pale and at least thirty years old; she even had touches of gray in her dark hair. Her manner was a little too brisk for Jem's taste, and he didn't like the way she made him feel — as if he had to be constantly apologizing for his habits and appearance.

But Miss Eames was also as smart as a whip, and so beautifully dressed that Jem couldn't help admiring her. As a thief, he had learned how to judge the value of every glove, shawl, watch, purse, hat, and handkerchief that he spied on the street, so he knew that Miss Eames was always well turned out. Even now she wore very superior garments.

Her white blouse was made of fine lawn worth at least one shilling and sixpence a yard. Her shiny little boots had been made to measure, and she had trimmed her blue skirt with the very best silk velvet.

"Come in, please," she said, retreating into a hallway paved with tiles. "We have finished our tea, but Mary will make you a new pot. And there's plum cake if you'd like some."

Jem's stomach growled. He had eaten only one slice of bread and dripping all day, so the prospect of plum cake made him feel suddenly faint with hunger.

"But what about their feet, miss?" the maid protested from behind Miss Eames. "They'll dirty the carpets . . ."

Miss Eames frowned. Before she could reply, Alfred said quickly, "We ain't fit to come inside, miss, it being so wet. I only stopped by to tell you summat you ought to know. It seems as how Jem were in Whitechapel earlier and passed one o' them shop-front theaters they got there—"

"Mr. Bunce!" An excited scream cut him off in mid-sentence. Jem realized that the singing had stopped, and was about to ask why when Birdie McAdam burst into the hallway, all glossy gold ringlets and rustling petticoats. She flung herself at Alfred, who stepped back and caught one of her outstretched arms.

"Mind, lass—me trousers is muddy," he warned. "You'd not want to ruin yer pretty clothes."

"Come and have some tea!" Birdie cried, then turned to Jem. "Come and have some cake!"

Jem glanced pleadingly at Alfred, who shook his head and murmured, "We cannot stay. We ain't fit for no parlor tea."

"Then eat in the kitchen!" Birdie exclaimed. By this time she was tugging at Alfred's hand, which looked very large and dirty next to her own. Jem couldn't believe how clean Birdie was. Her hair gleamed like brass; her silk ribbons were as shiny as silver plate; she had the pinkest fingernails, the whitest neck, and the most highly polished boots he'd ever seen.

She'd also grown a little since their last meeting, and was talking differently. More like a lady, he thought.

More like Miss Eames.

"Calm down, Birdie; you mustn't screech," Miss Eames chided. "What did I tell you about receiving visitors?"

"Mr. Bunce ain't no visitor; he's family," Birdie rejoined. Then, seeing Miss Eames purse her lips, she quickly corrected herself. "He *is* no visitor, I mean."

"Miss, if that boy comes in, he'll have to wash his feet," the maid interposed. She pointed an accusing finger at the brown footprint that Jem had already left on the checkerboard floor. "Either that or we put down some drugget."

"No—please—we ain't here to cause trouble." Alfred crumpled his hat with one hand as Birdie hauled on the other. "We came to deliver a message and will go directly when we're done."

"But don't you want to have a chat?" Birdie asked in a plaintive voice. "Don't you want to hear all my news?"

"Why, of course I do, lass," Alfred said. "That goes without saying . . ."

"Birdie, let Mr. Bunce deliver his message!" Miss Eames spoke sharply. "You mustn't *hound* people like that—it is not polite." Turning back to Alfred, she said, "What seems to be the problem, Mr. Bunce? Is Ned unwell? I notice he isn't with you."

"Ned's good. This ain't about Ned." Alfred hesitated, as if unsure of how to begin. Finally, however, he cleared his throat, took a deep breath, and launched into a full explanation. "Fact o' the matter is, somebody's bin using Birdie's name . . ."

5

OFF TO WHITECHAPEL

When Miss Eames heard Alfred's news, she was furious. "No freak-show manager is going to steal Birdie's name and get away with it!" she cried, before announcing her intention of tackling Mr. Lubbock herself. At once. In person. "If I leave now," she went on, "I might be able to stop the next performance. Mary! *Mary!*"

But the maid had vanished.

"She went to the kitchen," Birdie piped up.

Miss Eames clicked her tongue. "Then I must fetch my own hat and coat," she said. "Will you wait for a moment, Mr. Bunce?"

"Aye, but—"

"If Mary comes back, Birdie, tell her to hail a cab for us. Tell her I'll be down directly." Without waiting for a response, Miss Eames turned on her heel and scuttled up the stairs, which were fitted with a handsome carpet.

Jem looked at Birdie in dismay. "Won't there be no cake?" he whined.

"There's cake. Don't fret. I'll get you some." As Birdie released Alfred's hand to duck back into the drawing room, the bogler watched her go with a kind of melancholy wonder.

"She's a real lady now, ain't she?" he remarked once she was out of earshot. "It's hard to believe I found her scavenging in the mud when she were nobbut four years old . . ."

Jem didn't know what to say. Luckily, he didn't have to say anything, because all at once Mary came stomping back up from the kitchen. She was carrying a large basin of steaming water, which he eyed with alarm.

He had a nasty feeling that it was meant for his feet.

"Why, what are you doing with that?" Birdie demanded. She had reappeared suddenly, a piece of cake in each hand. "They'll not be staying, you know, so there ain't no cause to clean 'em up. And Miss Eames says you're to hail a cab."

"Hail it yourself," Mary retorted. Then she turned around and marched straight downstairs again.

Birdie sighed. "She hates me. I swear she'd like to put me out o' this house."

"You've not bin tormenting her?" asked Alfred, with a touch of concern. Birdie frowned, but it was Jem who answered—thickly, through a mouthful of cake.

"Of course not!" he said. "Wouldn't *you* hate Birdie if you was that maid? Mary looks to be from respectable folk, yet she must truckle to a street urchin that her mistress picked out o' the gutter like orange peel." Seeing Birdie's ferocious scowl, Jem grinned and winked. "*I'll* fetch a cab," he concluded. "I bin fetching cabs for a penny each at the London Docks. I'll find you a cab, don't fret."

And he did. It wasn't difficult. There were so many hackney cabs in the neighborhood that he didn't even have to run after one. All he had to do was stand at the bottom of the front steps and whistle.

Soon he and Alfred and Birdie were all safely tucked inside a four-seater carriage, waiting for Miss Eames.

"She always takes a mortal long time to get out o' the house," Birdie explained as she tied on her bonnet. Jem calculated that it was trimmed with real silk broad lace, worth a shilling a yard at least, and that her lavender gloves were made of the highest quality kid. "Her aunt's a good deal worse, though," Birdie continued. "Has to rise at dawn for the ten o'clock service at a church that's just down the street."

"Where *is* Mrs. Heppinstall?" Alfred queried. "Not poorly, I hope?"

"Oh, no. She's fit enough. She's out doing her charity work and should be home soon. I expect Miss Eames is leaving a note for her." Having finished adjusting the bow under her chin, Birdie raised her head and looked Jem straight in the eye. "But what *I* want to know is: What's a boy as works for a grocer in Islington doing fetching cabs at the London Docks?"

Jem flushed. He was trying to frame an answer when Miss Eames appeared at the door of the cab, carrying an umbrella. "Does the driver know where to go?" she asked Jem, who nodded. Then he reached down to help her climb in. By the time she'd settled herself on Birdie's left, opposite Jem, the cab was already moving.

But Birdie hadn't let all the fuss and flurry distract her.

"Well?" she pressed, her wide blue eyes still fixed on Jem's face. "What's the story? Did you part from Mr. Leach?"

When Jem didn't answer, Alfred said, "Aye. He did."

"I thought as much." Birdie gave a satisfied nod. "You don't never see a grocer's boy with bare feet."

Miss Eames flashed her a reproving look. "Double negatives, Birdie dear. You know what I've told you about 'don't never.'" Turning back to Jem, Miss Eames added,

"What are you doing now, Jem, if you're not a grocer's boy? Are you working for Mr. Bunce?"

"I sweep crossings," Jem growled.

"Oh, dear," said Miss Eames.

Birdie glanced at Alfred, who explained, "He only came to me this afternoon. I didn't know he were out on the street."

"But why not?" Miss Eames demanded. "Jem, why didn't you tell someone before this? You knew where we were—we could have helped you."

Jem swallowed. He was wriggling with discomfort and his face was bright red. Studying him shrewdly, Birdie asked, "Did you prig something?"

"No!" Jem glared back at her. "I ain't no prig! Not now I ain't!"

"He says he were turned out for eating a scrap o' cheese off the floor," Alfred quietly volunteered. "Says the grocer's wife took against him."

"She did," Jem mumbled. "I didn't steal nothing."

"So if you didn't steal nothing—I mean, anything— then why not go to Mr. Bunce for help?" Birdie inquired.

"Because Mr. Bunce don't live in the East End no more, and that's where I need to be!" As his gaze skipped from one puzzled face to the next, Jem felt utterly alone. He wondered scornfully if any of the others had ever been betrayed. "Sarah Pickles is *bound* to be living in the East End!" he spluttered. "*You* might not care about what she done, but I'll never forget it! And I'll make her pay for her treachery, even if I have to spend the next five years searching the whole o' London!"

There was a brief, shocked silence. The only sounds came from outside the carriage: the rattle of wheels, the clatter of hooves, the toot of a distant horn on the river. Jem waited as his three companions absorbed what he'd just said. No doubt they were thinking about him and how he'd once spent several minutes hanging like a dead pheasant, trussed and gagged, from a bogle's claws.

Though Sarah herself hadn't served him up to that bogle, she had sent him to the man who had—knowing full well what would happen next. And she had done it for money.

"I thieved for Sarah Pickles nigh on seven years," Jem spat, "and she sold me off like dog meat, at a few pence a pound."

"But I thought Sarah Pickles had disappeared," Miss Eames protested. She flashed Birdie an inquiring look. "I thought it was established that she must have been killed by some of her associates, as a consequence of betraying Jem."

Birdie hesitated. Jem gave a snort. It was Alfred who finally said, "Some think that. There's some as think otherwise."

"I ain't going to believe Sarah's dead till I see her rotten corpse in a coffin," Jem replied. "For she's cunning as a snake, and vicious with it. She's lying low somewhere is what *I* think, and I don't want to miss her when she raises her head."

Alfred turned his own head to stare out the window as Birdie remarked, in a skeptical voice, "So you think she's hiding in Whitechapel?"

"Or Shoreditch. Or Wapping. Or Bethnal Green." Jem folded his arms defiantly. "She allus had a good supply o' friends in that neighborhood, and a sufficiency o' chink to pay 'em with."

No one even tried to argue with him. Alfred was still gazing out the window. Miss Eames fidgeted with her umbrella handle, her brows knitted together in what looked like distress. Birdie cocked her head on one side as if weighing up what Jem had just told her.

At last she observed, in a thoughtful tone, "Sarah Pickles had you on a leash for seven years. Why do you still let her govern you?"

"I don't!"

"You do. You just said so. If it weren't for Sarah Pickles, you'd not be living on the streets o' Whitechapel."

"I ain't allus on the streets," Jem countered. "There's a cellar in Wapping I sometimes share. Tuppence a night, and no more'n four other sweepers in the bed."

"In the *bed?*" Miss Eames echoed. "Oh, dear me, no, that will never do." She appealed to Alfred. "Mr. Bunce, can you not find a corner for Jem in your own home if I promise to find him another job? I'm sure I'm not mistaken in thinking that a crossing sweeper's occupation is rather *low* for a boy of his intelligence. And I'm afraid that he may fall into old habits if he insists on revisiting old haunts."

Alfred shifted his attention away from the window at last. "Aye, like enough," he said gloomily, contemplating Jem with his usual morose gaze. "Though I ain't convinced he's got the makings of an errand boy. Or a coster's lad."

"If Ned can do it, I can!" snapped Jem, before realizing what he'd just let himself in for. "But I'd rather be a bogler's boy," he went on hurriedly. "You seen me work. I'm spry enough, ain't I? Seems to me I done well today."

"Why, what do you mean?" Birdie spoke sharply, stiffening against the sway of the carriage. Then she rounded on Alfred, who was sitting across from her. "You didn't go bogling with *him,* did you?"

As Alfred rubbed his nose, Jem's temper flared. "Well, and why not?" Jem demanded. "He's a bogler, ain't he?"

"Not any longer, though." Miss Eames was looking more and more upset. "Didn't you abandon that calling, Mr. Bunce? Didn't we agree that it was far too dangerous for the children involved?"

Alfred cleared his throat. "Aye, but—"

"What would *you* have done, then? Let that bogle eat another kid?" By now Jem was almost shouting. "Mebbe it wouldn't have troubled you none! Mebbe you don't care what befalls boot boys or scullery maids—only toffs and their kin!"

Birdie gasped. A red spot appeared on each of Miss Eames's pale cheeks. Alfred leaned toward Jem and snarled, "Don't you never speak to the lady like that or I'll box yer ears, so help me."

"And she *does* care," Birdie insisted. "Ain't I the proof of it? Miss Eames don't hold with snobbery o' that sort."

Jem muttered an apology. He was already feeling ashamed of himself. There was a long, awkward silence, laced with the crack of the driver's whip. Looking out the nearest window, Jem realized that they were already well past Leadenhall Street.

"Did you really kill a bogle today?" Birdie said at last. She was speaking to Alfred. "Where was it?"

"In a Newgate tavern."

"Newgate?" Birdie sounded surprised. "How did a Newgate taverner run you to ground in a court off Drury Lane?"

"Ask *him*," said Alfred, nodding at Jem—who confessed in a low voice, "A barmaid collared me outside the penny gaff. She were looking for you, Birdie, on account o' yer name being used by the tout at the door."

Birdie's face brightened. "Truly?"

"She'd read about you in the newspapers and wanted yer help. So I took her to Mr. Bunce, knowing as how you don't bogle no more."

Birdie suddenly looked downcast—and Jem couldn't understand why. Surely she wasn't pining after her old life as a bogler's girl? If so, Jem would gladly have swapped. He was still cleaning bits of cake out of his teeth with his tongue and savoring every morsel.

"The gall of it!" Miss Eames exclaimed. "Shouting Birdie's name on the street like that, as if she were a patent medicine! I suppose her name is plastered all over the bills and placards as well?"

Jem shrugged. He couldn't answer because he couldn't read. It didn't embarrass him to be reminded of this, but the same couldn't be said for Miss Eames—who gasped and looked mortified when she realized what she'd just said to him.

Before she could beg his pardon, however, the cab came to an abrupt halt.

"Whitechapel Road," boomed the cabman. "All out for Whitechapel Road."

THE IMPERSONATOR

Mr. Lubbock was still on his box outside the penny gaff. His voice had become a little hoarse. His silver lace was damp and bedraggled.

"Now exhibiting! The best show in London!" he bawled at a couple of factory girls who were hovering nearby. Then he spotted Miss Eames, and his eyes lit up. "Walk in, madam, walk in! A menagerie of mythical beasts! Curiosities from the farthest corners of the world!"

Miss Eames approached him. "Are you the manager of this establishment?" she asked.

"I am indeed!" Mr. Lubbock's fat, red face split into an unconvincing smile. "Josiah Lubbock, at your service."

"Well, Mr. Lubbock, I should like a word." Glancing at the nearby costers, Miss Eames added, "In private."

"A private viewing, madam? Why, certainly! It will cost a little extra, of course — especially since you've brought some companions with you . . ." Mr. Lubbock winked at Birdie but apparently didn't know what to make of Jem and Alfred. He shot them an uncertain look. "Let us say . . . ninepence? Or a shilling if you wish to touch the exhibits?"

"We are not here as patrons," Miss Eames replied crisply. "Kindly admit us, for I've no wish to discuss this matter with you in public."

The showman's smile faded. He cleared his throat as his gaze raked the surrounding street. Then he said uneasily, "Perhaps after the show, madam . . . ?"

"*Now*, Mr. Lubbock. Or I shall return with my solicitor."

"We ain't debt collectors, if that's what's worrying you," Jem added, just in case it was. And then Birdie stepped forward.

"If you don't let us in, I'll stand here and tell everyone *I'm* Birdie McAdam. Unlike that false Birdie you got in there." She pointed at the picture of the little girl cracking the whip as a gathering crowd of rough youths and hatless young women listened with great interest. "Don't try and say as how I ain't the genuine article," Birdie went on, "for

I've clear proof I am. Why, this here is Alfred Bunce the bogler, who can vouch for me!"

There was a murmur of surprise from the growing crowd of spectators. Alfred winced. Mr. Lubbock jumped down from his box (more nimbly than Jem would have expected) and mumbled, "We'd best go in. After you. Mind the step."

Miss Eames sniffed. She allowed him to push open the door to his shop, then briskly marched in ahead of him. Birdie followed close on her heels. But when Jem tried to follow Birdie, Mr. Lubbock flicked him aside with the bamboo cane.

Alfred grabbed it and said, "This boy is with me. Don't raise yer hand to him."

Mr. Lubbock apologized. He sounded shaken. Muttering something under his breath, he quickly herded his unexpected visitors into a long, narrow vestibule that contained an unmanned ticket booth and several glass cabinets full of preserved specimens. A doorway at the far end of the room was hung with blue plush. A trickle of light filtered in between all the bills and placards that covered the window.

"We'd best talk here," he remarked, locking the front door behind him. "It's more private."

"What's a . . . a 'ja-cul-us'?" Birdie suddenly asked. She had been inspecting the handwritten sign on one of the display cabinets—and all at once it dawned on Jem that she was actually reading it. Birdie McAdam had learned to read! He couldn't have been more astonished.

"A *jaculus* is a small, mythical dragon," Miss Eames explained, stopping next to Birdie. "This, however, appears to be a lizard with bat's wings attached to its shoulders."

"A remarkable discovery, is it not?" Mr. Lubbock began to mop his temples with a dirty handkerchief. "I obtained it from an old sea captain who spent fifty years roaming the West Indies. And here we have our selkie, and our griffin, and our Egyptian basilisk—"

"Mr. Lubbock!" Miss Eames cut him off so sharply that he jumped. "We are not *fools,* sir! Nor are we interested in the grotesque productions of a dishonest taxidermist!" She waved her hand at the exhibits, half of which were rotting away in jars of alcohol. "I can see for myself that this water horse is a stuffed seal with some kind of mane stitched to its head!"

"Madam—"

"There is only one impersonation that interests us, Mr. Lubbock, and that is the person who is passing herself off as Birdie McAdam."

Mr. Lubbock turned an even darker shade of puce. "Perhaps before we continue, madam, you'd care to introduce yourself," he said, straining to sound jovial. "I don't believe I caught your name."

"Eames. Miss Edith Eames." Drawing herself up to her full, not-very-impressive height, Miss Eames placed a hand on Birdie's shoulder. "And *this* is the real Birdie McAdam."

"Aha. Yes." The showman's smile became sickly and apologetic as his gaze dropped from Miss Eames's face to Birdie's. "Dear me, what a surprise! For I must confess, I had no idea that there *was* a real Birdie McAdam."

"Nonsense!" snapped Miss Eames.

"I assure you, I did not. I considered Birdie McAdam to be a mythical figure, like Spring-Heeled Jack."

"Can you not read, then?" Alfred growled. "She were in all the papers last summer."

Mr. Lubbock waved this objection aside with one pudgy hand. "Oh, but who can believe the press these days, Mr. . . . Mr. Bunce, is it?"

"Aye."

"One reads such fabulous tales of raised corpses, and mistaken identities, and three-headed pygmies . . . Why, it's hard to know *what* to believe! And when I heard about Birdie's remarkable deeds of valor, I naturally assumed that such a talented child could not possibly exist." Mr. Lubbock beamed at Birdie. "Were you indeed raised to kill bogles, m'dear?"

Birdie shrugged. "I helped to kill 'em."

"By singing?"

"That is no business of yours, sir!" Miss Eames barked.

"Ah, but it *could* be my business, if the little girl is willing. And very good business too." Addressing Birdie once more, Mr. Lubbock bent down and placed a hand on each of his knees. "I'm pulling in two pounds a night at present," he confided, "but if your voice is as sweet as your face, m'dear, the takings could double. And one-tenth of that sum could be yours."

Jem gasped. He immediately began to calculate percentages, even as he wondered if Mr. Lubbock could be telling the truth. Birdie's eyes widened. Alfred blinked.

Miss Eames, however, was unmoved.

"Don't be ridiculous!" she scoffed. "Why would Birdie want to work for you? She is studying with Signora Paolini and is destined for an illustrious career on the stage!"

"I'm sure she is, Miss Eames, but that doesn't mean she cannot earn her keep when she is *not* studying," Mr. Lubbock pointed out. "Why, what's to stop her from studying in the day and performing at night? I cannot see any objection to it."

Neither could Jem. He thought it an excellent scheme—and observed that Birdie, too, seemed struck by the idea.

"She would learn to crack a whip," Mr. Lubbock continued, "and to handle a snake and wrangle a pony—"

"A *snake?*" Jem interrupted, forestalling Miss Eames. "What snake?"

"It is a perfectly harmless python. Not at all venomous," Mr. Lubbock assured him. "As for our unicorn—why, she is the daintiest, most docile creature you ever laid eyes on! And our bogle's as deft as he is big. Very well trained. He knows what he's about."

Alfred snorted. "There ain't a bogle in the world can be trained," he said flatly.

"You'd be surprised, Mr. Bunce. Here—let me introduce you." Before Miss Eames could object, Mr. Lubbock scurried over to the plush curtain, which he pushed aside to reveal a much larger room with a raised platform at one end. In front of this platform were several rows of wooden benches. Behind it, the grubby plaster wall was covered with more colorful placards.

Jem decided that the single door to the left of the platform must lead backstage.

"Hi! Eduardo! Come here at once!" Mr. Lubbock cried. Then he turned to Alfred, who had followed him into the makeshift theater, and explained, "Our bogle is the scion of a renowned Italian family, skilled in all the theatrical arts. But he grew too heavy for clowning or tumbling, and has found his true calling elsewhere."

"You ain't got no box seats," Jem remarked, having satisfied himself that the room wasn't high enough to accommodate a gallery. His gaze snagged on several hooks in the ceiling. "Was this here a butcher's shop once?"

Before Mr. Lubbock could answer, a huge, hairy shape

emerged through the stage door. Even from a distance, Jem could see at once that it was a very large man in a brown fur suit made of rabbit or cat. The arms of the suit were enclosed by a pair of fur mittens, topped with claws made of horn or bone. Under one arm was tucked a detached head, complete with snout, tusks, and a hinged jaw.

Jem decided that the head was probably molded out of papier-mâché, or something equally light. The teeth were real, though — unless they had been fashioned from porcelain.

Miss Eames wrinkled her nose in disgust. "Really, Mr. Lubbock," she protested.

But the showman ignored her. Instead, with a theatrical flourish, he introduced Eduardo to "the *real* Birdie McAdam." Then he fixed his little blue eyes on Birdie again. "I'll warrant you'd make short work of *this* bogle — eh, m'dear?" he said.

"He don' look like no bogle I ever saw" was Birdie's response, as the man in the fur suit stared at her blankly. His big, bony, square-jawed face stuck out of his shaggy brown collar like a strange bloom sprouting from a flowerpot. His hair and eyes were even darker than Jem's.

"I don' unnerstand," he said to Mr. Lubbock. "Bedelia issa leaving?"

"No, no, you're not listening, Ed. This *is* Birdie Mc-

Adam. The *real* Birdie McAdam. Now, why don't you put on that head and show her what you can do?"

Eduardo opened his mouth, still looking puzzled. But then someone else broke into the conversation.

"What do you mean, 'Bedelia is leaving'?" a shrill voice exclaimed. "I'll have you know I ain't going *nowhere!* Not without a fight!"

Suddenly two more figures emerged from the backstage door. One was a dwarf wearing a false beard and a wax nose. He was dressed all in green, with a pointed green hat and knitted stockings. The other was a girl with a python draped over her shoulders. She was clad in a blond wig, a white dress, and a blue velvet sash. Jem decided that she was about sixteen years old.

"Why, Bedelia!" Mr. Lubbock exclaimed with forced cheerfulness. "The show's in ten minutes. Go and put on your slap — there's a good girl."

"Who is *she?*" Bedelia demanded as if he hadn't spoken. She was glaring at Birdie, who glared right back.

"I'll tell you who I am," Birdie retorted, folding her arms. "I'm Birdie McAdam, and *you* ain't. Why, you're nothing more than a cheap, false, parrot-voiced impersonator! And if you don't leave off what you're doing, I'll snatch you baldheaded — that's if you ain't *already* bald under that sorry excuse for a wig!"

7

THE PENNY GAFF

Bedelia turned to Mr. Lubbock. "What does she mean, I ain't Birdie McAdam?" the girl cried. "You can't do this! I were engaged for the entire London run!"

"Now, Bedelia . . ."

"Don't you 'Bedelia' me, Josiah Lubbock!" She rounded on Birdie again. "Who do *you* work for, then? Pottle? Bland? What shows have *you* done?"

Jem began to laugh. He couldn't help it. What with the wax-nosed dwarf, and the hairy giant, and the battling Birdies . . .

"She ain't here to take yer job," he told Bedelia, grinning from ear to ear. But Birdie quickly corrected him.

"I'm here to make her stop being me," Birdie said, "and I don't care if she loses her job as a consequence."

By now Bedelia was starting to look confused. It was her companion, the little man in green, who suddenly exclaimed, "You don't mean *you're* Birdie McAdam? The *real* Birdie McAdam?"

"Ain't that what I just bin saying?" Birdie replied crossly. Beside her, Miss Eames added, "This is a clear case of fraudulent impersonation. I shall take you to court if Birdie's name is not removed from your advertisements by tomorrow morning. Do you understand, Mr. Lubbock?"

Mr. Lubbock nodded. "Yes, of course," he assured her with another greasy smile. "I had no wish to cause offense. But might I just ask—"

"No, you may not," Miss Eames snapped. Bedelia, meanwhile, was gazing at Birdie in astonishment, open mouthed and goggle eyed.

"You ain't never the real Birdie," she protested. "You're so *young!* Ain't she young, Rupert?"

"She is," said the dwarf, nodding.

"I'm eleven years old," Birdie stiffly informed them.

"You're such a bit of a thing, though—ain't she, Rupert?"

"A scrap," the dwarf confirmed.

"And Rupert would know," Bedelia pointed out, "for he's worked with some o' the smallest, in his time."

Jem shot an inquiring glance at Rupert, wanting to hear more. But Miss Eames wasn't interested in Rupert's fairground memories. She reached for Birdie's hand and said, "I see no reason to stay. We've delivered our message. You will no longer profit from Birdie's name, Mr. Lubbock, or you'll be hearing from my solicitors. Good day to you, sir." She gave Birdie's hand a tug, then frowned when there was no response. "Come along, dear. What's the matter?"

"Nothing," Birdie mumbled. Catching her eye, Jem pulled a sympathetic face. He knew in his heart that she wanted to pet the snake, chat with the dwarf, and examine the exhibits. Why not? He wanted to do it himself.

Miss Eames, however, had no wish to stay. Not while a cab stood waiting outside. "We ought to get home," she told Birdie. "Whitechapel Road isn't exactly a respectable place to be. Is it, Mr. Bunce?"

Alfred shook his head. "Off you go, lass," he said to Birdie. When she pouted, looking mulish, he fixed her with a flinty gaze. "Do as you're told, now," he warned. "Miss Eames knows what's best for you." Then he turned and motioned to Jem. "You too, lad. Come along."

"One moment, Mr. Bunce." Stepping forward, Mr. Lubbock managed to insert himself between Alfred and the door. "I wonder if *you* might be interested in a public appearance? On competitive terms, of course."

Alfred scowled. "Get out o' me way," he rasped.

"You're a bogler, Mr. Bunce. You've made a name for yourself. People would pay to see you at work." Before Alfred could do more than sniff, Mr. Lubbock gestured at Bedelia. "A double act, perhaps? You wouldn't have to do much. Your main contribution would be your name; my associate would take care of the rest. Why, she could be your new apprentice!"

Jem bristled. "*I'm* his new 'prentice. I'm a bogler's boy," he said.

"Indeed?" For the first time, Mr. Lubbock studied Jem with genuine interest. But Alfred shook his head sternly.

"I ain't going on no stage," he declared, "and neither is Jem."

"Then may I make another suggestion?" As Alfred side-stepped him, trying to follow Miss Eames into the vestibule, Mr. Lubbock began to talk very quickly. "Have you ever considered how valuable a bogle would be? People pay enormous sums to see tigers and elephants—only think how much they'd pay to see a real, live bogle!" Before Alfred could sidle away, Mr. Lubbock grabbed his arm. "I'm acquainted with the owner of a traveling menagerie, and I'm sure that, with his help, we could devise a means of caging and keeping any bogle you might catch during the course of your daily rounds—"

"Listen here, Lubbock." Alfred wrenched himself free, then planted his finger on the showman's chest. "In the first place, you can't trap a bogle. Try and you'll perish."

"Yes, but—"

"In the second place, I don't bogle no more. It ain't a healthy occupation."

"Mr. Bunce—"

"And last of all, I don't work for liars." Alfred suddenly turned his attention to Jem, using the same dark, piercing look that he'd used to quell Birdie. "Liars is nothing but trouble," he declared, very slowly and clearly. "They promise you money and it never comes. When they make a mistake, they allus blame you for it. You should remember that, lad. They ain't worth the time you spend on 'em."

Jem grunted. He didn't know what else to do. As an accomplished liar, he felt that Alfred was being a little harsh. But he couldn't exactly say so.

"I'm not lying, Mr. Bunce," Mr. Lubbock protested. "Why would I want to saddle myself with a vicious creature if it wasn't going to make us both a fortune? Which it would, sir, I promise you. On my mother's life—"

"D'you know what bogles eat?" Alfred interrupted. "Do you know what you'd be feeding 'em?"

Mr. Lubbock glanced at Bedelia, who shrugged. Beside her, Rupert said vaguely, "They'd be partial to a bit o' meat, I daresay?"

"They eat children," Alfred growled. Then he touched his hat in farewell. "You don't keep bogles, sir; you kill 'em," he concluded. "Good day to you. I'll see meself out."

He moved away so quickly that he was in the street before Jem could catch up with him. Miss Eames was already outside, tearing a placard off a wall. It was drizzling. A line of people stood waiting for the penny gaff to open. The watery reflections of nearby gas lamps gilded the damp cobblestones.

"Here!" said the man at the front of the line, when he saw what Miss Eames was up to. "What's your game, then?"

"The next show is canceled," Miss Eames informed him.

"Canceled?"

"You have been misled. Birdie McAdam will not be performing here tonight."

Miss Eames was so absorbed in her work that she seemed not to notice the sudden clamor of disappointed theater patrons. Jem heard it, though. And so did Birdie.

They exchanged an anxious look as several drunken loiterers moved toward Miss Eames, loudly complaining.

"Ye're ten minutes late, and now ye're saying ye'll not open at all?" somebody bellowed. Whoever he was, he sounded Irish.

Alfred grabbed Miss Eames's wrist. "Come," he said,

pulling her toward their hansom cab, which was waiting just down the street. Birdie slipped behind Miss Eames and began to shove her along. Jem tried to distract the Irishman.

"It's Josiah Lubbock you want. He's the manager o' this here gaff," Jem announced. He pointed at the shop door, where the showman was skulking. "That's him there — see? He'll tell you why there ain't no show tonight."

As the crowd rounded on Mr. Lubbock, erupting into a chorus of complaints, Jem turned and made for the hansom cab. He could hear Miss Eames giving Alfred's address to the cabman but didn't stop to wonder why until he was safely tucked away in the vehicle, opposite Alfred and Birdie. Only when the cab had started to move, heading west down Whitechapel Road, did Jem feel safe enough to speak.

"Why are we going to Alfred's place?" he asked Miss Eames. "I thought you was heading home?"

Miss Eames looked at him in surprise. Her complexion was blotchy, her skirt was splashed with mud, and her hair had come loose, falling in damp wisps from beneath her hat — which sat crookedly on her head. Jem was relieved to see her looking so disheveled. It made her less intimidating somehow.

"Oh, I couldn't let you walk," Miss Eames replied. "Not barefoot. Not in this weather." As Jem blinked, she added, "You *will* take Jem for the night — will you not, Mr. Bunce? He cannot be left on the street."

"Aye," Alfred rumbled, sounding resigned. "I'll take him."

"I'm sure we'll be able to find him a suitable position," Miss Eames went on. "He is not *completely* unskilled, after all."

"Mebbe he can sell fly papers," Birdie suggested. She was regarding Jem in a slightly resentful way, her arms folded, her eyes narrowed. "Mebbe he can work as a Catch-'Em-Alive Boy."

"Mebbe," said Alfred. But Jem didn't want to sell fly papers. He wasn't about to walk around London with a loaded fly paper tied around his cap, singing, "Catch all the nasty beetles and flies, catch 'em from teasing the baby's eyes."

"I ain't no hawker!" he snapped. "I'm a bogler's boy now!" Appealing to Alfred, he continued, "We killed a bogle today. Don't that make me a bogler's boy?"

"Not if I ain't a bogler," Alfred replied shortly.

"But you are!" Jem exclaimed. "How can you sit there with a bogler's bag on yer knee and claim you ain't a bogler?"

"I'm a *retired* bogler." Alfred frowned at Jem. "That's what you're to say, next time anyone comes to you with tales o' missing scullery maids and such. D'you hear?"

After a moment's hesitation, Jem nodded. He didn't have much choice. He was wet, tired, and hungry, with no shoes, no job, and barely a penny to his name. He wasn't in a position to argue with Alfred.

"And if you're to stay with me, you must pull yer weight," Alfred went on. "First thing you can do is sweep the place out, since you left yer broom there. If you don't know how to cook, Ned'll teach you. Aside from that, there's water to haul and a fire to keep stoked." Before Jem could say that he would be happy to do all these things, Alfred warned, "But if you ever bring home another prospect like you done today, you'll be out o' there faster'n a swift can fly. Understand?"

"Yes," Jem mumbled.

"The last thing I need is you pointing me out to every stray barmaid as comes along. Why, I moved halfway across London to prevent it!" Leaning forward suddenly, Alfred glowered at Jem. "And another thing—I'll not have you chasing Sarah Pickles."

"But—"

"It's too dangerous. *She's* too dangerous, living or dead." Something about Alfred's tone made Birdie shiver and Miss Eames wince. "If she's dead, then those as killed her won't take kindly to your nosing about," Alfred continued. "And if she's living . . . well, I'll not have you vanish into thin air like all them other poor souls as crossed Sal over the years."

"But she sold me as bogle bait!" Jem protested.

"Aye, and you're lucky to be alive," the bogler agreed. "Which is how I want you to stay. *Alive*. Else I ain't got no use for you."

He waited as Jem swallowed, clenched his fists, and finally said, "All right."

"Long as you're under me roof, you'll not chase Sal?" Alfred pressed.

"No," Jem answered. And he was telling the truth — up to a point. How could he chase Sarah while he was under Alfred's roof? It wasn't as if she lodged there.

Jem knew that when he did find Sarah, it would be somewhere else in London . . .

8

The Missing Apprentice

*R*at-tat-tat-tat!

A knock on the door awakened Jem the next morning. For an instant he didn't know where he was. But then he raised his head, rubbed his bleary eyes, and realized that he was in Alfred's room, under a pile of old clothes.

"Ned?" he squawked as the rapping continued. *Rat-tat-tat-tat!* Judging from the pale light creeping through the window, it was still very early—yet Ned Roach was nowhere to be seen. His boots were gone. There was no one on his paillasse.

It occurred to Jem that a coster's boy like Ned might

have to rise before dawn if he wanted to reach Covent Garden Market in time to grab the choicest fruit.

Rat-tat-tat-tat.

"Whassarr . . . ?" Alfred grumbled from somewhere deep in a nest of grubby bedclothes. Jem pushed back his own covers and stood up. He was still wearing his canvas trousers and blue shirt, but had carefully washed his feet upon crossing Alfred's threshold the previous night.

Alfred had insisted on it.

"I'm a-coming," Jem growled. He staggered over to the door, dodging strips of fly paper on his way. When he lifted the latch and pulled the door open, he found himself peering at a total stranger. "Who are you?" he asked crossly. "What do you want?"

"Hugh Purdy's my name." The stranger tipped his cap, which was made of leather. He also carried a leather tool bag and wore leather pads tied to the knees of his trousers. "I'm looking for Mr. Alfred Bunce," he said. "Miss Lillimere sent me."

Jem grimaced. He glanced over his shoulder at Alfred, who was sitting up in bed, running his hands through his hair.

"There's a cove here wants to see you," Jem told him. When Alfred groaned, Jem turned back to Hugh Purdy. "A little early, ain't it?"

"I got a job this morning," Purdy replied, "and I'm afeared to go up there without Mr. Bunce comes along." As Jem hesitated, conscious of Alfred grunting and coughing in the room behind him, Purdy took off his cap. He was a wiry little man with an angular, clean-shaven face, a thatch of mouse-colored hair, and skin as leathery as his tool bag. Jem judged him to be about thirty years old.

"I'm a plumber and glazier," the man continued, "and I lost my apprentice on a roof yesterday morning." Seeing Jem blink, he added, "Billy didn't fall, I'd swear to it. For I searched until nightfall, but there weren't no trace of him thereabouts." Purdy shook his head in bewilderment. "When it got too dark to keep searching, I stopped for a pint at the tavern nearby—and that's when Mabel told me about the bogle in her basement."

By this time Alfred was more or less upright. He had pulled on his trousers and was dragging his old green coat over his nightshirt. Jem also noticed that the neighbors were beginning to show an interest in Alfred's unexpected visitor. One or two doors had opened in the passage outside. Several pairs of eyes were watching Hugh Purdy's every move.

"You'd better come in," said Jem, having decided that Alfred would probably prefer to discuss his bogling business in private. He ushered Purdy over the threshold, then pulled a grotesque face at the nosy old woman across the hallway before slamming Alfred's door shut.

"I'm sorry to rouse you so early, Mr. Bunce," Purdy was saying. He had fixed his bemused gaze on the flapping strips of paper overhead. "I'm putting lead on a roof, see, and must have it done by the end o' the week. But I can't do it without a boy, and won't take another boy up there till I discover what happened to the first . . ."

Alfred coughed, hawked, and spat. He wasn't looking very well.

"Why d'you think a bogle's to blame?" he asked. "Could the boy not have run off?"

"Not Billy," the plumber replied. "Billy's a stouthearted lad, as keen as mustard. He had no cause to run, and no desire to."

Reaching for his pipe, Alfred studiously ignored Jem, who was kicking his bedclothes tidily into one corner. "You sure he weren't taken? There's some folk do that, when they need boys for thieving, or begging. They grab 'em where they find 'em."

"On a rooftop?" Purdy's tone made it clear what he thought of that idea. "Billy's a big boy, sir. Ten years old and sturdy as a stump. Yet I didn't hear a sound—not a single cry or clatter. One instant he were fetching sheets o' lead, and the next . . ." Purdy trailed off, shaking his head again. But Alfred said nothing.

He was busy packing his pipe with tobacco.

"I ain't never heard of a roof bogle," Jem observed at

last, to break the lengthening silence. Still, however, Alfred didn't speak.

It was the plumber who finally said, "I once heard tell of a chimney bogle taking kids from a mill near Sheffield. So when Mabel mentioned your visit, Mr. Bunce, it crossed my mind that—"

"Billy might have bin took by a chimney bogle," Alfred interrupted. He had pulled a box of matches from his pocket.

"Exactly!" The plumber sounded relieved that Alfred hadn't scoffed at the notion. "For there's any number o' chimneys up there, and precious little else."

Alfred heaved a sigh. He struck his match, lit his pipe, and greedily filled his lungs with smoke. Then he sat on his bed and asked the plumber, in a voice tranquilized by tobacco, "Have the folk in the house bin troubled at all?"

"No, sir, for it's empty. All but brand-new. Once the flashing is done, everything inside is to be painted."

"Where *is* this house?" said Jem as Alfred pensively puffed away.

"On Holborn Viaduct," Purdy replied. "Near the railway bridge."

Alfred frowned. "Is that—?"

"Near the tavern? It is."

Jem was pleased to see Alfred frown. It meant that the

bogler was interested enough to be disturbed—or perhaps confused. It meant that he was hooked, Jem thought.

Like a fish.

"That's very strange," rasped Alfred. "You'll not see bogles so close together, as a rule. They tend to be solitary creatures . . ."

Purdy shrugged. "You'd know best," he said. "I ain't had no experience with bogles."

"What about the chimneys in the house?" was Alfred's next question. "Do *they* draw well?"

"That I can't tell you. Far as I know, they never was lit. Some of 'em don't yet have mantels."

Alfred gave a grunt. Purdy watched and waited. Then Jem, who was very hungry, decided to poke at the fire. Though it had been reduced to a heap of glowing embers, he felt sure that if he rearranged the coals and blew on them hard enough, he might be able to boil a kettle.

"I ain't a young man, Mr. Purdy," Alfred said at last. "How tall is this house o' yours?"

"Five stories. Including the basement." When Alfred grimaced, Purdy assured him, "I've a sturdy ladder and ropes aplenty, and the slates up there is clean as a whistle. No moss or bird's mess on 'em."

Alfred still looked unconvinced. So Jem, who was now squatting in front of the fire, poker in hand, said, "*I'm* spry enough. *I* can go up there."

"Not without me, you can't," Alfred retorted.

"I'll pay extra." Though Purdy wasn't begging, exactly, there was an urgent edge to his voice. "Mabel parted with eight shillings — I'll pay ten."

"Ten!" It was a princely sum. Jem stared at Alfred, wide eyed.

The bogler smoothed his mustache thoughtfully.

"Billy is the son of an old friend," Purdy went on. "He's the best boy I ever had and has lodged with my family these six months past. It makes me heartsore to think—" He stopped suddenly, then swallowed a few times before proceeding. "If a bogle took him, I'll not rest till it's dead. Billy deserves nothing less, poor lad."

Jem knew that Alfred wouldn't have the heart to resist this plea but decided to grease the wheels a little, regardless. "Even if there ain't no bogle," he told Purdy, "you'll still have to pay costs. A shilling down, and a penny for salt."

"Fivepence," Alfred interrupted. He shot Jem a reproving look. "*Fivepence* for a visit. And a penny for salt."

"I'd be happy to pay the shilling," Purdy began, before the bogler cut him off.

"I ain't in the habit o' speeling me customers. It's sixpence all up if the bogle don't show."

"And the bus fare on top o' that," said Jem.

Alfred scowled as Purdy gave a surprised laugh. "He's

a downy one, ain't he?" the plumber observed, eyeing Jem with reluctant admiration. "The lad bargains like a Thames ferry man."

"He weren't raised right," said Alfred. Then, having resigned himself to the inevitable, he added, "Could you wait for us downstairs, Mr. Purdy? I need a minute or so to make meself decent."

"Of course! Anything you want, Mr. Bunce." The plumber's face creased into a wide, relieved smile. He had very good teeth, Jem noticed. "There's a baker's shop around the corner. What if I was to stop in and buy us a couple o' Bath buns for breakfast while you're dressing? We could eat 'em on our way."

Jem didn't even have to nod; his stomach spoke for him. Alfred muttered something about being very much obliged. Then Hugh Purdy left the room—and Alfred made sure that the door was firmly shut before rounding on Jem, saying, "I'll have no more o' that, d'you hear?"

"More o' what?"

"Them gammoning, griddling ways you garnered from Sal Pickles. If you can't be honest, there ain't no place for you here."

"What do you mean?" Jem was deeply offended. "I never tried to gammon nobody! I were haggling is all."

"You was driving up the price and speaking out o'

turn," Alfred snapped. "I'll *never* take advantage of no desperate soul that's a-grieving for some lost child. Sal might have, but I ain't her. And neither are you."

Jem was assailed by the sudden memory of how he had once helped to rob a woman's house while she was making her regular weekly visit to her dead child's grave. It was a sour and shameful recollection, but he told himself, as he always did, *It were Sarah as made me do it. She's the one as led me astray.*

And she deserved to suffer the consequences.

"Besides which, you ain't here to talk. You're here to listen and to learn," Alfred was saying. When Jem opened his mouth, the bogler immediately cut him off. "Ned's smart enough to know that he don't know *nothing*. Birdie's the same. You'd better follow their lead, or we'll be parting ways by nightfall. I don't want you saying one word to that plumber without leave from me. Understand?"

Jem swallowed hard. Then he nodded.

"Good." Alfred picked up one of his boots. "Now take that jug next door and see if Mrs. Ricketts can spare us a drop o' hot shaving water . . ."

9

ON THE ROOF

Though Jem had heard of the Holborn Viaduct, he'd never been there. He knew that it had been built, quite recently, across the valley lying between Fetter Lane and Newgate Street. He also knew that it was supported on the back of a remarkable bridge. But when he finally reached this famous bridge, he could see very little of it. From the top, it was just a wide stretch of busy road flanked by iron balustrades and bronze statues.

Jem particularly liked the statues of the four winged lions. The other four statues were of gigantic women wearing bed sheets. They didn't interest him much. He preferred to look at the women hurrying past them, wrapped in sensible coats and shawls.

He was hoping to see the same woman he'd glimpsed the previous afternoon, near the omnibus stop down the road. He was convinced that if he spotted this woman again, he'd be able to put a name to her face.

It bothered him that he couldn't remember who she was.

Buildings were being constructed all around the viaduct, wherever older houses had been knocked down to make way for the new stretch of road. After passing Saint Sepulchre's Church, heading west, Hugh Purdy pointed to where the Saracen's Head Inn had once stood. Skinner Street was also gone, he lamented, as were Haberdashers Court and Turnagain Lane. A railway station was being erected near the bridge, with a grand hotel attached to it.

"You wouldn't recognize this place," said Purdy, shaking his head as he surveyed all the hoardings and rubble. "I growed up near here, on Catherine Wheel Court, and *that's* gone too. Like they put a scythe through Snow Hill."

The plumber finally stopped in front of a large terrace that was going up on the south side of the viaduct, near Saint Andrew's Church. It was a tall, handsome building made of fresh-laid bricks and newly carved stone. The front door hadn't been painted, but all the windows were glazed—including the shop windows downstairs. A load of banisters had been dumped near the main staircase. No one had yet sanded the floors, papered the walls, or installed any fireplace mantels.

Everything inside was coated with a thick layer of plaster dust.

"Do bogles leave tracks?" Jem asked Alfred as Purdy ushered them into the vestibule — where the floor tiles were a mess of powdery footprints.

"Not as a rule," Alfred replied. "But that don't mean a thing." He sniffed the air like a bloodhound as he followed Hugh Purdy into the first room. Here, someone had left a mangy broom and a wheelbarrow. The fireplace was just a square hole in the wall. The floor in front of it was covered in footprints, all of them made by hobnail boots.

"Can't see no traces here," Alfred observed after hunkering down to peer up the flue. When Purdy asked him what traces he would expect to find if a bogle was in residence, Alfred shrugged and said, "Depends on the bogle. Some might leave a stain or a smell. Most don't leave nowt at all."

Jem sneezed. The only things *he* could smell were sawdust and plaster, with a little linseed oil thrown in. It was the same in the next room, and the one after that. As they slowly ascended, past door after door without knobs or architraves, Alfred checked every fireplace in the building — and found nothing in any of them.

"If there's a bogle haunting the roof, then it's staying up near the chimney pots," he finally declared. "Else I'd be feeling its presence, which I ain't."

"You'd *feel* it?" said Purdy with a touch of alarm. "How?"

Alfred shrugged. "You'd feel it too," he replied. "Everyone's mood allus slumps when there's a bogle about." By this time he was kneeling by a fireplace in one of the attic rooms, where the brick walls hadn't yet been plastered over, and where the huge, heavy roof beams were still exposed. There were several discarded tools on the floor near him. Jem eyed them wistfully, knowing that the hammer had to be worth at least a shilling, and the chisel double that.

But he resisted the urge to pick up even a nail punch, since Alfred would almost certainly tell him to put it down again.

"If you want to inspect the roof, Mr. Bunce, you've only to step out onto the slates," Hugh Purdy remarked, pointing at a nearby dormer window. It was circular, like a ship's porthole, and framed a view of the elaborate stone balustrade that ran along the edge of the roof. "I've put a ladder out there and can tie a rope around your middle. But you'll see for yourself, there's plenty to hold on to . . ."

Alfred rose to his feet. Jem dashed past him and climbed up onto the windowsill. Below it was a wide gutter that separated the balustrade from the sloping roof. To his right, a ladder had been propped against the slates, leading up to the roof's apex. To his left was a bank of chimneys, practically within touching distance.

The lowering gray clouds seemed almost as close as the chimneys. Jem wondered how long it would be before the rain started, making it too wet to go crawling across a pitched roof.

"Oh, this ain't so bad!" he announced. "I seen *much* worse than this!" While working for Sarah Pickles, he had often broken into houses by lifting roof slates. Sometimes he had even done it in the middle of the night. Climbing onto a balustraded roof in broad daylight, with a ladder to help him and no slimy pigeon droppings to slip him up, seemed like pleasant work in comparison. "Let *me* go out," he begged Alfred, who had joined him at the window.

But Alfred shook his head. "Wouldn't be safe."

"Yes, it would! I'm a good climber!"

"That ain't here nor there." As Jem opened his mouth to protest, Alfred growled, "It's the bogle as worries me, not the climbing. We don't want to lay our bait afore we set our trap." Having silenced Jem, he turned to the plumber. "Where did you last see yer boy? Can you show me the exact spot?"

"I can," said Purdy, dropping his tool bag. Next thing he was out on the roof, tying a length of rope to the balustrade. Once this rope had been attached to Alfred's waist, the two men began to inch their way along the gutter, while Jem lay across the windowsill, straining to see as much as he could without actually setting foot outside.

"Last time I saw Billy, I were up there, working," Purdy explained, pointing at the roof's peak. "He came down the ladder to fetch more lead. Then his singing stopped, and when I next looked up . . ." He trailed off with a sigh.

Alfred stiffened. "You heard him *singing?*"

"I did. He had a fine voice."

The bogler frowned. Jem knew that the bogle would have been drawn to Billy's voice.

"So he didn't go nowhere near that chimney?" was Alfred's next question.

"No."

"Where was yer lead?"

"I left it there. In a box." This time Purdy indicated a spot halfway between the ladder and the window. Alfred squinted at this patch of gutter. Then he asked, "Are you sure the boy didn't go back inside?"

"He had no cause to. I checked the box later, and saw lead enough in it."

"But would he have gone to relieve himself?"

Purdy hesitated. At last he said, in a slightly sheepish tone, "There's gutters for that, or we'd be up and down all day."

Alfred gave a grunt. Jem wanted to inquire about solid

waste but didn't dare, not after the way he had been scolded for speaking out of turn that morning. Instead, he peered around at the gleaming expanse of gray slate, the narrow chimney pots, the half-finished flashing, and the little turrets on the balustrade, wondering where a bogle could possibly have hidden itself. Had the missing apprentice *really* been eaten? It seemed so unlikely—and not just because there were no obvious boltholes on the roof. Jem found it hard to believe that a bogle was lurking nearby because he didn't feel gloomy or hopeless. Even under such low, brooding clouds, the roof seemed like a peaceful spot, far removed from the dirt and clamor of the street.

Jem had slept in far worse places.

"Besides, Billy wouldn't have gone off without asking," Purdy was telling Alfred. "And if he did, where is he now? I looked in the cellar. I looked in the coal hole. *He ain't in this house*, Mr. Bunce."

"What's that?" Alfred said suddenly.

His wandering gaze had snagged on something. Jem leaned even farther out of the window, desperate to see what had alarmed the bogler. Only by craning his neck and shading his eyes was he finally able to make out a kind of grating, which was set into the thick wall that divided the house beneath them from the one next to it.

"That ain't no down pipe," Alfred continued, steadying himself against the balustrade. "What's it for?"

"Oh, that," said Purdy. "That's a ventilation shaft."

"A what?" Alfred didn't sound any wiser, so the plumber tried to explain.

"It troubled me, too, until I mentioned it to a friend o' mine. He's a flusher in the sewers and told me there's a great tangle o' pipes and tunnels built into the viaduct. That there"—Purdy nodded at the grating—"is a shaft as lets out sewer gas from under the street."

"Sewer gas?" Alfred echoed. He glanced at Jem, who grimaced.

"There's one in every party wall built along here," Purdy related. "My friend tells me there's gratings set into the road as well. And shafts in the lampposts." He shook his head admiringly. "Ain't nothing like this viaduct in all the world."

Jem stared at the spot where Purdy's box of lead sheets had been positioned. To reach it, Billy would have had to climb down the ladder and turn his back on the grating, which would have been about ten feet away from him.

Having seen a bogle in action, Jem had no trouble imagining what might have happened next. And he shuddered at the thought of it.

Alfred sighed. "That there is where yer bogle came from," he announced, with a nod at the ventilation shaft. "Straight up from the sewers and straight back down again."

He paused for a moment, chewing on his bottom lip. "I'm sorry," he said at last. "'Tis the worst stroke o' luck I ever saw. The Board o' Works should have consulted a Go-Devil Man afore building bogle runs into these here houses."

"But—but ain't that hole too small, Mr. Bunce?" Purdy was gaping at him in disbelief. "Why, Billy himself could barely fit through it, let alone the bogle as ate him!"

"Never think any hole's too small for a bogle," Alfred replied. Then he turned and headed straight toward Jem, planting his feet with great care as he clutched the balustrade.

Jem reached out to help him back inside.

"Wait! Where are you going?" Purdy exclaimed. "What about the bogle? We have to kill it!"

Alfred shook his head. "I can't. Not up here."

"We couldn't lay down no salt," Jem observed, thinking aloud. "The roof's too steep." When he saw Alfred's nod of approval, he felt quite pleased with himself.

"But it's got to be killed, Mr. Bunce!" Before Alfred could even respond, Purdy abruptly changed tack. "If it lives in the sewers, could we not trap it down there?" he demanded.

Alfred paused, then shrugged. He was straddling the windowsill. "Mebbe."

"Then that's what we'll do." Purdy spoke with energy

and purpose. "I'll have a word with my friend Sam Snell, the flusher. He'll get us in. That's if you don't object, Mr. Bunce?"

"I've worked the sewers before," Alfred said wearily.

"Good." Purdy seemed to think that the matter was settled. He didn't bother to ask Jem how *he* felt about sewers. Neither did Alfred, but that didn't surprise Jem.

After being underfed and overworked by his last two employers, Jem wasn't expecting Alfred to treat him like anything but a dumb animal.

Just as long as he don't truss me up for slaughter, Jem thought on his way back downstairs.

One day, he reminded himself, Sarah Pickles was going to pay for doing that.

10

SAINT SEPULCHRE'S CHURCH

Hugh Purdy insisted that they all go straight to the Viaduct Tavern. "Sam Snell allus drinks a pint there after his morning shift," Purdy said. "It's the best place to catch him, this time o' day." He then offered to buy Alfred a brandy while they were waiting for the flusher. "I daresay you need one, after your spell on the roof."

Alfred agreed. So it wasn't long before he and Jem were sidling into the taproom of the Viaduct, trying to ignore the looming bulk of Newgate Prison nearby. It astonished Jem that people could swill down their gin within yards of such a terrible place. How could they not feel guilty and hunted? It was like having a judge breathing down your neck.

"Why, if it ain't Mr. Bunce!" A familiar voice greeted them as they stepped into a room that Jem barely recognized. The crowds had melted away; the gas lamps were burning very low; the air smelled stale and sour. But Mabel Lillimere was in her usual spot behind the bar, wiping and shelving pint pots. "And Mr. Purdy, too!" she piped up. "So you found each other! I *am* glad. Here . . ." She reached under the bar and produced a bottle of brandy. "You'll not be paying a penny in *this* establishment, Mr. Bunce. I'm to tell you as how Mr. Watkins just hired his new potboy and won't be fretting about his safety, thanks to you and your 'prentice."

Alfred grunted. Jem grinned. Purdy, meanwhile, was peering around the room, which was almost deserted.

"Is Sam not in yet?" he asked. "I'll have my usual, by the by."

"I ain't seen Sam, but I expect to," the barmaid told him. She had already measured out Alfred's brandy and water. "Anything for the lad, Mr. Bunce?"

Delighted, Jem opened his mouth to order a quart pot of Dutch bitters. But Alfred spoke first.

"A dram o' cider," he said, before knocking back his brandy in one gulp.

Jem glowered at him.

"How did you fare on that roof?" asked Mabel. She seemed very well informed. As Hugh Purdy explained what had happened, Mabel listened intently. And though her eyes never left his face, she didn't spill a single drop of the various orders she was dispensing.

When the plumber finished, she nodded slowly. Then she turned to Alfred.

"There's someone needs to consult you, Mr. Bunce," she declared. "He's sexton at the church across the road."

"*Sexton?*" Jem echoed, almost choking on his cider. His experience with churchmen had never been good. They seemed to do nothing but preach at him—perhaps because he'd spent so much of his life picking pockets.

Though Alfred didn't say a word, his expression became wary.

"I can take you over there while Mr. Purdy waits for his friend," Mabel continued. "Mr. Froome would be *so* grateful. He's a lovely man, sir, and mortal worried."

"About what?" Alfred growled.

"Why, about his missing choirboy!" Mabel was already untying her apron. Before Alfred could protest, she turned her face to the nearest door and shouted, "Edgar! Where are you? Come here at once!" To Purdy, she said, "Edgar will look after you while I'm gone, since I'll not be more'n a minute away." Then she raised her voice again. "Edgar! You're to mind the bar, d'you hear?"

"I hear," Edgar replied, lumbering into view. He was a boy of about twelve, large and rawboned, with red hands, bloodshot eyes, and coarse, gingery hair. He wore a calf-length apron spattered with grease.

"I'll be back directly," Mabel told him. She produced a bonnet from some unseen locker, then stepped out from behind the bar. "Edgar's our new potboy," she informed Alfred, dragging her bonnet onto her head. "He's strong for his age, and cheap at the price. But he can thank *you* for his job, Mr. Bunce. We'd not have dared hire him if you hadn't killed that bogle!"

Jem was amused to see how meekly Alfred followed Mabel out of the tavern. With her hand tucked under his arm, she steered the captive bogler straight across Giltspur Street as if he were no older than Jem. He seemed unable to resist her. Though he dragged his feet and muttered under his breath, his dour expression was no match for the barmaid's bustling confidence.

Jem trailed after them. He kept his eyes peeled but saw no familiar faces on his way to Saint Sepulchre's. The church sat in a modest yard behind a fence of iron railings. Its main entrance lay farther down Newgate Street, beneath an elaborate porch. Here, an elderly man in a rusty black coat and knee breeches was sweeping dead leaves off the flagstones. He didn't see Mabel until she was almost on top of him.

"Why, it's Miss Lillimere!" he said in a cracked and quavering voice like the bleat of a broken reed instrument.

His hair was white, as were his side-whiskers. But he wore no beard or mustache. "Ye're too late for the morning service, lass."

"I didn't come for that, Mr. Froome." Releasing Alfred, Mabel laid a hand on the old man's arm. "This here is Mr. Alfred Bunce, the Go-Devil Man. He kills bogles for a living."

"The Go-Devil Man . . . ?" Mr. Froome peered at Alfred with small, pale, rheumy eyes. Alfred stared back morosely, adjusting the weight of his sack.

In the lengthening silence, Jem's gaze began to wander. He noticed that the ceiling of the porch was covered in extravagant carvings: shields, roses, doves, angels. They were all damp and soot blackened.

"Ye're a bogler?" Mr. Froome asked abruptly, just as Mabel was opening her mouth to prompt him.

"I am," Alfred replied.

"He killed a bogle in our cellar yesterday," Mabel volunteered. "And since you're missing a boy, Mr. Froome, I thought as how you might need Mr. Bunce."

The sexton blinked. Jem wondered if he was a little deaf, or senile. But then the old man cleared his throat and said to Alfred, "I once met a bogler in Lincoln. Name of Chaffey. D'ye know him?"

Alfred shook his head.

"Strange feller. Gypsy blood. Worth every penny,

mind." Leaning on his broom, the sexton seemed to escape for a moment into memories that left his eyes misty and his mouth slack. It wasn't long, however, before he shook off his reverie and asked, "How much do ye charge, Mr. Bunce?"

Alfred recited his fees in a low rumble, while Mabel edged past him. "I have to go," she said apologetically once he'd finished. "Edgar's so new, I don't trust him at the bar. But you'll not be needing me, I'm sure. Why, you're old enough to manage your own affairs!"

She chuckled at her own wit as a smile cracked across Mr. Froome's wizened features. "Allus a pleasure, Miss Lillimere," he assured her, touching his forehead as if he were tipping a hat. She responded with a nod and a wave, then headed back down Newgate Street.

Jem was watching her go when Mr. Froome said to him, "Ye're not from this parish. I'd know if ye were."

"I'm with Mr. Bunce." Jem cocked his thumb at Alfred. "I'm his 'prentice."

"What's yeer name?"

"Jem Barbary."

The old man nodded. He seemed satisfied. Moving a little stiffly, he tucked his broom under his arm, turned on his heel, and shuffled into the church. "I'd best show ye the crypt," he declared.

Alfred and Jem exchanged a doubtful glance before setting off after him.

"Is that where the child went missing? Down in yer crypt?" Alfred asked the sexton's retreating back—which was bent with age and ridged like a ship's keel.

"'Tis where the poor lad was last seen," Mr. Froome answered. His voice echoed slightly, bouncing off a very high, vaulted ceiling that was held up by two rows of columns. Jem was surprised at how big and white and empty the church was inside. No one was sitting in the pews or kneeling in front of the altar. No one was cleaning the brass.

"Show some respect," Alfred muttered, whisking the cap off Jem's head. He had already removed his own hat, which was now squashed under one arm. His boots squeaked loudly as he followed the sexton—who soon came to a halt by the southwest wall, where a short flight of stairs led down to a low arch fitted with an iron gate.

"We've no mortal remains tucked away here now," Mr. Froome remarked, putting aside his broom to fumble with the keys that hung on a chain around his neck. "Most of the old bones were took out in the fifties, on account of the cholera. The rest were moved to Ilford Cemetery when they dug up half the churchyard not long ago."

"Good," Jem mumbled. But Mr. Froome didn't hear him.

"The state of the foundations grows more sorry with each passing day. There's talk of backfilling the crypt, though I've heard such talk these twenty years and seen nothing come of it." Mr. Froome unlocked the gate and pushed it open, causing rusty hinges to squeal. "At present, I use the crypt for storage. Wood scraps. Old gravedigging tools. Things of that nature."

"Then why was the boy down here?" Alfred wanted to know. When the sexton didn't immediately reply, he began to ask the question again. "Why was —"

"Our choirmaster sent him down," Mr. Froome interrupted. "By way of punishment, or so I'm told. For singing sharp."

A brief silence fell. Alfred grimaced. Jem felt glad that *he* had never joined a parish choir. Then Mr. Froome observed, "We'll be needing a light."

"I have one," said Alfred. He produced his dark lantern as Jem peered into the undercroft, which looked very old and dirty. Ribbed vaults sprang from squat, stone columns. Irregular piles of junk were silting up corners. The floor was damp, and the air smelled of rot and mice and mold — and something else.

"Are you sure there ain't no corpses down here?" Jem asked nervously, forgetting that he was supposed to keep his mouth shut. Suddenly Alfred's lantern flared, pushing back the shadows.

"Not that I know of," Mr. Froome replied. To Alfred, he said, "Our choirmaster claims he released the boy. 'Tis my belief Mr. Tindall simply unlocked the gate and walked off without a second glance, being the sort of feller who has eyes only for his organ and ears only for his music." Watching Alfred scan the crypt, Mr. Froome coughed and added delicately, "Ye'll understand, Mr. Bunce, that our rector believes the boy ran away. He'll have no truck with the notion of bogles."

"Gentlemen never do," said Alfred. Then he stiffened. "What's that?" he barked, pointing at the crown of an archway embedded in a distant wall. It was partly concealed by the planks of wood propped against it.

"That?" said Mr. Froome. "Why, that's the old Newgate tunnel."

"The what?"

"The tunnel to the prison." Seeing Alfred's blank expression, Mr. Froome tried to explain. "Back in the old days, the sextons of this church would ring a hand bell outside the condemned cell at Newgate on the night before a hanging. But the crowds used to gather so early that they blocked the path of anyone leaving the church too late. So this secret tunnel was built." As Jem shuddered, staring aghast at the murky void, Mr. Froome suddenly broke into verse. "'All ye that in the condemned cell do lie,'" he intoned, "'prepare ye, for tomorrow ye shall die. Watch all, and pray, the hour

is drawing near, that ye before the Almighty must appear.'"
When his voice cracked, he stopped and cleared his throat.
"I've forgot most of the text," he admitted. "It was recited in
full for the prisoners' solace. But I never was charged with
the duty myself, thanks be to God."

"It came from in there," Alfred said flatly.

The sexton gaped at him. "What?"

"The bogle. It's a-waiting down that passage." Alfred
nodded at the tunnel, a mirthless half smile tweaking the corner of his mouth. "Yer boy's dead and gone, Mr. Froome,"
he announced, "for that there is a bogle's den if ever I
saw one."

THE CRYPT BOGLE

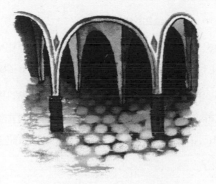

Alfred laid down his ring of salt not far from the tunnel's entrance. He wouldn't let Mr. Froome shift any bits of rubbish around, explaining that he didn't want the bogle disturbed. So the mouth of the tunnel remained half blocked by a broken pew back.

Jem was told to wait on the stairs until Alfred was ready.

"And what should *I* do, Mr. Bunce?" asked the sexton. "Stand by with an andiron? Or mebbe a pickax would be better . . ."

"Bogles is fast movers, Mr. Froome," Alfred replied. "If

I was you, I'd keep me distance. I'll tell you when it's safe to come back."

The old man seemed to accept this. He gave a thoughtful nod, then offered to fetch Alfred's fee. "If ye've no objection, Mr. Bunce, I'll record this payment in our books as 'expenses pertaining to vermin,'" he said. "For the rector won't question a rat catcher's hire."

"I ain't got no problem with that, Mr. Froome."

"And I'll fetch a pair of boots while I'm about it," the sexton added, patting Jem's head on his way up the stairs. "For I mislike seeing a lad in work go barefoot. And there's a good supply of old boots in the vestry, thanks to our parochial mission."

Jem perked up when he heard this. He had been sitting very quietly, trying to ignore the tremor in his hands and the sweat on his brow. For some reason he was far more anxious about this job than he'd been about the last. But the offer of free boots made him feel much better.

It was a month at least since he'd worn through his previous pair.

"You ain't to hawk them boots," Alfred warned him once they were alone. "I know Sarah Pickles used to make all her boys beg 'em off charities to sell or pawn, but I'll not have you do it."

"I weren't about to!" Jem replied, stung. He would

have said more if Alfred hadn't put a finger to his lips and muttered, "Not another word, now. Here's yer looking glass. There's yer position. Don't take yer eyes off me — and *don't let yer guard down*. Understand? This is the third bogle we've found in the neighborhood, and there ain't no telling how many more might be lurking nearby."

Jem swallowed. By this time his heart was pounding so hard that he feared it would burst through his rib cage. "You mean — you mean you think there's more'n one in the tunnel?" he squeaked. But Alfred silenced him by pushing Birdie's mirror into his hands.

Soon Jem was stepping carefully into the ring of salt while Alfred positioned himself beside the tunnel entrance. A wash of daylight spilled down the stairs in front of Jem but didn't reach the shadowy regions behind him, where Alfred stood with his salt and his spear. Only the dark lantern illumined Alfred's coattails, waistcoat buttons, and long, bony, solemn face.

Jem's hands were shaking so much that he found it hard to frame Alfred in his little square of glass — or to recognize the bogler's signal when he saw it. He thought Alfred's nod was caused by his own tremor. But when Alfred hissed, and nodded again, Jem realized that he was supposed to start singing.

So he did.

"The night afore Larry were stretch'd,
The boys they all paid him a visit;
A bit in their sacks too, they fetch'd—
They sweated their duds till they riz it."

Jem's voice wobbled like jelly. Something about the crypt frightened him far more than the tavern cellar had. Was it that ominous tunnel to Newgate? Had the corpses once buried here left a lingering miasma? Or was the hidden bogle somehow making him feel like this?

Telling himself not to be so craven, Jem took several deep, calming breaths before launching into the second verse of his song.

"For Larry were allus the lad,
When a friend were condemned
*   to the squeezer,*
He'd pawn all the togs that he had
Just to help the poor boy to a sneezer."

A scraping noise suddenly reached Jem's ears. It was the tiniest sound, but it caused him to shift his gaze slightly from Alfred's reflection to the wooden planks propped across the tunnel's mouth.

Something was creeping through a black space between these planks. The light was so poor that at first Jem thought he'd spotted a huge spider. But then he realized that the hairy, jointed legs silently fanning out were, in fact, giant fingers. And they were connected to four long, hairy arms, which slowly unfolded like carpenters' rules as they emerged from the darkness.

Jem paused and swallowed, then continued to sing.

> *" 'Pon me conscience, dear Larry,' says I,*
> *'I'm that sorry to see you in trouble,*
> *And yer life's cheerful noggin run dry,*
> *And yerself going off like its bubble!' "*

The body attached to the arms was a great hairy bladder, propped up on legs like a toad's and crowned by a head bigger than a bull's. The bogle's horns weren't like a bull's, though; they were as barbed and twisted as weathered chunks of thorn hedge. Its snout was long, with flaring red nostrils and a double row of huge, dripping, steely fangs. Its eyes were on fire.

Jem tried not to look. He was having trouble breathing. But he managed to stammer out another verse.

> *" 'H-hold yer tongue in that matter,' says he,*
> *'F-for the neck-cloth I don't care a button,*
> *And by this time tomorrow you'll see*
> *That yer Larry will be dead as —' "*

Alfred lunged. Jem shrieked. He dropped his mirror as he threw himself straight over the salt and into a forward roll — and another — and another. He completed four somersaults, bowling along like a hoop, until he fetched up against the opposite wall, upside down with his legs in the air.

Behind him, something exploded.

He heard the crackling roar and saw the green flash. He even felt the heat. But by the time he'd slid sideways and righted himself, the flame had been snuffed out. Nothing was left of the bogle except a huge black scorch mark — and a truly awful smell of burnt hair.

Even the salt had turned brown.

"I don't like the look o' that," Alfred said hoarsely. He was standing at the edge of the circle, his mustache singed and his face dusted with soot. When he disturbed the salt with the toe of his boot, it made a sizzling noise. "Don't you touch it, d'you hear? It might be poison."

"I won't," Jem mumbled. He staggered to his feet, vaguely aware that his left knee was smarting. "I dropped the looking glass," he quavered. "I — I don't know where it is."

"Mebbe it's broke," said Alfred, who was now rummaging through his sack. Jem blanched. He knew that a broken mirror meant seven years' bad luck.

But when he finally *did* find the mirror, it wasn't in

pieces. It had turned into a pool of black glass, which had fused to the floor.

"What does that mean?" he asked Alfred as they surveyed it together. "Is it good luck or bad luck?"

"It's bad luck for me," Alfred replied, wiping his face with his neckerchief, "since I must buy another."

Jem flushed. "I'm sorry," he croaked. He felt sick and dizzy and ashamed.

Alfred shrugged. Jem wanted to ask if the cost of the next mirror would be deducted from his own wages. He wanted to suggest that they hang any future glass on a string around his neck, to prevent further mishaps. He wanted to find out if Birdie had ever broken a mirror, and if not, whether a broken mirror was grounds for dismissal.

But he wasn't given the chance to speak, because Alfred began to hustle him upstairs—where the sexton was patiently waiting.

"Well?" asked Mr. Froome. He carried a pair of brown boots and was flanked by two men: Hugh Purdy and a blond giant who wore a fantailed hat. Jem assumed that the stranger must be Purdy's friend the sewer flusher.

"It's done," Alfred told Mr. Froome. He then nodded at Purdy before shifting his gaze to the flusher, who had a silver tooth, pierced ears, and a tattoo on his wrist.

"Sam Snell at yer service, Mr. Bunce," the flusher announced with a wide grin, shaking Alfred's hand enthusiastically. "I never *did* think I'd meet a genuine Go-Devil Man, though it's bin a dream o' mine since I were nobbut a young shaver!"

Alfred blinked. Then Sam Snell released him and turned to Jem, saying, "So you're the brave lad as hunts down them bogles, eh? I'd ha' given me right arm to do the same, as a boy, but went to sea instead."

He proceeded to shake Jem's hand vigorously, his blue eyes twinkling and his silver tooth glinting. Jem couldn't help smiling back. He'd been feeling so bad about the broken mirror that he welcomed any praise he could get. And he'd always admired seamen.

"You're a scrap of a child to be facing down bogles," the flusher continued. "And a mite green around the gills, besides. Mebbe you need a shot o' liquor." He appealed to his friend. "We should buy 'em a drink, Hugh!"

"Nay," said Alfred. He looked a little distracted, as if something was preying on his mind. "We have to go now. Unless we're needed in the sewers, Mr. Purdy?"

"Uh—no. Not yet." The plumber explained that Sam would have to speak to his foreman, and his foreman to an inspector, before Alfred would be allowed inside the Holborn Viaduct. "But Sam ain't expecting no trouble. He says if they had boys working the sewers—which they don't— they'd have hired a bogler long since."

The flusher nodded fervently. "I've said all along there's

bogles, but no one's had the spine to take it to the Sewers Office."

"I see." Alfred seemed anxious to quell the talkative flusher (who may have been a little drunk, Jem thought). "Well, you know where to find me if you hear any more," the bogler said to Purdy, before addressing Mr. Froome. "There's traces in the crypt you should be wary of. I've doused it in holy water, but I wouldn't touch it without gloves."

"I understand," said Mr. Froome. "And I'll be careful."

"Have you ever heard owt from Newgate Prison?" Alfred went on. "About young'uns escaping from the cells, or some such thing?"

"I have not."

"Then you'd best keep yer ears open." Seeing the sexton blink, Alfred sighed and explained, "That there tunnel is a perfect bogle's lair, and might be sheltering others where it joins the prison. Even if it's bin emptied, I'm inclined to think a second creature might move in. For this corner o' town ain't like no other. There's more bogles here than I've ever come across in one place, and it troubles me. Very much."

"Oh, dear," Mr. Froome quavered. Then he gave Alfred his fee and Jem his boots, remarking to Jem as he did so, "I hope these fit. There's a stocking in each."

"Thank'ee, sir." Jem bobbed his head, almost teary

with gratitude. He couldn't understand why he was feeling so shaken. The bogle was dead. He was alive. And Alfred wasn't the type to beat an apprentice for breaking a mirror.

Yet Jem felt like sobbing his heart out just because he'd been given a new pair of boots.

Puzzled and mortified, he pulled them on while Alfred said his goodbyes to the others. But when at last they emerged onto Newgate Street together, Jem said to Alfred, in a very small voice, "Is a dead bogle as bad as a live one for making you low spirited?"

Alfred shot him a quick, measuring glance. "Not as far as I know."

"Mmph." Jem fell silent. Alfred waited. He and Jem both donned their hats, walking toward the nearest bus stop through the milling crowds. Jem's feet felt oddly clumsy, wedged into their casings of stiff leather.

At last Alfred observed, "Birdie never broke no looking glass, but she once dropped a flask o' brandy into a cesspit."

Jem brightened. "She did?"

"Aye. *And* tried to claim the bogle took it." Alfred gave a snort of laughter. "Ask her yerself when we get to Bloomsbury. She'll tell you I ain't lying."

"We're going to Bloomsbury?" asked Jem, diverted by this news. "Why?"

"Because I don't understand what's happening here." Alfred's eyes narrowed as he scanned his surroundings, almost as if he expected to see bogles slithering along the gutters. "Bogles ain't like pigeons," he said. "They don't travel in flocks. So why is this corner o' London crawling with 'em?" Without waiting for an answer, he continued, "Miss Eames is book learned. *She* might know why. And she might know what to do about it, besides. For I tell you, lad"—he shook his head gloomily—"I'm flummoxed."

12

Jam Tarts for Tea

Bogles don't hunt in packs," said Alfred. "I ain't never seen more'n one bogle every half a mile, even along the river. So what's three of 'em doing within a stone's throw o' Newgate Prison?"

He was sitting in a flowery little parlor, full of books and pictures, stuffed birds, embroidered cushions, spindly furniture, clocks, tassels, and crocheted doilies. Jem and Birdie were with him, as were Miss Eames and her aunt, Mrs. Heppinstall. They were gathered around a low mahogany table laid with a linen cloth, a silver tea service, and a plate of jam tarts.

Jem had already eaten three of the tarts. He had also drunk two large cups of sugary tea. In fact, he'd been so busy stuffing his mouth that he'd hardly said a word since arriving on Miss Eames's doorstep. He'd said "Hello" to Birdie on first entering the house. He'd said "Yes, please" when offered a jam tart by Mrs. Heppinstall. And he'd muttered a few vague words of approval after hearing from Miss Eames that all the posters with Birdie's name on them had been removed from Josiah Lubbock's penny gaff.

"I went there this morning, just to make sure," she'd told her two visitors before shepherding them into the parlor.

But it was Alfred who'd done most of the talking. Very slowly and carefully, stopping occasionally to sip his tea or shake his head, he had described his adventures around Newgate Prison in great detail before finally coming to the point. "In all yer reading," he asked Miss Eames, "did you ever stumble upon a *pack* o' bogles, hunting close together? For I never did." Seeing Miss Eames frown, he added, "Could they be foreign, d'you think? Or Scotch?"

"Scotch?" she echoed, then leaned forward to put down her teacup. She was beautifully dressed, as usual; Jem calculated that the blue-velvet trimming on her jacket was worth at least eight shillings a yard. "In all honesty, Mr. Bunce, Scotch bogles tend to be lonely guardians tied to particular places," she replied. "Like the Baisd Bheulach, for instance, or even the Loch Ness Monster. However, I've read about some creatures who are mentioned always in the plural. The *sluagh*. The *brollachan*. The Dunters and the Red Caps, which infest certain border castles—"

"Aye, but do they haunt in clusters, or is it one for each castle?" Alfred interrupted. "And if they *do* mix, do they all look the same, or differ as much as a pig differs from a duck?"

Miss Eames blinked.

"Why, Mr. Bunce, what a *very* odd question," said Mrs. Heppinstall, who had been listening with great interest as she poured the tea. She wore a black gown, a gray shawl, and a white lace cap. Her silvery hair formed two little bunches of ringlets over her ears. "What on earth do you mean by that?"

"Jem knows." Alfred nodded in Jem's direction. "He saw 'em. Why don't you tell Miss Eames what they was like, lad?"

Jem had to swallow a mouthful of pastry before he could oblige. "The cellar bogle looked to be made o' black gelatin," he said thickly, spraying crumbs everywhere. "The crypt bogle had a wolf's head, and a monkey's arms, and a toad's legs—"

"They was like chalk and cheese." Alfred cut him off before he could finish. "If they hadn't bin, I'd have started wondering if I'd even *killed* the first. On account of how close it were living to the second."

"I see." Miss Eames nodded, pursing her lips. Meanwhile, on the couch beside her — which was upholstered in a green damask that Jem valued at three shillings and sixpence a yard — Birdie McAdam was wriggling about like a worm on a hook, impatient to have her say.

"Mebbe all o' them bogles was cast from their old haunts," she suggested. When the others stared at her blankly, she turned to Alfred. "You just said there's houses coming down and houses going up over by Newgate Street," she reminded him. "And new railway tunnels and sewers being laid . . ."

"Aye," Alfred confirmed.

"Well, what if that's flushed out the bogles?" Birdie argued. "Like roaches when you shift a bin?"

"Yes, of course!" Miss Eames brightened. "That *would* make sense!"

"Clever girl," Mrs. Heppinstall said fondly, patting Birdie's arm.

But Alfred didn't look convinced. "Even if all the new work *is* flushing bogles out o' their dens," he objected, "that don't explain why they ain't spreading out, instead o' clumping together."

"Perhaps it's territorial," said Miss Eames. Alfred grunted. Jem reached for another jam tart.

Then Mrs. Heppinstall gently inquired, "Would you care for something else, Jem? A tongue sandwich, perhaps? Jam tarts don't build sturdy bones."

Jem's mouth was already full, so he nodded. Mrs. Heppinstall immediately rang the little silver bell at her side, as Alfred continued in a glum, slightly anxious tone, "What's worrying me is where this might lead. If there's so many bogles about, what's to stop 'em living in the same lair? Suppose I do another job and find there's more'n one to deal with? What then?"

Birdie hissed. Jem shuddered.

Miss Eames frowned again. "But, Mr. Bunce," she said, "I thought you had abandoned bogling? Except in this one instance, of course . . ."

"I swore I'd clear out Holborn Viaduct," Alfred retorted stubbornly. "And that's what I'm a-going to do. But if I take Jem down the sewers and find two bogles instead o' one, what then?"

"Let *me* go!" Birdie cried. She began to bounce up and down, making springs creak and petticoats rustle. "I'll distract one bogle while Jem lures the other! We can work as a pair!"

"You'll do no such thing," Miss Eames said in a crisp, reproving voice.

"You can't stop me!" Birdie shot back. And before Mrs. Heppinstall— or even Alfred—could protest, she added,

"If you don't let me go, I'll walk out! I shall! And you won't never see me again!"

"Birdie, *dear* . . ." Mrs. Heppinstall bleated, as Miss Eames matched Birdie's scowl with her own.

"Nonsense!" snapped Miss Eames. "Don't be foolish, Birdie. Where on earth would you go?"

"Mr. Bunce'll take me back. Won't you, Mr. Bunce?" Birdie fixed a pair of big, blue, beseeching eyes on Alfred, who dragged a hand over the pouches and hollows of his face, muttering something inaudible.

Jem said nothing. Though he was anxious about his own little hard-won corner of Alfred's room, he knew that if Birdie laid claim to it, he wouldn't stand a chance. All he could do was glare at her, hoping that she would come to her senses. Why would anyone wearing silk hair ribbons and lace-trimmed petticoats want to live in a tiny attic room full of red dust?

She was mad, he thought.

Then the maid entered. And before Mrs. Heppinstall could ask for a tongue sandwich, her niece suddenly re-marked, "Take the children upstairs, Mary. Jem wants to see Birdie's room, I'm sure."

Jem blinked at her. Birdie exclaimed, "No, he don't!"

"I wish to talk to Mr. Bunce," Miss Eames declared. "In private."

"But—"

"Do as you're told, lass." At last Alfred decided to intercede, raising his voice from its usual low rumble and fixing Birdie with one of his hard, dark looks. "This ain't yer house," he said. "Seems to me you've lost respect since you come here. I thought I raised you better."

To Jem's surprise, Birdie didn't answer back. Instead, she colored, rose, and began to walk out of the room, straight backed and fuming. Jem leaped up to follow her — though not without grabbing another jam tart.

"And, Birdie?" Miss Eames called after her. "Remember what I told you about double negatives."

"Double negatives," Birdie muttered under her breath as she stomped into the hallway. "I'll give *you* double negatives!" Though Jem couldn't see her expression, he knew from her tone that she was furious.

Mary watched them both trudge upstairs with a smug look on her face.

"D'you think I'll get that sandwich?" Jem asked Birdie once they had left the first landing behind. He was amazed to see that the stair carpet ran all the way to the upper floor — and that there were just as many pictures and fans and mirrors covering the walls in this private region of the house as there were in the more public spaces downstairs.

"If it's food you want, you'd be better off in the kitchen," Birdie growled. She led him into one of the best bedrooms, which contained a shiny brass bedstead heaped with feather pillows, a large chest of drawers, an array of china figurines, a fireplace, a chair, a washstand, a dressing table, a looking glass, and a paraffin lamp. The walls were papered in a floral design that matched the curtains. An Axminster carpet lay on the floor.

"Is this *your* room?" Jem was astounded. "I thought you slept in the attic!"

"I did, at first," said Birdie, heading straight for the fireplace. "But then they moved me here."

"No wonder the maid hates you." Jem gazed around, shaking his head in wonder. "You're addled," he announced. "Why kick up a fuss when you got all this? I'd rather live here than at Alfred's."

"That's because you don't understand what it's like." Squatting in front of the grate, Birdie took a brass-handled poker and thrust it straight up the chimney. "You think it's all jam tarts and silk shifts, but it ain't. They won't let you do *nothing* without permission. They tell you how to talk and walk and sit and stand—"

"What's that you're doing now?" Jem interrupted. She seemed to be dislodging a loose brick. "If you're trying to bring down the chimney, I'll not be a party to it."

"Don't be stupid." Birdie's tone was scornful. "This is how I eavesdrop. The flue leads straight up from the dining room, so if the folding doors are open, I can hear everything they say in the parlor."

"Oh." Jem munched on his jam tart as Birdie wriggled into the fireplace. She then put her ear to the hole she'd made, ignoring Jem, who began to inspect the contents of her room. The cane-seated chair was worth about three shillings, he guessed. The washstand had a marble top. Birdie's brushes were backed with horn, and she had a workbox inlaid with mother-of-pearl.

"They're talking about Ned," Birdie suddenly revealed from her listening post. "*She* wants to know why Ned can't help. Mr. Bunce is saying Ned would lose his job if he missed a day."

"Which is the truth," said Jem. He picked up a little silver casket, checked inside, and saw that it was full of sugar pastilles. For some reason, the discovery made him furious. "You're off yer head, wanting to leave this place and live in a dirty garret!" he spluttered.

"*You* chose to live in an East End cellar," Birdie rejoined.

"Only because I'm looking for Sarah Pickles!"

"Shhh!" Birdie flapped her hand at him. "They're talking about me now . . ."

But Jem had already fallen silent. Something was stirring in the back of his mind. Sarah Pickles . . . garrets . . .

Birdie gave a sudden squeal. "Miss Eames says I can do it!" she crowed. "As long as she comes too!" When Jem didn't respond, Birdie turned around to see why. "Did you hear? We'll be going down the viaduct together!"

"Shhh!" Jem was holding his temples with both hands. The name was on the tip of his tongue. It was so close, he could almost smell it . . .

"What ails you?" Birdie demanded. "Is it a headache?"

"Eunice Pickles!" Jem blurted out.

"What?"

"Sarah's daughter! Eunice Pickles!" Jem gazed at her wildly, amazed that he could have forgotten about Eunice. "I seen her in the streets around Newgate! She's living there, I'd swear to it! And if *she's* there . . . why, then, *so is her ma!*"

13

THE PROPOSITION

That night Jem dreamed of Sarah Pickles. He dreamed that he was hiding under the bed in her garret lodgings, which he'd only ever visited twice in all his years of faithful service. The first time, he'd gone there with her son Charlie to collect some tools for a break-and-enter job in Islington. The second time, he'd been sent there all alone with a delivery of silver plate.

On both occasions, Eunice Pickles had been hovering in the background, fat and frumpy and silent. She'd had the look of someone who spent all day sweeping floors and boiling bacon. But in Jem's dream, she was trying to lure him out from beneath the bed with a plate of jam tarts, as Sarah waited behind her, ax in hand.

Then Jem felt something coil around his ankle, and realized that a bogle had broken through the floorboards . . .

"Aaaah!" He woke with a cry and sat bolt upright.

"Nightmare?" asked Ned, who was perched on a nearby stool, tying his boots.

Jem nodded, dry mouthed. It was still very early. Alfred lay snoring on the other side of the room, under a pile of coats and blankets. Ned hadn't lit the lamp because a pale gray wash of light was leaking through the window.

"You'll need to stoke the fire," Ned observed. "*And* empty the bucket."

"I know," rasped Jem.

"What was the dream about?"

"None o' yer business."

"I'll wager it had bogles in it."

Jem scowled. It irritated him that someone who'd been scouring mud flats for a living only six months before should suddenly look so prosperous and respectable. Despite his missing teeth and scarred hands, Ned knew how to present himself. His mop of dark curls was always neatly combed now. His square-cut face was always buffed clean, and every tear in his shirt had been expertly mended. He wore new boots, a new cap, and a new blue coat with three brass buttons.

He'd even become more talkative, thanks to long days spent selling fruit off the back of a barrow. And though he was barely eight months older than Jem, he was already much larger.

Jem couldn't help feeling that he'd been outstripped. That was why he reached for his own new boots, which he thought were much finer than Ned's. But before he had a chance to pull them on, someone knocked at the door. *Rat-tat-tat-tat.*

Ned glanced over at Alfred, then asked Jem, "Is he expecting company?"

Jem shrugged. Ned sighed and went to answer the door, which swung open to reveal Josiah Lubbock. The showman had abandoned his purple topper and silver lace; instead, he wore a plain tweed lounge suit and a bowler hat.

"Good day to you!" he said cheerfully. "Am I right in thinking that this is the residence of Mr. Alfred Bunce?"

"Uh—yes," Ned replied.

"But he'll not want to see *you*," Jem added.

"Oh, I wouldn't be so sure of that," said Mr. Lubbock. "Not until he hears my proposal." He began to shoulder his way past Ned as Alfred stirred and coughed on the other side of the room.

"Here!" Jem jumped up. "What d'you think you're doing? No one asked you in!"

Ignoring him, the showman addressed Alfred. "Mr. Bunce, I have a proposition. If you allow me to accompany you on your next job, and bring at least one paying customer with me, there'll be a ten-shilling fee in it for you." Mr. Lubbock removed his hat as Alfred sat up in bed, unshaven and bleary eyed. "People pay handsomely to watch dogs kill rats," Mr. Lubbock went on, "and would pay even more to see you kill a bogle."

Alfred hawked and spat. "How in the devil did you find me?" he croaked.

"Why, I heard Miss Eames give your address to the cabdriver the day before yesterday." Mr. Lubbock seemed completely unfazed by all the bits of paper dangling overhead. Even Alfred's disheveled, red-eyed, half-dressed condition didn't appear to trouble him. He simply plowed on, oblivious to Jem's scowl and Alfred's coughing and Ned's sudden restlessness.

"I must go or I'll be late," Ned murmured to no one in particular, then slipped into the hallway and shut the door behind him.

Mr. Lubbock didn't so much as pause to take a breath.

"Since then I've been sounding the market, Mr. Bunce, and I can assure you that there *is* an audience for bogle baiting. One naturalist of my acquaintance—who originally came to me expressing an interest in my preserved griffin—has promised to stump up a whole *pound* for the privilege of a ringside seat." Before Alfred could do more than yawn, Mr. Lubbock added, with an ingratiating smile, "I thought it only fair to split this sum down the middle, you understand."

"Hah!" Jem gave a snort. "Which is to say, yer friend promised *two* pounds, and you'll be pocketing three-quarters of it!"

"Oh, no, no." Mr. Lubbock wagged a finger at him. "That's not the way I conduct my business, young man."

Alfred, meanwhile, was climbing stiffly out of bed. His nightshirt was flapping around his bony white ankles. "The answer is no, Mr. Lubbock," he said.

"But surely—"

"Bogling's dangerous. Too dangerous for spectators."

"Oh, come now," Mr. Lubbock chided. "How dangerous can it be if you have children working with you?"

Jem scowled. He wanted to ask Mr. Lubbock how *he* would react if cornered by a bogle. Then he saw Alfred's expression and decided not to speak after all.

"I don't pull untrained kids off the street and set 'em to work," Alfred said through his teeth. He shuffled past Mr. Lubbock, making for the door. "Besides, bogles don't like crowds."

"It wouldn't be a crowd," Mr. Lubbock assured him. "Two or three people at the *most*—"

"Even one is too many." Alfred grabbed the doorknob. "Good day to you, Mr. Lubbock," he said, then pulled the door open—and nearly jumped out of his skin.

Two familiar figures were standing on the threshold.

"Mr. Bunce!" Hugh Purdy exclaimed. His raised fist suggested that he'd been about to knock. Beside him, Sam Snell was holding his fantailed hat in both hands but was otherwise fully decked out in his flushers' gear: a blue oilskin coat, fishermen's boots, and leather gauntlets.

While Alfred stared at him, Purdy continued, "We're that sorry to rouse you so early in the day, sir, but you told us to look you up when we heard more. Which we have."

"Our Inspector o' Sewers has given us leave to take you down the tunnels," Sam Snell interposed. "So we was wondering if you'd care to do it now, Mr. Bunce?" Catching sight of Josiah Lubbock, the flusher added genially, "And anyone else you might care to bring along is more'n welcome, o' course."

"Indeed?" said Mr. Lubbock. But Alfred rounded on him.

"You ain't invited," Alfred snarled. "Get out o' here."

"Sir—"

"Now!"

Startled, Purdy and Snell both stepped back to clear

a way for the showman, who made a dignified, if slightly hurried, exit. "Mr. Josiah Lubbock, at your service," he informed the other two visitors—perhaps in the hope of securing their names. Alfred, however, was already hustling Purdy and Snell into his room.

After slamming the door in Mr. Lubbock's face, he turned to them and said, "Don't pay *him* no mind. He's a liar."

Hugh Purdy nodded politely, prepared to drop the subject. His friend, however, was more inquisitive.

"What did he want?" asked Snell.

"Nowt." Alfred's tone was brusque. He addressed the plumber. "Where are you expecting us? And when?"

"Oh." Purdy's face fell. "Can you not come now?"

"There's someone else needs to be fetched first, and that might take time." Alfred didn't elaborate, but Jem realized that he was talking about Birdie.

As the plumber sighed, his friend said, "We'll meet you at twelve o'clock, then, after I finish me shift. Under the bridge is the best place."

Alfred nodded. He was eyeing Sam Snell's waterproof clothes. "We ain't got no sou'westers," he pointed out.

The flusher dismissed this concern with a wave of his hand. "You'll not likely need 'em."

"And there's to be a lady with us," Alfred finished. Jem

saw the two visitors exchange a surprised look. But even this news didn't put a dent in Sam Snell's good humor.

"Why, and I'd be proud to escort any lady as would show an interest!" he declared with a grin. "Only tell her not to wear her Sunday best."

"I'll do that," said Alfred. He had the slightly impatient look of someone who wanted a moment's peace to dress and shave and empty his bladder. But before he could invite his guests to leave, one of them launched into yet another plea for help.

"There's something else I must ask you, Mr. Bunce, while I've got yer ear," Sam Snell announced. "I've a friend as works at Smithfield Market who's bin a-fretting over stories told by some o' the lads there, about a missing butcher's apprentice."

"Oh, aye." Alfred didn't sound very encouraging. Jem's heart sank.

Not another one, he thought.

"There's all manner o' railway sidings under the new market, where porters unload carcasses from the trains and transport 'em straight up to the main building in hydraulic lifts," the flusher explained. "And though it's a busy place, day *and* night, it ain't without its quiet corners—"

"They've got a bogle under the market? Is that what you're saying?" Alfred interrupted.

"Well, sir, that's what Bob's a-wondering, now he's heard there's a plague o' bogles just down the street." Snell went on to inform Alfred that his friend Bob Ballard had heard reports of "summat strange" near the sidings—and that a trucker's boy had last been seen picking up meat scraps from the Smithfield platforms.

"I understand." Alfred cut him off, rubbing his furrowed brow as if he had a headache before turning to the plumber and asking, "Is that what the folk round Newgate call it? A plague o' bogles?"

Purdy nodded. "In the Viaduct Tavern they do," he replied.

Alfred shook his head morosely. "It's the truth," he muttered. "I ain't never seen nowt like it before . . ."

"But you'll come, sir?" Sam Snell's tone was both eager and breezy, as if he had no doubt whatsoever that Alfred would oblige.

Something about his unyielding confidence must have influenced Alfred, who heaved a weary sigh of resignation and growled, "I'll come. Tell yer friend I'll come tomorrow morning."

Snell beamed his thanks. "Bob'll be right grateful," he assured Alfred, "for his own son is 'prenticed at the markets, and Bob's wife won't let the lad set foot there since hearing about them missing boys . . ."

Jem grinned sourly as Snell chattered on. How nice it

would be to have a mother who cared about your safety! No one cared about Jem's safety. No one had bothered to ask him how he felt about tackling another bogle. Alfred hadn't even consulted him about taking Birdie along with them.

It didn't matter, though. That was what Jem told himself. The important thing was that they were returning to the neighborhood around Newgate Street.

For it was there, beneath the unsuspecting noses of London's largest collection of magistrates, that Sarah Pickles had cleverly chosen to hide herself.

14

Into the Viaduct

From down on Farringdon Street, the viaduct bridge was a dazzling sight. Its ironwork was a tangle of flowers and dragons, picked out in red and gold. Its pale stone plinths were carved and gilded. At either end of the bridge, the two staircases connecting Farringdon Street with the road above it were encased in a pair of elaborate, five-story buildings, each of which looked to Jem like a cross between a palace and a big white wedding cake.

But the iron gates beneath the arch weren't quite so ornamental. They were barred like prison gates, with a lock on them that could have kept out an army of elephants. "Sam's ganger has the key," said Hugh Purdy, who had arrived at the bridge just minutes before Alfred's small crew. After being introduced to Miss Eames and Birdie, the plumber explained that he'd parted company with Sam Snell earlier that morning—but that Sam would be bringing his ganger, Nathaniel Calthrop, to meet them all.

"What is a 'ganger'?" Miss Eames inquired. She and Birdie both wore dark, sturdy fabrics: brown holland, gray tweed, black worsted. Each of them carried a pair of Wellington boots in a drawstring bag made of canvas. Birdie's hair had been pinned up under a small, untrimmed bowler hat.

"Why, a ganger is a foreman," Purdy replied, just as a series of thumps and clicks startled everyone. These noises seemed to be coming from the wooden doors behind the iron gates. Then the doors swung inward, revealing Sam Snell and a plump little man with an enormous red mustache.

Both men were dressed from head to toe in waterproof clothing.

"Come in, come in!" Sam Snell exclaimed, unlocking the gates from the inside. "This here is Nat Calthrop. Mr. Calthrop, this is Mr. Bunce, and Mr. Purdy, and . . . um . . ." He trailed off as he spotted Miss Eames, who promptly stuck out her hand and said, in a brisk and manly way, "Miss Edith Eames. How d'you do?"

Snell shook hands vigorously, grinning with delight.

His boss didn't look quite so pleased. With his jaundiced skin, orange mustache, sour expression, and squat, round shape, Calthrop made Jem think of a giant lemon. The ganger nodded at Purdy and grunted at Alfred. Jem received only a suspicious glare. When Miss Eames smiled, Calthrop mumbled a greeting. But he stared at Birdie in dismay.

"Naebody said aught about a wee lass," he protested.

"Oh, she'll not be a bother," Snell assured him cheerfully. "Don't you fret, Mr. Calthrop. I'll look after her."

"I can look after myself!" Birdie retorted, much to Snell's amusement.

"Is that so?" he said with a chuckle. Then Calthrop asked him if he wanted to spend all day loitering on Farringdon Street, and Snell said no.

Soon they were marching up a short flight of narrow stairs, following Calthrop's safety lamp into the depths of the viaduct.

Jem was amazed at what he saw as he trudged along. He'd been expecting something small and damp and dirty, but the brick-lined tunnel into which they finally emerged was about six feet wide by ten high, with a solid stone floor. Along one wall ran a bundle of pipes and cables, which Sam Snell identified as gas and water mains, telegraph wires, and pneumatic tubes. In the arched ceiling, gratings admitted pools of light from the street above. The sewers, Snell explained, were at the bottom of another, vaulted chamber that lay below their feet.

"And beneath *that* is the low-level sewer, which crosses under the viaduct, along Farringdon Street," the flusher concluded. "But that ain't connected to the viaduct ventilation shafts."

"If yeer boggart climbed onto a roof, as Sam claims, it maun bide in the subway sewer," Calthrop volunteered.

"Aye, but *where* in the sewer?" said Alfred. Jem could understand his concern. The subway looked endless, and the sewer beneath it had to be just as long. How were they going to find the exact location of Purdy's unfinished house from down in this dark, underground burrow?

"If someone lifts me up, I can peek through that grate over there," Jem offered. "Mebbe we'll get our bearings if I do that."

Sam Snell burst out laughing. "Why, there ain't no need for circus tricks, lad!" he exclaimed. "We got every street and house number marked along here, so the connections can be cut in an emergency." He then lifted his safety lamp, illuminating all the words and numbers painted on the northern wall.

"How clever," said Miss Eames in an admiring tone. "So we simply have to find the correct number and go straight down from there?"

"Through the nearest manhole. Aye," Calthrop agreed.

"It ain't far." Suddenly Hugh Purdy spoke up. He had been peering at the house numbers. "No more'n a hundred yards or so to the west, I'd say."

"Then off we go!" his friend declared happily. It was Calthrop, however, who took the lead again.

They moved off in a single file, past drainpipes and belltraps that connected the road above to the sewer below. Calthrop didn't say a word, but Sam Snell entertained everyone with an account of the remarkably large rats that infested the sewers. He also kept reassuring Miss Eames that she had nothing to fear from coal or sewer gas. "For we tested the air with Davy lamps this very morning and found nothing amiss. Why, I could light a pipe in perfect comfort!"

Jem wanted to ask why, if there wasn't any gas, the air still smelled faintly of sewage. But before he could speak, Birdie nudged him and whispered, "Did you see Eunice Pickles on yer way here?"

He shook his head.

"If I knew what she looked like, I could watch for her myself," said Birdie. "Does Mr. Bunce know?"

Again Jem shook his head. "And don't you tell him, neither."

"Shhh!" Up ahead, Alfred turned to hiss at Jem. "Shut

yer mouth! Ain't no way o' knowing how many bogles lurk down here. D'you want to lure one out too soon?"

Jem fell silent, blushing. A few minutes later, they reached their destination, which was marked by a number painted on the northern wall. Alfred began to light his dark lantern as the two flushers cast around for the nearest manhole.

Calthrop was the one who found it.

"Why—what's this?" he spluttered. "The cover's off!"

Snell looked mystified. Miss Eames said, "Perhaps the bogle is to blame."

"The boggart, aye—or some bauchling sneckdraw of a flusher!" Calthrop grumbled.

Meanwhile, Alfred crouched beside the dark hole and peered into it, wrinkling his nose at the smell, as Jem asked Sam Snell in a shaky voice, "Won't we be needing oilskins down there?"

"Not if you stay on the platform." Snell explained that a shelf had been built along one side of the subway sewer for ease of movement. "In the low-level sewer, you'd be up to yer knees in water," he said, "but the viaduct sewers is the friendliest I ever saw."

"Even so, Birdie and I should probably put on our rubber boots," Miss Eames declared. Before she could open her drawstring bag, however, Alfred said, "Wait."

"But—"

"I can't see nowt from up here. And no one's a-going down no sewer till I've had a good look at it." Alfred turned to Calthrop. "That shaft we saw on the roof o' the house—it starts under here?"

The ganger nodded. He explained that each ventilation shaft ran from the arched ceiling of the sewer, sideways over the house vaults, and then up the party walls. So yes, he said; the opening of the shaft must be close to the manhole.

"There's a ladder to climb, if ye've a mind to it," Calthrop added. "But 'tis a very *long* ladder, ending on a very narrow ledge."

Alfred grunted. Then he dropped his sack, clamped his teeth around the handle of his dark lantern, and lowered himself into the sewer. Soon he was out of sight—much to Jem's consternation.

It didn't seem to Jem that they should be splitting up. Not down in the dark, among the bogles.

"Are you a bogler yerself, Miss Eames?" asked Sam Snell after a slightly awkward pause.

"No, Mr. Snell, I am a folklorist," Miss Eames replied. "I have a scientific interest in bogles. I study them."

"Ah." Snell nodded, though Jem wasn't convinced that the flusher had entirely understood her. It was Hugh Purdy who said, "You've come to investigate the plague, I dare-say?"

Miss Eames blinked. "The what?"

"The plague o' bogles hereabouts," Purdy reminded her.

"Oh." Miss Eames looked a little flustered, Jem thought. "Well . . . naturally, it concerns me . . ."

"I've bin a-thinking on it myself," Purdy continued, "and wonder if it might be accounted for by the Fleet River. Which runs just beneath here — don't it, Sam?"

"That it does," Snell confirmed, nodding enthusiastically. "Through the low-level sewer along Farringdon Street, all the way to the Thames."

"Is that true?" Birdie had been squatting at the edge of the manhole, trying to catch a glimpse of the sewer beneath it. Now she glanced up to address Nat Calthrop. "Is there a river under Farringdon Street?"

"Aye," said the ganger. "And a burn under Smithfield Market, running along Cowcross to the old Fleet Ditch. And another under Newgate Street —"

"*Newgate* Street?" Jem exclaimed, before catching Birdie's eye.

"And all of 'em's connected through the Fleet," Purdy concluded. "Which is where them bogles might live, when they ain't moving about in the streams and sewers."

He shot an inquiring look at Miss Eames, who opened her mouth, then shut it again. Birdie sat back on her heels, awestruck. "I never knew about no underground rivers!" she marveled, before leaning forward to address Alfred—who was on his way back up the ladder. "Did you hear that, Mr. Bunce? Mr. Purdy says as how all the bogles might be gathering hereabouts on account of a river beneath Farringdon Street!"

Alfred didn't respond. He was too busy trying to haul himself out of the manhole without dropping his lantern. It was Miss Eames who observed thoughtfully, "A lot of English folk monsters *are* found in lakes and streams. Eachies and grindylows, for example."

"So mebbe it's the river-sewer we ought to be searching," Birdie suggested as Hugh Purdy reached down to help Alfred out of the manhole.

"We'll be searching no sewers," Alfred rasped. "Not today."

"Why not?" The plumber frowned. "Ain't there a bogle down below?"

"Oh, there's a bogle. Mebbe more'n one. But the platform is too narrow."

"For the ring o' salt, you mean?" asked Jem.

"Aye." Alfred straightened, peering around in the gloom. "We must do the job up here, where there's space enough to lay a trap." Then he glanced at the two flushers and said, "The fewer folk is on hand, the better."

Calthrop sniffed. "Ye dinnae want us here?"

"It might take a long time," warned Alfred.

"Then I'll bid ye good day, for I maun attend to my business." Calthrop gave his keys to Sam Snell. "You can let yeer friends out. And I'll have those keys back on the morrow, at first peep."

"Yessir." As his ganger began to clomp away, Snell turned to Alfred. "I cannot leave you in the subway unescorted, Mr. Bunce. It's against the rules. But I'll stand wherever you wish."

"Over there, then. With Miss Eames," Alfred replied. "And you, lad—I want you just here. Where I can see you." He gave Jem a prod. "Birdie? I'll be putting you in the trap today, if you've no objection."

"Oh, *no!*" said Birdie. "I've no objection at all!" And as Alfred fished around in his sack, looking for the bag of salt, her face split into a wide, happy grin.

Jem was amazed. He himself was beginning to feel very frightened, for Alfred's warnings were echoing around the inside of his head. *Mebbe more'n one ... This corner o' town ain't like no other ... Ain't no way o' knowing how many bogles lurk down here ...*

What if he had to face two bogles at once? Or three? Or four? Or fifteen? What if they hunted him down like a pack of wolves?

Even Alfred wouldn't be able to fight off a whole *stampede* of bogles ...

15

An Unpleasant Surprise

Jem skulked against the north wall of the subway, staring at the uncovered manhole about twenty feet away. Behind him, at a safe distance, Sam Snell, Hugh Purdy, and Miss Eames were waiting and watching. Alfred had stationed himself against the opposite wall, to Jem's right. In front of them both, on the other side of the manhole, a safety lantern stood at Birdie's feet.

The ring of salt encircled her, sparkling like a diamond necklace.

Then Alfred nodded at Birdie. Though her back was turned to him, she saw his nod reflected in the mirror she was holding. And she immediately burst into song.

"I am a brokenhearted milkman, in grief I'm arrayed
Through keeping of the company
Of a young servant maid,
Who lived on board and wages,
The house to keep clean
In a gentleman's family near Paddington Green."

Birdie's voice echoed off the walls like the chiming of silver bells. Jem was astonished at how clear and strong and sweet it was. She didn't sound like a street singer; not anymore. Every note cut through the air as cleanly as a knife blade, without a trace of breathiness.

"She was as beautiful as a butterfly
And proud as a queen
Was pretty little Polly Perkins of Paddington Green."

Beyond Birdie's small, straight, narrow figure lay an empty void. Alfred had thought it unlikely that anything unexpected would creep up on her. There were too many adults in the way, he'd said. Nevertheless, he'd told Jem to keep his eyes fixed on the dim space in front of Birdie, while Alfred himself watched the manhole.

So Jem was forced to ignore the only thing he really wanted to look at, as Birdie trilled away like a canary in a coal mine.

"She'd an ankle like an antelope and a step like a deer,
A voice like a blackbird, so mellow and clear,
Her hair hung in ringlets so beautiful and long;
I thought that she loved me, but I found I was wrong."

Staring down the tunnel ahead of him, which was lit at regular intervals by the gratings in the roof, Jem wondered gloomily if his brief spell as a bogler's boy was now over. With Birdie back on the job, he would almost certainly be relegated to some kind of supporting role — and how much would that be worth, in shillings and pence? Not much, he suspected. Why, Alfred might decide he didn't even *need* another apprentice. And if that happened, Jem would find himself on the street again. Because why would Alfred want to keep a boy who couldn't pay his way?

If you weren't useful, you were expendable. That had always been Jem's experience.

Of course, it was possible he wouldn't have to face being sacked. He might be killed first, right here, in the viaduct. They might *all* be killed by a ravening horde of bogles . . .

Suddenly he gasped. This surge of despair, he knew, wasn't natural. He realized that the bogle must be very close. Then he heard Birdie's voice falter — just for an instant — before she bravely began to sing again.

"She was as beautiful as a butterfly
And proud as a queen
Was pretty little Polly Perkins of Paddington Green."

Jem couldn't resist glancing at the manhole. What he saw made him catch his breath. Something was squeezing through the hole — something that looked like gravel coated in pitch. But it didn't spread out into a widening pool. Instead, it reared up and up, swiftly and silently, until it was taller than Alfred, and as broad as it was high. It had a misshapen lump of a head, pierced by several deep, dark holes that might have been eyes, or mouths, or ears; Jem couldn't tell. Its limbs were blunted stumps, which would suddenly erupt from unlikely spots on its torso before dissolving back again. With each step it took, its legs would disappear and reemerge, disappear and reemerge . . .

It looked molten yet solid — deformed yet shapeless — like a black satin bag full of rocks. And it didn't make a sound as it heaved itself toward Birdie, whose voice remained steady and firm, though Jem could see light dancing on the mirror that trembled in her hand.

"When I asked her to marry me,
she said, 'Oh, what stuff!'
And told me to drop it, for she'd had quite enough

Of my nonsense . . . At the same time,
I'd bin very kind,
But to marry a milkman she didn't feel inclined."

Slowly the bogle advanced. One stump entered the magic circle—then another, then another. Jem's heart was in his mouth. Though he stood frozen and speechless, he was shouting at Alfred inside his head: *Kill it! Kill it now!* But Alfred didn't move. He was waiting for the bogle to drag its last haunch into the ring of salt.

And Birdie was waiting for him to give her a signal.

"She was as beautiful as a butterfly
And proud as a queen
Was pretty little Polly Perkins of Paddington—"

Alfred lunged. Somebody screamed. Birdie threw herself out of the ring as Alfred tossed a handful of salt. Jem yelled, "Birdie! Wait!" because she had kept running, down the tunnel, out of sight.

Then the bogle whirled around, a dozen limbs sprouting from its body. Jem ducked. He didn't see Alfred's spear hit home, but he felt its impact. The bogle seemed to explode, sending rocky fragments bouncing off the walls like shrapnel. The shards clanged on pipes and thudded to the floor. Half a dozen of them struck Jem on his arms and head, burning him like hot coals.

He could hear Alfred swearing.

"Birdie? *Birdie!* Where are you?" cried Miss Eames. She was already brushing past Jem, heading for the magic circle. But Alfred's arm suddenly shot out to bar her way.

"Wait. Don't touch that muck," he warned roughly. Jem saw that a tarry puddle was turning to dust on the floor.

"Birdie!" Miss Eames called again. *"Are you there?"*

"I'm here," Birdie replied. She had stepped out of the shadows into a pool of light. Her face was as white as the salt on the floor. "And I ain't hurt."

"I am," said Jem, examining a gash on his hand. "It's going black at the edges."

"Show me," Alfred demanded. Soon he was rubbing fresh salt into Jem's wounds, which included a burn and two cuts. The salt stung so badly that Jem tried to pull away, hissing. But Alfred was stronger than he looked.

"Give it a minute," he rumbled, his fingers clamped around Jem's wrist. "If the salt don't work, we'll try a little holy water."

"That could have been very dangerous," said Miss Eames, sounding shaken. "I had no idea those things could erupt like volcanoes. Has it happened to you before, Mr. Bunce?"

"Aye."

"Then you should not have left these children within the blast radius. Why—only look at Birdie's hat! It has a terrible scorch mark on it."

"Oh, that ain't nothing." Birdie spoke impatiently. "What about Mr. Bunce? He's the one as needs attention!"

It was true. Alfred's green coat was covered in burns. There was a cut on his face that was turning black, like Jem's. But a pinch of salt, applied to the wound, seemed to bring some relief. Alfred's strange, spreading bruise immediately vanished, and a normal-looking scab began to form. Soon he was swigging brandy from his flask while Birdie packed up his bag and Miss Eames made notes in a little red book.

It was Jem who first noticed that Sam Snell and his friend hadn't moved. Once the pain of his injuries had eased a little, Jem became conscious of his surroundings again. He saw that the scattered chunks of bogle had turned to drifts of black dust. He saw that Birdie knew exactly how to wrap Alfred's spear. And he saw that the plumber and his friend were still rooted to the spot, slack jawed and silent, as if turned to stone by sheer horror.

"Mr. Snell?" said Jem. "Mr. Purdy? Are you all right?"

There was no response from Sam Snell. But Hugh Purdy snapped to attention as if someone had doused him in cold water. He touched his friend's arm, then muttered soothing words of reassurance until Sam Snell finally roused himself from his trance.

It wasn't long before the flusher was talking nonstop, stammering and spluttering, as he led the others back toward the viaduct entrance.

"I swear, I ain't never seen nothing like that there . . . no, and won't never forget it, neither. What a terrible great thing, Mr. Bunce! And what a noise it made, at the end! The lads won't believe me when I tell 'em . . ."

No one tried to interrupt him. Alfred wasn't talkative at the best of times, and rarely had much to say after killing a bogle. Birdie was busy dodging Miss Eames, who kept trying to inspect her skin and clothes for black marks. Hugh Purdy looked stunned. Jem was exhausted. He found himself lagging a few steps behind the others, pining for a sip of brandy. His wounds were still smarting, and he wondered if they were the cause of his sudden fatigue.

". . . And what a brave little lass she is, Mr. Bunce." Up ahead, Sam Snell was still rambling on. "Brave as any soldier, and with *such* a voice! Why, she'd make her fortune on the stage. I thought as how she were frozen with fear, standing there like that, but then — phht! Off she went, fleet as a squirrel —"

"And it's a mercy there wasn't no other bogles, or she might have run straight at 'em." Alfred spoke sharply, cutting Snell off in midsentence. "Jem! What are you doing, dawdling back there? D'you see summat?"

"No," said Jem. The words had barely left his mouth when a bright glint caught his eye. Tucked away beneath one of the low pipes attached to the wall, gleaming in the light that filtered through an overhead grating, lay a large gold coin. "Here's a sovereign!" he exclaimed. "It must have fallen down from the street!"

"A sovereign, eh?" Sam Snell began to chatter away as Jem squatted to retrieve the coin. "Well, make sure it's a good'un. There's many a coiner will drop his cache when being pursued, in the mistaken belief that them grates lead straight to the sewers—"

"There's a shilling, as well!" Jem interrupted. Having picked up the two coins, he felt along the floor beneath the pipe, in search of others. Then a pang of dejection went through him. Of *course* there wouldn't be any more. And the coins he already had were probably counterfeit, as the flusher had warned . . .

"JEM!" Birdie screamed. "LOOK OUT!"

But Jem didn't need to look. He'd recognized the misery overwhelming him. He'd heard the scrape of a manhole cover. And knowing what he knew, he didn't waste time glancing around.

Instead, he sprang up and began to climb the wall, using the layered pipes as purchase. When he reached the topmost pipe, he glanced down. He saw giant teeth snapping at his heels. He saw Alfred and Birdie running toward him. He saw the manhole extruding a massive gray worm, which grew longer and longer as he edged away from it.

"*In six months she married, this hardhearted girl,*" Birdie sang frantically, "*but not to a viscount, and not to an earl . . .*"

The bogle lunged. Jem leaped from the pipe and grabbed an overhead grating. Then he swung his feet up so that they wouldn't dangle, and screamed at the top of his voice.

Above him, a female pedestrian stopped in her tracks. "Why, what's this?" she said, bending over to peer through the bars of the grate.

At that instant, Jem heard a deafening *BANG*—and was engulfed in a cloud of red steam.

16

A Brief Respite

Within ten minutes of killing the second bogle, Alfred was swilling down brandy in the Viaduct Tavern.

Everyone else had joined him there—even Miss Eames. "I don't normally frequent such establishments," she'd murmured upon gingerly seating herself at a corner table, "but I feel in need of a little brandy after such a dreadful shock." Jem knew just how she felt. He would have ordered a cream gin for himself if Miss Eames had let him. Instead, he had to be satisfied with a glass of cider, which didn't steady his shaking hands. Every so often he found himself gasping for air, like someone drowning in a heavy sea.

Hugh Purdy paid for the cider. He did it wordlessly, by pushing his money into Mabel's apron pocket. What he'd seen in the viaduct had rendered him speechless; he hadn't made a sound since stumbling into Farringdon Street. His friend Sam Snell, on the other hand, couldn't seem to stop talking. It was Snell who'd proposed that they visit the tavern—Snell who had ordered the first round of drinks—Snell who now started to pepper Mabel with details of their recent exploits, as she served out nips of gin and pints of porter.

"I tell you, lass, I nearly died o' fright, watching the poor lad hang from that roof like butcher's meat, and the monster snapping at his heels. But then Mr. Bunce, here—why, he let fly with his spear, and caught the thing in its soft parts, and *BOOM!* It blew apart like a dead man's belly!"

"Oh, *please*, Mr. Snell!" Miss Eames protested, covering her mouth with a wispy white handkerchief. Alfred turned on the flusher with a snarl.

"There's ladies present. Where's yer manners?"

But Snell had already begun to apologize. "Begging yer pardon, miss—only I'm that churned up, I don't know what I'm saying. To think there's such perilous creatures in the subway, and I never once saw 'em before! Ain't no accounting for it."

"Yes, there is," Birdie said impatiently. She had been allowed her own little glass of port wine, but it had been so heavily watered that it was pale pink. "The reason you never saw 'em is that you never had no kids with you."

"That's true. I never did." Sam Snell acknowledged this freely. "As for you, lass—you was the bravest of us all! Standing there, still as death, while the boggart drew closer and closer—"

"Will you shut yer mouth?" Jem said sharply. The very thought of bogles made him break into a cold sweat. No matter how much he wanted to forget it, that moment he'd spent clinging to the roof of the tunnel would stay with him forever. He could still feel the bogle breathing down his neck. He could still see the distant sky trapped behind an iron grating.

Then he felt Birdie squeeze his hand under the table, and he realized that he shouldn't be showing everyone how disturbed he was. Alfred would have no use for a frightened apprentice.

Snatching his hand away, he cleared his throat and said to Birdie, in a hard, bright voice, "You sound better'n ever. Like a real nightingale."

"That she does!" Sam Snell saluted Birdie with a raised pint pot. "I ain't never heard a sweeter songbird. You ought to be on the stage, lass." Before Birdie could reply, he turned to Jem, adding, "And so should you. Why, the pair o' you would make a fine double act! The girl could sing and the boy could tumble."

"Don't be ridiculous!" Miss Eames snapped. She looked ill at ease and kept eyeing the other patrons suspiciously— even though many of them appeared to be quite respectable. (Jem had already spotted a couple of inky clerks.) "I think we should go," she continued. "Birdie will benefit more from a hot dinner than she will from an extended session in a public house."

"We can't go yet," Jem protested. "For Mr. Bunce ain't bin paid."

As Hugh Purdy began to fumble in his pocket, mumbling an apology, Alfred scowled at Jem. "It ain't yer place to be dunning for me," the bogler chided. "Mr. Purdy will settle in his own good time."

"Which is now," said Purdy, pushing a handful of coins across the table. "You'll forgive the delay, Mr. Bunce. My head is full o' pictures I'd as soon forget. I keep thinking about Billy, and wondering which o' those things . . ."

He trailed off, grimacing. Mabel laid a sympathetic hand on his shoulder. "You did all you could for him, rest his sweet soul," she said. "The bogle's dead now. And you'll not be losing no other boys the way you did Billy."

"I'd not be too sure o' that," Alfred growled. Having finished his drink, he asked Mabel for another. Then he turned to Miss Eames. "In all the years I've bin bogling, I ain't never seen nowt like I did today. Summat's wrong. And I can't account for it."

"Mebbe it's the underground river—" Birdie began, before Alfred interrupted her.

"Nay." He shook his head. "That river's bin here longer'n London has, and I never killed but two bogles in this quarter over the past six years."

"I ain't saying the river *caused* the plague," Birdie retorted. "I'm saying mebbe the river is where bogles like to live. And since there's bin so much digging and building in this part o' London—"

"Aye, we spoke o' that." Alfred cut her off. "But what about all the other work across the city? What about the Embankment? What about the Thames subway? Ain't no plague o' bogles down by Blackfriars Bridge."

"How do *you* know?" asked Jem. As Alfred eyed him narrowly, he continued, "There might be, only no one's told you about it."

A brief pause ensued. The tavern was filling with ink-spattered printers and blood-spattered butchers. The air was becoming smoky, and the noise level was rising.

Jem wondered, in an absent-minded way, if Sam Snell or Hugh Purdy might agree to stump up for another cider— or even a mutton chop.

"I've been doing some research into this corner of the city," Miss Eames suddenly remarked, "and was alarmed to discover that it sits on what is effectively a giant graveyard."

Seeing every face at the table swing toward her, she went on to explain, "The Romans buried their dead here. There are also cemeteries at Christchurch, and Saint Sepulchre's, and Newgate Prison—"

"That don't signify," Alfred interposed, frowning. "What bearing does that have on the bogles?"

"Well," Miss Eames replied, "it occurred to me that they *might* make a habit of raiding old graves."

"Like the resurrection men," said Mabel. She had been hovering behind Hugh Purdy with a large brown jug, listening with great interest to the talk around the table. Now, as the plumber shot her a puzzled look, she decided to make her own contribution. "There was a lot o' bodysnatching hereabouts in the old days, on account o' the hospital being so near," she revealed. "Why, the surgeons from Saint Bart's used to buy drowned corpses just up the street, in the Fortune o' War Tavern. A special room was set aside for the purpose. I've seen it myself."

Jem wondered what on earth body snatchers had to do with bogles. Alfred must have been wondering the same thing, because he regarded the barmaid quizzically for a moment, then turned to Miss Eames and said, "Bogles don't eat corpses. They like their meat fresh."

Miss Eames flinched. Before she could protest, however, Birdie spoke up again. "Bogles don't live in packs, neither, Mr. Bunce. But they've formed a taste for company in this here part o' London — so why not a taste for corpses as well?"

Jem was struck by the logic of this argument. When he glanced at Alfred, he saw that the bogler was also impressed, though still not wholly convinced.

"Aye, but Saint Sepulchre's graveyard is empty now," Alfred pointed out. "The sexton told us it were dug up, not long ago, and all the remains shifted to Ilford."

"*All* the remains?" said Birdie. "Could little bits not have been left behind?"

Jem opened his mouth to ask if she thought that the bogle living in Saint Sepulchre's crypt had been foraging in the churchyard for stray fingers and toes. But he never got the chance to speak. Suddenly Miss Eames stood up, looking a little paler than usual.

"It's time we went," she announced. "I see no profit in addressing such a grisly subject when everyone is so overwrought." She began to sidle past the plumber, who had already jumped to his feet. "Come, Birdie. We'll catch the omnibus, I think."

Birdie scowled. "I don't want to go!"

"You do as you're told, and don't give Miss Eames none o' yer lip," said Alfred. He, too, had risen from his seat, though not because he was on his way out. He'd done it because Miss Eames was standing. "Here," he added, fishing around in his pocket. "This is yer share o' the fee. You earned it, lass."

Birdie's angry flush faded as Alfred pressed six shiny pennies into her palm. Jem saw Miss Eames open her mouth, then shut it again.

He cleared his throat. "What about me?" he asked. "Don't *I* get sixpence?"

"You'll get a fat ear if you don't shut yer mouth," rasped Alfred. Then he slapped Jem's arm with his hat brim. "And don't sit there like a lump when there's a lady on her feet."

Glowering, Jem stood up. He waited in silence as Miss Eames took her leave. "I'll give the whole matter some thought, Mr. Bunce," she promised, before she and Birdie withdrew, "but it's my strong belief that you should attempt no more bogling expeditions until we solve this mystery."

Sam Snell soon followed her, explaining that his wife was expecting him at home. Then the plumber offered his apologies; he had a duty to Billy's ma, he said, and would need to break the sad news to her as quickly as possible.

It wasn't long before Alfred and Jem found themselves alone at the corner table, surrounded by loud, laughing, tipsy strangers. By this time Alfred was on his third brandy and water. He sat hunched over it, his expression morose, his dark gaze turned inward.

At last Jem said, "I lost that sovereign. And the shilling too. I dropped 'em when the bogle went for me—and ran out o' that pipe too fast to pick 'em up again."

Alfred didn't reply. Instead, he reached into his pocket, pulled out a shilling, and flicked it at Jem without even glancing in his direction.

Jem caught the coin with one hand, then stared at it in amazement.

"Why—why, thank you, Mr. Bunce," he stammered, just as Mabel appeared at his side.

"Another brandy, Mr. Bunce?" she queried. When he nodded, she continued, "I forgot to mention that a gentleman was here earlier, asking about you. Name o' Josiah Lubbock. He said you were acquainted with him."

Jem gasped. Alfred peered up at her from under his bushy eyebrows and said, "What did *he* want?"

"He wanted to know where to find you," the barmaid answered. "He said if I had the particulars of any jobs you might be engaged for, he could meet you there."

Alfred sniffed. Jem exclaimed, "He must have bin listening at yer door, Mr. Bunce! This morning, after you threw him out!"

"I told him I don't discuss my customers' affairs," Mabel went on. Her clear gray eyes were searching Alfred's face. "And I didn't take the shilling he offered me, neither." As Alfred blinked and reached into his pocket again, she colored and stepped back. "Oh, no, Mr. Bunce! I'd not take a *penny* from you."

Alfred mumbled his thanks, looking embarrassed.

"And the next time I see Mr. Lubbock, I'll be giving him a piece o' my mind!" the barmaid concluded, before hurrying away to fetch Alfred's fourth brandy.

"I'll have a cream gin here, if you please!" Jem called after her, tapping the table with his shilling.

"Oh, no, you won't," said Alfred.

"But I'll pay for it meself!" Jem assured him. "I've means enough to do it!"

"If you buy spirits with that there shilling, I'll take it back," Alfred warned. Then his head snapped around as he heard the sound of a throat being cleared just behind him.

"Ah . . . Mr. Bunce?" a familiar voice quavered.

It was Mr. Froome, the sexton.

17

Meeting the Matron

Alfred's face fell. His shoulders slumped.

He closed his eyes.

"Ye'll forgive me for interrupting," the sexton said in his creaky voice, "but I came at a lady's request. She wants a word, Mr. Bunce."

The bogler opened one eye, then the other. They raked Mr. Froome up and down, from the top of his thick, white mane to the soles of his dirt-encrusted boots.

"What lady?" Alfred growled.

"A respectable woman I've known these five years or more. The widow of a bankrupt printer from Bath. Nowadays she's a nurse at Christ's Hospital School, around the corner."

At the sound of the word "school," Alfred groaned and rubbed his face with one hand. Jem asked, "Is it a boys' school or a girls' school?"

"A boys' school," said Mr. Froome. "And two boys are missing."

"Why, Mr. Froome!" Mabel's voice suddenly broke into their exchange. She had reappeared with Alfred's order. "How are you faring? Well, I hope?"

"All the better for yeer kind inquiry, Miss Lillimere," the sexton responded, with a stiff little bow.

"You'll be wanting your usual, I expect?"

"No, lass, I'll not stay long. I came to fetch Mr. Bunce, if he's willing to step across the road for five minutes."

"Oh." The barmaid glanced curiously from the sexton to the bogler as she placed a full glass on the table. "I hope nothing's amiss at the church?"

"Nothing that would concern Mr. Bunce," Mr. Froome assured her.

"Good," said Mabel. She was too polite to ask any further questions. Watching her hurry away, the sexton remarked, "'Tis sinful to see a girl like that working in a place like this."

Alfred didn't comment. Instead, he asked, "Is yer friend at the church now, Mr. Froome?"

"She is, Mr. Bunce."

"In that case, I can spare her five minutes." Alfred then drained his glass, lurched to his feet, and heaved his sack up onto one shoulder.

Jem followed him out of the tavern without saying a word. It seemed strange that Alfred had agreed to talk to a prospective client after what had just happened in the viaduct. Jem knew that Miss Eames wouldn't approve. But he also knew that nothing *he* said would make any difference. So he kept his mouth shut, even though he felt sick at the thought of confronting another bogle.

Out in Newgate Street, the crowds were thick and noisy. Jem peered at every face that passed him but didn't spot Eunice Pickles. Mr. Froome immediately turned right, into Giltspur.

"Where are we going?" asked Jem. Then he saw that the sexton was veering toward a little stone booth attached to the north end of Saint Sepulchre's, overlooking the churchyard. This curious addition, which looked like the base of a lopped tower, was fitted with a single door and several windows.

The door stood open.

"Our old watch house was built to guard the graves at night, on account of all the bodysnatchers hereabouts," Mr. Froome explained. "And since Mrs. Kerridge is afeared of being seen, I thought it best that she wait for you where no one ever comes." Prompted by Alfred's confused expression, the sexton added quietly, "It not being her free day, she risks dismissal for leaving the school grounds."

Alfred gave a grunt. He then crossed the watch house threshold just ahead of Jem, who almost bumped into him when the bogler stopped abruptly. As his eyes adjusted to the dimness, Jem saw the reason behind Alfred's sudden halt.

The room they'd entered was so small that if Alfred had taken a step farther, he would have collided with the woman who was waiting there.

"Mrs. Kerridge, this is Mr. Alfred Bunce, the Go-Devil Man," Mr. Froome announced from the street. "Mr. Bunce, this is Mrs. Alma Kerridge, a nurse from the school across the way."

"We're called matrons now, Mr. Froome," said Mrs. Kerridge. She had a harsh voice and a clipped way of speaking. Her figure was short and sturdy, and she'd wrapped it in a gray woolen shawl. Though Jem couldn't see her very well in the dim light; he could just make out a round face under a snow-white cap. "I've not much time, Mr. Bunce, for I'll be missed soon," she went on as Mr. Froome disappeared from sight. "The fact is, we've had two boys vanish in as many weeks, and I'm at my wits' end. One was friendless — a charity boy — but the other has family who will *not* believe he ran away. I'm disinclined to believe it myself, Mr.

Bunce, no matter what the warden might think." Suddenly she spied Jem skulking in the shadows. "Why, who is this? Is he with you?"

"Aye," said Alfred, sounding a little dazed. "Jem is 'prenticed to me."

"Indeed." Mrs. Kerridge studied Jem for a moment with a penetrating gaze before shifting her attention back to Alfred. "In all honesty, Mr. Bunce, we've had runaways in the past. Some boys pine for home. Some are flogged and bullied till they abscond, or refuse to come back after their holidays. But John Cobb was too timid to flout the rules. And Cornelius Sturn had nowhere else to go."

"How old are they?" Alfred gruffly inquired.

"Nine and twelve."

"And where was they last seen?"

"John was last seen somewhere between the buttery and the kitchen. As for Cornelius . . ." Mrs. Kerridge paused, then sighed. "I cannot tell you. All I know is that he vanished after supper."

"In the evening?" asked Alfred.

"In the evening, yes. They both disappeared very late in the day." As the bogler pondered, frowning, Mrs. Kerridge watched him with her bright, piercing eyes — and Jem watched Mrs. Kerridge, silently giving thanks that he wasn't a student at her school. There was something formidable about Mrs. Kerridge. And all her talk of flogging and bullying didn't appeal to him either.

"I've one more thing to tell you, Mr. Bunce," she suddenly confessed. "For some time now, several of the matrons and some of the kitchen staff . . ." She trailed off, then squared her shoulders, took a deep breath, and continued. "We've a notion that some kind of *presence* may be roaming the school at night. It is for this reason that I approached you."

"What kind o' presence?" Alfred wanted to know. "Has anyone seen it?"

Mrs. Kerridge didn't answer his question. Not directly. "At first I thought it might be a 'fazzer,'" was her roundabout response. "There's a tradition of senior boys scaring the younger ones at night. They call it 'fazzing.' I don't hold with it, of course, but I cannot *always* be watching them." Her hard gaze once again darted toward Jem, who shifted uneasily beneath it. "Having satisfied myself that the boys weren't responsible," she went on, "I began to wonder if the place was haunted. In the old days, the Greyfriars used to bury their dead under the school, when it was still a monastery. And there's any number of boys in the infirmary graveyard."

Jem shuddered. *Not only floggings, but ghosts as well,* he thought. *Ugh!*

"Then I encountered Mr. Froome yesterday," Mrs. Kerridge concluded. "He told me about the creature in his crypt, and I decided to seek your help. Mr. Froome was kind enough to alert me when he saw you in the neighborhood." Hearing Saint Sepulchre's bells toll the hour, she said crisply, "I cannot stay. Will you undertake this work? I'm told that your fee is six shillings, and a penny for salt."

"It's six shillings for *every bogle*," Jem corrected. "And fivepence if there ain't none."

Mrs. Kerridge raised a delicate eyebrow at Jem. Alfred, meanwhile, had set down his sack. "You didn't answer me, ma'am," he reminded her. "Has this thing bin seen?"

"Not seen. Only heard," Mrs. Kerridge replied. "A strange, dragging, shuffling noise."

"No smells or stains?"

The matron regarded him levelly. "It is a school, Mr. Bunce," she said. "There are always smells and stains."

Jem snorted with amusement. He couldn't help himself. Mrs. Kerridge looked at him and asked, "Where do *you* go to school?"

Jem stiffened. He glanced nervously at Alfred, who muttered, "He don't."

"A pity." Mrs. Kerridge eyed Jem's bare calves, dirty knees, torn shirt, and uncombed hair, as if ticking off a mental checklist. At last she turned back to Alfred. "You didn't answer me, either, Mr. Bunce. Will you take the job? There are forty-five boys in my ward, and another six hundred in the school. If bogles eat children, as Mr. Froome claims, then you hold all those young lives in your hands, sir."

Alfred took off his hat and scratched his head.

"I'll not claim that the warden will be grateful to you," Mrs. Kerridge went on. "He refuses to listen to any concerns that might damage the school's reputation. If I were to mention bogles, he would dismiss me in an instant. And say afterward that I was spreading lies to seek revenge." She sniffed, then took a step forward so that she was standing toe to toe with Alfred. "But *I* shall be indebted to you henceforth," she declared, "as will all the other matrons, save one—who prides herself on her breeding and, as a consequence, won't concede that bogles exist."

Still Alfred wasn't persuaded. He glanced at Jem, who stared back mutely, waiting and watching. Though Jem wasn't eager to go bogling again, he couldn't help but wonder if recent events might work to his advantage. After all, Alfred had just stumped up a whole shilling. Who knew how much more the bogler might fork out if Jem had to brave unnumbered bogles without Birdie's help?

"We'll pay double," the matron suddenly offered, in a businesslike manner.

"Done." Alfred capitulated. It wasn't really surprising, Jem thought. Even Miss Eames would have found it hard to withstand the matron's iron will. "But I can't promise nowt," Alfred continued. "I'll have a look, and if I think you've a bogle, we'll proceed from there."

Mrs. Kerridge nodded. "In that case, you must oblige me with a subterfuge," she said. "I shouldn't be here, as you probably know. Will you wait a few minutes until I return to my duties? Then present yourself at the entrance in Butcher Hall Lane, off Newgate Street, and give my name to the porter."

"I'll do that," Alfred promised.

"If asked, you're to say you catch rats." Mrs. Kerridge's gaze flickered toward Jem for a moment, as if concerned that he was listening. "It pains me to resort to such a falsehood," she admitted, "but circumstances demand it. You'll not get past the gates if you tell the truth."

"No, ma'am. I understand that."

The matron nodded again, still regarding Jem. "Have you no coat, boy?" she inquired of him.

Jem blinked, then shook his head.

"A child needs a coat, now that winter's coming." Mrs. Kerridge seemed to measure him with her eyes. "Christ's Hospital is a charitable institution. Perhaps I can supply you with something suitable." Seeing that Jem was struck dumb, she didn't wait for a "thank you" but tightened her shawl around her stocky frame and addressed Alfred. "I'm very grateful, Mr. Bunce," she said. "And I'll see you again shortly."

All at once she was marching across the street, away from Alfred and Jem—who didn't immediately follow her. Jem felt winded, as if he'd just run into something hard.

Alfred looked stunned.

"Miss Eames ain't going to like this," Jem finally observed.

"If Miss Eames has a problem, she can take it up with Mrs. Kerridge," the bogler retorted.

Then he reached down and picked up his sack.

18

The Bluecoat Boys

What's this?" said Alfred.

He had stopped to peer down at a grating in the middle of the schoolyard. Mrs. Kerridge, who was walking ahead of him, turned and answered, "That's the Ditch. We call this entire playground the Ditch." She gestured at the wide expanse of cobblestones, which was flanked on all four sides by large, handsome buildings. "It covers the ditch that used to surround London in the old days. Now the ditch is merely a drain, of course."

Alfred gave a grunt. Beside him, Jem eyed the grating

nervously, wondering how many bogles were lurking beneath it. One? Two?

A hundred?

"Over there are the Grammar and Mathematical Schools," Mrs. Kerridge went on, flapping her hand first at one massive wing, then at another. These great piles of stone looked very stern and imposing in the gray, wintry light. But the boys weaving in and out of their arched doorways looked ridiculous — or so Jem thought. He was thankful that *he* didn't have to wear yellow stockings or a silly blue tunic.

With a pang of dismay, he remembered the matron's promise to find him a new coat. Surely it wouldn't be one of these strange, old fashioned smocks?

"Must the boys wear their uniforms out on the street?" he couldn't help asking. Mrs. Kerridge studied him for a moment. Now that she was back in her own little kingdom, she seemed more formidable than ever. Her cheeks were ruddy, her step was brisk, and her gray hair lay flat on her temples, like thin slabs of iron, beneath the starched pleats of her cap.

"A boy must wear his uniform even during his holidays," she finally declared. Seeing Jem wrinkle his nose, she added, "It builds character to be constantly fighting off the taunts of apprentices and errand boys."

Jem wasn't so sure about that, but he made no comment. It was Alfred who said, "Where do the boys sleep?"

Mrs. Kerridge motioned to an elaborate stone gateway at the southern end of the quadrangle. "The dormitories are through there, off the cloisters."

"And the kitchen?" asked Alfred.

"Under the Great Hall. I'll show you."

The Great Hall was an enormous Gothic structure that looked like a church. It had stone buttresses, a tower at each corner, and ranks of stained-glass windows three stories high. As they approached the building, Mrs. Kerridge explained that its back wall stood in the London Ditch, and that it was sitting over the cellars of the old Greyfriars refectory. "There's a lot of cellar space under the hall," she said. "I've heard tell that runaway boys were once placed in dungeons, where they were chained up and poorly fed. But that was sixty years ago, before the hall was built. So it's hard to say whether the cellars and dungeons are one and the same." Suddenly she stopped in her tracks. *"Master Ferris!"* she rapped out. "What have you there, pray?"

She was addressing a large boy of about fifteen, whose wispy fair curls were at odds with his big, beefy head.

"A stick, Matron," he mumbled.

"A *stick?*" She sounded appalled, as if the boy had said

"dead snake." "Are you permitted to *run* with *sticks*, Master Ferris?"

"No, Matron."

"No, you are *not*." Mrs. Kerridge held out her hand. "If you like sticks, Mr. Tice would be only too happy to acquaint you with his cane. Is that what you want?"

"No, Matron."

"Then give the stick to me. And get along with you." For a moment she watched the boy as he lumbered off. Then she turned to Alfred and said, as if nothing had happened, "John Cobb was very near the cellars when he disappeared. I'll take you to the buttery and show you what our arrangements are. The school is between meals at the moment, so we shouldn't be in anyone's way."

Alfred said nothing. He glanced at Jem, who rolled his eyes. Then they followed Mrs. Kerridge into the Great Hall—which turned out to be a colossal room built above a warren of smaller ones. Jem caught only a glimpse of the main refectory. It was a dazzling sight, all stained glass, ribbed vaults, galleries, chandeliers, and row upon row of tables. At one end of this room, the staircase that led down to the buttery was also very handsome: wide, well lit, and intricately carved. But the buttery itself was a disappointment. It was just a small space full of shelves, neatly stacked with crockery, glass, silver, linen, and pewter.

Jem was much more impressed by the smell of baking from the kitchen.

"At every meal, three of the senior boys are appointed head cellarman, bread monitor, and clerk of the dairy," Mrs. Kerridge explained. "Then *they* appoint a salt boy, a cloth boy, a beer boy, a potato boy, and so forth."

"A potato boy?" Jem echoed. "What's that?"

"A boy charged with serving potatoes." Mrs. Kerridge spoke in a flat voice more withering than any sneer. "And a very popular job it is, too."

Jem wasn't surprised. If *he* had been a potato boy, he would have eaten one potato in every three.

"John Cobb was plate boy the night he disappeared. He had to distribute clean plates, then collect and scrape the dirty ones. So he was one of the last boys left here." Mrs. Kerridge sighed as she spotted a patch of grease on the floor. "A scullery maid saw him deliver a load of dirty plates to the kitchen, but he never returned to the buttery from there. And no one's seen him since."

"Would you show me the kitchen, ma'am?" said Alfred.

They descended another set of stairs, emerging into a massive space under a high ceiling that was held up by broad, granite pillars. Even in the midafternoon it was a busy place. Fires were burning, pots were boiling, and legs of mutton were being basted. Jem counted three cooks and six kitchen maids, together with a young boy in an apron, hauling coals.

Since the boy wasn't wearing a silly blue smock, Jem assumed that he was a servant rather than a scholar.

"The scullery is over there," Mrs. Kerridge said to Alfred. "I'll show you." She led him past a fat cook and a thin maid. Jem shuffled along behind Alfred, amazed at the number of ovens, ranges, and shiny copper pots that were needed to supply the school with three hot meals a day. Great vats of stewed fruit could have fed a whole army. There was so much flour scattered about, he felt as if he were in a mill.

At one point Mrs. Kerridge stopped to address a young slavvy, whose apron was spotted with grease and whose fine, black hair was falling out from beneath her crumpled cap. "The floor in the buttery needs cleaning," Mrs. Kerridge informed her. "Kindly see to it, Minnie." Then the matron moved on, weaving her way between scurrying figures until she reached the far side of the room — where a long, narrow passage led to a scullery. Opening off this passage were several dark doorways. "Those are our larders and storerooms," Mrs. Kerridge told Alfred. "One of them contains the brine trough, and another the meat safe—"

"*Hello?*" Alfred interrupted, raising his voice. "*Is any-*"

body in there?" When no one replied, he addressed Mrs. Kerridge. "Don't move," he instructed. "I'll not be wanting company. You wait here too, lad."

Jem nodded. He had no desire to explore the dingy passage, which looked much older and damper than the rest of the kitchen. So he stood back while Alfred advanced into the shadows, wondering how the matron would react if he asked her for a spoonful of black-currant jam.

"I might fetch that coat," Mrs. Kerridge suddenly remarked. "If I can safely leave you here all alone, Jem?"

"Yes'm," Jem replied.

"I'll not come back to find that you smell of treacle or candied ginger?"

Jem shook his head. "I ain't a thief," he said shortly.

"Good. For thieves go straight to hell."

Mrs. Kerridge then bustled away, promising to return very soon. Jem watched her go with a sullen look. It angered him when people simply *assumed* that he would steal things—especially when they knew nothing about his past life. Was it so obvious that he had once picked pockets? Why did everyone seem concerned that he would resume his bad habits, even though he now had a perfectly respectable job hunting down bogles? Had his work for Sarah Pickles left some kind of indelible mark on him, like a brand?

Perhaps he *was* marked. Perhaps he was permanently spoiled and twisted, thanks to Sarah. Thanks to that shuffling, two-faced, evil—

All at once he gasped as a brilliant idea flashed into his head.

"Here!" A sharp voice punctured his fit of abstraction. "You're in me way, you dozy lummox!"

Jem gave a start. He realized that he was blocking the path to the scullery, and that the grease-spattered slavvy was trying to get by. She was staggering under a huge load of dirty pots.

"Begging yer pardon, miss," he mumbled, taking a step back.

"They ain't never hiring *you?*" she demanded contemptuously.

Jem shook his head.

"Good," she snapped, then lurched past him into the damp, dark passage. Jem wondered if she would ever come out again. Did bogles eat big girls? Minnie was scrawny, but she also looked tough. And she was old enough to wear a corset . . .

"Minnie! Oi, Minnie!" one of the kitchen maids suddenly bawled. Next thing she was hurrying after the slavvy, waving an omelette pan. Just as the two girls erupted into a screaming battle somewhere out of sight down the passage, Alfred emerged again — as if chased out by all the noise.

"Well?" said Jem.

Alfred sniffed. His face was long and sour under the drooping brim of his hat. His dark gaze scanned the busy kitchen, jumping like a flea from body to body. "We'll come back tonight, when it's quiet," he growled. "That bogle won't be out and about till all this commotion ceases."

"So there *is* a bogle?" asked Jem.

"Oh, aye. Far as I can tell." Alfred addressed a passing cook. "Begging yer pardon, ma'am, but there's a larder down yonder with nowt in it. Can you tell me why, when the others is packed to the ceiling?"

"On account o' the stench. A sewer lies beneath, or dead monks, or summat." The cook frowned at him. "What's *your* business here?"

Alfred adjusted the weight of his sack, grimacing. He seemed uncomfortable with the notion of telling a lie. It was Jem who answered, "Mrs. Kerridge hired us to kill vermin."

"Oh." The cook nodded, apparently satisfied. Then she trudged away. Watching her, Alfred muttered, "We'll need both o' you for this — you and Birdie. Else I'll not take the risk."

"Miss Eames won't like it," Jem pointed out.

"Miss Eames won't like a school turned into a larder," Alfred retorted. Then he sighed and said, "We'll go straight to Bloomsbury and challenge her. With luck, she'll be persuaded in time for us to come back this evening. With Birdie."

"Uh — Mr. Bunce?" Jem had his speech all prepared but found it harder to begin than he had expected. After clearing his throat, he finally stammered, "M-may I stay here while you go? For I've business in this neighborhood."

Alfred fixed him with a skeptical eye. "Business?" he echoed.

"There's a girl I saw hereabouts and wish to see again." Jem hoped to mislead Alfred without actually lying to him — and when he saw Alfred's mouth twitch, he knew he'd succeeded. "If I went knocking on doors in search of her, I could ask about bad smells and missing children," Jem continued, watching Alfred closely. "I could find out how far the monsters range in these parts."

"Aye," the bogler conceded. "You could."

"And mebbe win you more business," Jem finished, just as Mrs. Kerridge approached them. She was carrying a rust-colored jacket, cut short and narrow. Her face was flushed with triumph.

"I think this might fit you, Jem," she announced. "The

sleeves are too long, and a little shiny with use, but a stiff brush and a few stitches will fix that. It's worsted wool, so it will not lose its shape after washing. Here—why not put it on?"

She held out the jacket as Alfred wearily inclined his head. "You'll want a new jacket if you wish to impress a young lady," he had to admit. "Go on. Take it."

As far as Jem was concerned, this was all the permission he needed to hunt down Eunice Pickles.

19

Plain Dealing

Jem's serge coat had horn buttons and a silk lining. There wasn't a patch or a darn anywhere on it. Mrs. Kerridge had turned back the cuffs a little, to shorten the sleeves. She had even sewn his name into the collar.

When he entered the Viaduct Tavern wearing his new coat, Mabel Lillimere exclaimed, "Why, what's this? Has the Lord Mayor come to pay us a call?"

Jem grinned. "Handsome, ain't I?" he said, raising his voice above the din at the bar. The taproom was noisier than ever; Mabel was already hoarse from shouting.

"Fine as fivepence," she loudly agreed, pushing a pint pot toward a hatless navvy covered in brick dust. "How did you come by such a garment? I know it ain't from Mr. Froome."

Jem's smile faded. Was she accusing him of theft? "Mrs. Kerridge gave it to me."

"The matron? From the Bluecoat School?" Seeing Jem nod, Mabel narrowed her eyes. "Don't tell me there's a bogle in amongst all o' them boys?"

As Jem opened his mouth to reply, his gaze snagged on a familiar face at the other end of the counter. Josiah Lubbock was as red as sealing wax and sweating profusely. He smiled at Jem, then raised his glass and his voice and said, "I hear you're something of an acrobat. Have you ever thought of going on the stage?"

Jem gave a snort. He was holding on to the bar for dear life, as larger patrons tried to elbow him out of the way. "No offense, Mr. Lubbock, but I'd not be beholden to you if I could help it," he bellowed. "I'd not trust you well enough." Then he turned back to Mabel. "Begging yer pardon, miss; did you ever see a woman in here, thirty-five or close to it, plump and pasty, with a spotty face and a walleye? She used to call herself Eunice Pickles, though she might have taken another name."

Mabel stared at him for a moment, looking surprised.

"Mousy hair," Jem continued. "Red nose. Sulky expression."

She shook her head regretfully, then addressed the patrons lined up in front of her. *"Anyone here know a Eunice Pickles? Spotty and fat, with a walleye?"*

Jem waited hopefully, but the only response was a chorus of negatives. Some of the men chaffed Mabel, claiming that *they* would never dally with such a homely creature.

Mabel cast Jem a harassed, apologetic glance.

"Where is Mr. Bunce?" a voice murmured in Jem's ear. It was Josiah Lubbock. Having abandoned his place at the other end of the bar, he had battled through the crowd to reach Jem's side. "He's not ill, I hope?"

"No," Jem replied shortly. "But he'd be sick as a cat if he laid eyes on you now, lurking about like a prigging valet. Why don't you mind yer own business?"

"That's exactly what I *am* doing," said Mr. Lubbock. "I'm minding my own business by attempting to expand it."

"By leaching off others, you mean," Jem scoffed. He was about to wriggle away when a brilliant notion struck him. *This slang cove wants to make use o' me,* he thought, *but what if I make use of him, instead?*

"I hear you vanquished two bogles in the Holborn Viaduct this morning," Mr. Lubbock went on, smiling his greasy showman's smile. "Or so I was informed by that watchmaker over there, who had it from the barmaid—"

He stopped suddenly as a bell began to toll outside. Everyone in the taproom paused to listen. When Jem saw several of his neighbors cross themselves, he realized that the Newgate Prison bell was ringing — and that someone was about to be hanged in the prison yard.

"May God have mercy," the navvy muttered.

And an old man said, "It don't seem right, the way they're scragged nowadays. Ain't no ceremony to it, with no crowds and no notice, and us here lushing down blue ruin, too ignorant to salute the poor soul's passing, since we don't even know what he's done."

There was a rumble of agreement. Then Mabel, who was hauling at a beer tap, remarked, "All the licensed victuallers hereabouts is poorer since they stopped public hangings. It was good business, I'll say that."

"Because folk need a spectacle!" Mr. Lubbock insisted, addressing the room at large. "Especially if it involves bloodletting. Why, ever since the days of the ancient Romans, people have been demanding blood sports. And they'll pay good money to see rat baiting, or cockfighting." He winked at Jem, who jerked his chin at the door.

"We need to talk," Jem mumbled. "In private."

Mr. Lubbock nodded. Then he drained his glass, slapped it down on the sticky surface in front of him, and eased his way through the press of bodies around the bar.

He finally caught up with Jem in the street, where the foot traffic had slowed to a dawdle. Everyone was listening to the Newgate bell — even the costers.

"I've a proposition for you," Jem announced. "A mutual agreement, like."

"Fire away," said Mr. Lubbock.

Jem cleared his throat, trying to ignore the sudden pang of guilt that assailed him. He knew that Alfred wouldn't approve of his plan. But then again, it was a *good* plan. And it wouldn't harm anybody.

"There's a plague o' bogles hereabouts," Jem began, with a nod at the tavern door. "You may have heard the folk in there fretting over it."

"I haven't," Mr. Lubbock replied. "But carry on."

"We've killed four bogles in this quarter already. What I'm about to do is go knocking on doors, to ask about missing children."

"And you'd like me to help?" said Mr. Lubbock.

"I would."

"In exchange for . . . ?"

Jem didn't reply immediately. He was too busy thinking. At last he declared, "If you find a missing kid, you'll find a bogle, like as not. From there, it's up to you."

Mr. Lubbock pursed his lips and regarded Jem shrewdly. "You want me to tout for your master?"

Jem shrugged.

"If I find him clients, and cry up his services, it's only fair that I profit from my efforts," Mr. Lubbock pointed out.

"A small, select audience of spectators could help defray the cost of the bogler's visit. Why, I could offer his clients a cut of my takings, with which they might pay his fee!"

"You could," said Jem. Though he didn't like the idea, he realized that it would benefit poorer people who couldn't afford a bogler. And if Alfred refused to cooperate—well, that wasn't Jem's fault, was it? Jem had never once tried to claim that Alfred would agree to the plan.

It was shifty behavior, of course. Jem knew that. But it was no more shifty than Josiah Lubbock.

"We might have a notice put up in that window, seeking information about children missing locally." Mr. Lubbock gestured at the Viaduct Tavern. "I'm sure the delightful Miss Lillimere would oblige us."

"Mebbe," Jem had to admit. "Though I'll wager there's some round these parts as cannot read."

"Then others could read it to them." The showman spoke with complete confidence. "I could apply to the landlord. I could appeal to his charitable and neighborly instincts."

Jem pulled a sardonic face.

"I could say to the landlord, 'Mr. Watkins, will you join me in ridding Newgate of a scourge more terrible than typhoid? I am proud, sir—proud and eager—to be walking the streets in search of these unholy, bloodsucking vermin.'" Mr. Lubbock cut a sidelong glance at Jem before concluding, in a sly voice, "I suppose you don't need me to approach the Bluecoat School? Since we already *know* it's infested."

Jem sighed. The man was incorrigible.

"So are you interested?" Jem asked wearily. "If not, I'll be on me way."

"To look for Eunice Pickles?"

Mr. Lubbock smirked. Jem's heart skipped a beat. "What do *you* know about Eunice Pickles?" he demanded fiercely.

"Only that you're keen to find her. A middle-aged lady, I believe? Pale and plump and walleyed?"

They stared at each other for a moment. Mr. Lubbock seemed quite pleased with himself. Jem was wondering if he'd made a big mistake.

He'd been hoping to introduce the subject of Eunice Pickles casually, as an afterthought. Yet the showman had such an instinct for ferreting out secrets that he'd already grasped the importance of Eunice Pickles. He seemed to sense that she was the real reason behind Jem's search for missing children.

It was maddening.

"Her ma owes me a debt," Jem said at last. "And since I ain't the only one she's dodging, it's likely she's changed her name."

"I see." Mr. Lubbock nodded as if this all made perfect

sense. "And should I happen to find her, what's it worth to you? Once she's paid her debt?" Seeing Jem blink, he elaborated. "A five-shilling finder's fee, perhaps?"

Jem nearly laughed out loud. Suddenly he felt quite at home—and ready to deal with a man who understood that you could put a price on anything.

It occurred to him that Mr. Lubbock and Sarah Pickles would have got along very well.

"No." He shook his head, even though he knew that he was bargaining over a cut of nothing at all. "That's more'n she owes me."

"Two shillings?"

Jem snorted.

"A quarter of what you collect, then," said Mr. Lubbock. "That seems fair."

Jem agreed, with feigned reluctance. "But you ain't to warn either of 'em," he growled. "Eunice or her ma."

Mr. Lubbock raised his brows. "Are they aware that you work for a bogler?"

"No."

"Do I have your permission to name Mr. Bunce, then?"

"It would be better if you didn't. She knows him, too."

"Very well." Having satisfied himself on this point, the showman tackled another. "And may I ask what Miss Eunice's mother looks like?"

"Like a leg o' mutton gone bad," Jem spat. Then he realized that he shouldn't let his hatred show — not to Josiah Lubbock. "She's old, and fat, and wrinkled like a prune," he went on, more calmly. "Her hair's gray and she favors coal-scuttle bonnets."

"And she hails from?"

"Bethnal Green."

Mr. Lubbock inclined his head. "Then I'll keep my ears pricked for East End vowels," he promised, "and my eyes peeled for coal-scuttle bonnets."

"You can take the north side o' Newgate," Jem instructed, pointing up Giltspur Street. "I'll take the south."

"And meet again where? At the tavern?"

"At Mr. Bunce's crib. Tomorrow morning." Jem wasn't going to utter a word about his appointment with Alfred at nightfall. He had no intention of arriving on the matron's doorstep with Josiah Lubbock in tow. "But don't bother to show yer face if you ain't got nothing to offer," Jem added. "For I'll not be inclined to let you in."

"Oh, I always have something to offer," Mr. Lubbock replied serenely. Then he simpered at Jem. "I'm glad you've had a change of heart, by the by."

Jem frowned. "A change of heart?"

"About not trusting me well enough to be beholden to me."

"You've a good memory," Jem conceded, ignoring the twinkle in the showman's eye. "But make no mistake, sir: I still don't trust you. And I ain't beholden to you." He held out one dirty hand, fixing Mr. Lubbock with a bright, challenging look from beneath the brim of his baggy brown cap. "This here is plain dealing. Tit for tat. We'll both get something out of it and walk away clean."

"That we will," Mr. Lubbock confirmed. Then he shook Jem's hand, adjusted his bowler, and headed off down Giltspur Street.

Jem hurried away in the opposite direction, toward Warwick Lane.

20

Looking for Eunice

Jem began his search on Warwick Lane because he'd last seen Eunice heading in that direction. To Jem, Warwick Lane looked like the kind of street that Sarah Pickles and her daughter had always occupied in Bethnal Green. It was narrow, dirty, airless, and faintly threatening. But the farther he went, the more clearly he saw that a city slum wasn't quite the same as a rookery in the East End.

For one thing, the buildings in Warwick Lane were taller and older than most East End buildings. And though some had fallen into disrepair, it was clear even to Jem that many of them had once been very fine—unlike the buildings in Bethnal Green. What's more, the city crowds were sprinkled with lawyers and physicians and merchants, while the streets of Bethnal Green were largely peopled with poor folk: seamstresses, boot makers, navvies, pickpockets.

The city businesses were more prosperous too. Jem's first stop on Warwick Lane was a printing office, which was papered with bills and bursting with books and pamphlets. All the men in this office could obviously read, from the refined young clerk ordering a gross of leaflets to the burly typesetter with big shoulders and ink-stained hands. When Jem stuck his head through the door, he took one look and instantly retreated, before anyone inside could tell him to hook it.

He knew that Eunice Pickles would never set foot in such a place.

So he revised his original plan, deciding to concentrate on public houses. The Bell, on the western side of the street, was an old-fashioned coaching inn built around a cobbled court. It was several stories high, with here and there an outbreak of long, wooden balconies that were stacked one above the other, like theater galleries. People hung over the balustrades, smoking and spitting, while others slouched at ground level, surrounded by straw and horse manure. A clutch of old dog carts moldered near the stables, which were as bad as anything in Bethnal Green.

Jem entered the Bell's courtyard from Warwick Lane,

through a large, square opening high enough for a man on a horse. The taproom was immediately to his right. It should have been a cheerful place, because its windows formed a wall of glass that overlooked the courtyard. But when Jem walked in, he saw that the glass was so dirty, and the bar itself so old and sooty, that it wasn't cheerful at all.

The potboy didn't know anything about missing children. Nor had he heard of Eunice Pickles. As for his patrons, they were all from out of town. So Jem abandoned the bar and did a quick circuit of the courtyard. Here he found a few locals, including a groom, a cook, and a knife grinder.

But none of these people could help him.

The Old Coffee Pot was Jem's next port of call. It stood near the entrance to Newgate Market, which occupied a small square tucked away behind Warwick Lane. Most of the butchers had recently moved to the new markets at Smithfield, so the pavilion in the center of the square was all but deserted. Even the clock on its cupola had stopped. The tavern was busy enough, though — and when Jem spoke to the untidy blond barmaid (who screeched her orders like a parrot as she slung quart pots around as if they were teacups), she was surprisingly helpful.

"Why, yes," she said. "We had a lad go missing here only last week. He were a printer's devil, and tried to pay for a pint o' porter with a bad shilling. When I challenged him on it, he ran away, with a good many customers in pursuit. But no one could catch him. They say he vanished into thin air."

"He ducked down into the vaults below the market stalls," an eavesdropping patron interrupted, "and we never did find him."

"I daresay he kept hidden in some dark corner, then seized his chance when he could," was the barmaid's theory.

But Jem wasn't so sure about that. "There's *vaults* under the market?" he demanded.

"So I've heard," said the barmaid, "though I ain't never seen 'em. They're old storage cellars, from the days when Newgate had a market beadle and a slaughterhouse, and more horse-drawn railway vans coming in and out than there's fleas on a dog." She admitted that she'd not heard of any other strange disappearances but promised to spread the word.

Unfortunately, she couldn't recall ever having laid eyes on Eunice Pickles.

By the time he left the Old Coffee Pot, Jem was halfway convinced that there had to be bogles under Newgate Market. So he went to make inquiries at the Sun and Last Inn, which opened directly onto the market square. Here he heard about the printer's devil all over again, though no one seemed to know much about the underground vaults. Someone *did* mention an apprentice called Tom Peel, who had gone missing a month or so previously from a brass foundry in the old College of Physicians, just down the road. But then someone else pointed out that Tom had been a ne'er-do-well who had spent all his time threatening to stow away on a ship bound for America. And it was generally agreed that if he hadn't gone to sea, the boy had probably been murdered.

He was that kind of lad, according to the landlord. A bad lot.

Since Jem couldn't find anyone at the Sun who recognized his description of Eunice Pickles, he moved on down Warwick Lane, past something that must have been the old College of Physicians. It had a great domed roof held up by massive stone pillars, and looked rather like a bank, or a church. But it was also dingy and dilapidated, with only the brass foundry and a squalid collection of butchers' shops cluttering up its inner court.

Most of the butchers who worked there were drinking in a nearby tavern called the Three Jolly Butchers. Its landlord, Mr. Quick, didn't know Eunice Pickles. He did, however, know Tom Peel. Tom had been a regular patron but had died of the grippe in a Portsmouth hospital. "I swear 'tis true," Mr. Quick said, "for I had a letter from his poor

mother, who could not get Tom's indenture money back."
In other words, Tom Peel had not mysteriously vanished
after all—though Mr. Quick knew of three other children
who had. "Name o' Moggs," he explained. "When their
mother died, she left 'em all alone in the world. The eldest
daughter did piecework at home, making hairnets, while the
boy cleaned boots. But one day they all disappeared and
have not been seen since." After a moment's thought, he
added, "People say they went to a workhouse. What I say is:
Why did they leave their tools behind? All their needles and
brushes were still in the cellar, along with their clothes and
their bedding—"

"They lived in a *cellar?*" Jem interrupted sharply.

"Like beggars in Saint Giles," Mr. Quick confirmed.
"And paid two shillings a week for the privilege." He shook
his head in disgust. "Their lodgings were falling down
around their ears—and still are. The sooner they demolish
that old cesspit, the better. 'Tis a blot on the neighborhood,
for all its past fame."

He was referring to the Oxford Arms, which stood a
little farther along Warwick Lane, down a short passage. It
was another galleried coaching inn, even bigger than the
Bell, but its rooms were now let to long-term tenants and its
stables were stuffed with costers' carts. When Jem arrived
there, he found two women tearing each other's hair out in

the cobbled yard, as dozens more leaned over the balcony railings, urging them on. The fight ended when one woman was flung into a stack of baskets and burst into tears. The victor stomped off, muttering darkly.

There was a murmur of disappointment from the audience.

Meanwhile, Jem was scanning the face of every spectator, fully expecting to spot Eunice Pickles. But he didn't; she wasn't there. Disappointed, he then began to inquire after the missing Moggs children, darting around to catch people before they drifted back into their grimy, tumble-down rooms.

"Indeed, I spoke to that family once or twice," a skinny Welsh girl finally admitted. She was a fur puller by trade, so her clothes were covered in cat hair, and she had a dreadful cough. "They lived in the old beer cellar, but they're gone now. And not a soul has lived there since."

"Why not?" asked Jem.

"Duw, and would you show me who'd want to?" She shuddered. "You might as well crawl into a grave."

She then pointed at a wooden hatch set into the ground near the old bar. Lifting this hatch, Jem saw a rickety ladder leading down into a black pit. The stench that wafted up was sickening—a mixture of stale beer, mold, sewage, and something else.

Jem didn't bother to go any farther. A single sniff told him all he needed to know. He dropped the hatch and retreated.

"You might have a bogle down there," he said. Seeing the Welsh girl's bewildered expression, he added, "One o' them murdering monsters as skulks in the dark."

"A knocker, is it?"

"Mebbe." Jem wasn't familiar with all the different kinds of bogle. Not like Miss Eames. "I know a Go-Devil Man, if you want it killed. You can reach him through Mabel Lillimere, at the Viaduct Tavern."

"But no one ever goes down in the cellar. Why would we need a Go-Devil Man?"

Jem snorted. "Bogles eat kids," he replied, "and there's a deal o' kids in these parts. I'd not be surprised if the sewers was crawling with bogles. So you'll want to cover this trapdoor with summat heavy, afore they start spilling out like a plague o' rats." As the girl goggled at him in a witless kind of way, he decided to change the subject. "D'you know a woman called Eunice Pickles?" was his next question.

Once again, he drew a blank. The fur puller had never seen Eunice. Neither had any of her friends. It was very disheartening—and since the light was starting to fade, Jem decided to abandon his search, at least for the moment. Instead, he wandered back into Warwick Lane, where he bought an eel pie for his supper.

He ate it on his return trip to Newgate Street.

By this time he was feeling a little drained. It had been a long day, full of incident. Though bogling was in many ways easier than sweeping—and far, far easier than stealing purses—it wasn't a job for someone who valued his independence. Jem wasn't used to having his every move watched and judged. He didn't like being told what to do. That was why he hadn't flourished as a grocer's boy.

Yet now he had to obey orders like a military man or suffer the consequences.

Not that he was complaining. As he walked along in his new coat and boots, his pockets jingling with change and his mouth full of pie, he felt more prosperous than he ever had before. Suddenly he could see why other people sometimes looked ahead, hoping for better things. After all, Birdie McAdam was now living the high life. And she had once been a bogler's apprentice, just like Jem.

But then again, Birdie was special. Jem knew that. Sarah Pickles had told him all about Birdie's predecessors: the boy who had gone to gaol, the boy who had run away to sea, the boy who had been killed by a bogle. According to Sarah, Alfred Bunce had burned through his apprentices like matchsticks until he'd found Birdie McAdam, singing on the banks of the Limehouse Canal. Birdie had lasted six long years at Alfred's side, and was now eating teacakes off fine porcelain every afternoon. Of *course* she was special.

Jem wasn't. And that was something he had to re-member, for it would do him no good to think otherwise. Though he might have had a bit of luck for once, it would run out eventually. It always did. And when that happened, he would find himself on his own — as usual.

There was no point putting his faith in anyone else.

Upon reaching Newgate Street, he hesitated. It was al-ready growing dark. Across the road, to his left, he could see light spilling from the windows of the Viaduct Tavern. There was a new bill posted in one of the windows, but Jem couldn't see it clearly from where he was standing. And he didn't want to edge any closer, in case Josiah Lubbock was waiting inside.

So he turned up his collar, pulled his cap down low, and headed straight for Christ's Hospital School.

21

A LARDER BOGLE

Alfred had his strategy all worked out.

"Far as I can tell, the bogle came from that empty larder off the scullery passage," he declared. "But a larder ain't big enough for *our* purposes, so we'll use the scullery instead."

He was standing in the school kitchen, which was dark and deserted. Though the air still smelled of baking and the tabletops were still damp, none of the kitchen staff had stayed up to welcome him. All the cooks and maids were in bed now. So were the students, the beadles, the matrons, the masters—and every porter bar one.

Mrs. Kerridge couldn't leave her dormitory of an evening, so she had made certain arrangements with the night porter, Mr. Sowerby. It was Mr. Sowerby who had admitted Alfred and his friends into the school. It was Mr. Sowerby who had hidden them in an infirmary waiting room while candles were snuffed and fires doused all over the school grounds. And it was Mr. Sowerby who had finally ushered his unofficial guests across a small yard separating the infirmary from the Great Hall, when he'd judged that the coast was clear.

He was a pudgy little man with small features and a soft voice. Even though he wore a dark blue uniform, he didn't look very threatening. It was hard to imagine him driving unwelcome visitors from the school gates.

"Is there owt ah can bring thee, Mr. Bunce?" he inquired, hovering on the kitchen threshold. He carried a lamp in one hand and his cap in the other. Though his tone was mild and his expression placid, he kept rocking restlessly from foot to foot, like someone anxious to be on his way.

His balding head gleamed with perspiration.

"I don't need nowt from you, Mr. Sowerby, thanks all the same," said Alfred.

"Except the fee," Jem interposed. He had positioned himself beside Birdie, who was clad in what he had privately labeled her "bogling outfit": a tight-fitting dress, a bowler hat, and sturdy black boots. Miss Eames wore something similar, though her outfit was made of gray tweed instead of navy-blue cashmere.

"Seek me out at the gate when the job's done, and tha shall have thy fee," Mr. Sowerby advised. "Mrs. Kerridge arranged it so."

"Very well." Miss Eames spoke crisply. "Thank you, Mr. Sowerby. You may go now, if you wish."

"That ah will, for ah mun get back. Thank'ee, miss." The porter promptly vanished, taking his lamp with him. The only light now came from Miss Eames's lantern—and from the embers that still glowed in every fireplace.

"That feller were scared witless," Jem observed, pleased that he wasn't the only one sweating like a cold pint of beer. Birdie, though pale and solemn, was as dry as chalk. Alfred seemed quite calm, in a grumpy sort of way, while Miss Eames (being a lady) didn't appear to perspire when she was anxious.

Instead, she became a little overbearing.

"Kindly refrain from making remarks like that, Jem," she scolded. "It is not seemly to draw attention to another person's moment of weakness." Before Jem could do more than pull a sour face, she turned to Alfred. "What is your plan, Mr. Bunce? Do you want us in the scullery?"

"Not yet," Alfred replied. Then he addressed the two children. "'Tis a long room, and a narrow one. I'll be laying a ring o' salt at each end, then standing in the middle, by the door."

Jem blinked. Birdie exclaimed, "There'll be *two* circles?"

"Aye." Alfred paused, then added, "In case there's two bogles."

"Oh," said Birdie.

"It ain't likely," Alfred went on, "but we must be prepared."

"And how do you propose to prepare for two bogles?" Miss Eames demanded with an edge to her voice. Jem could tell that she disapproved of the whole enterprise. When he looked at her stiff posture, her white face, and the fierce way her black brows were knitted over her flashing eyes, he was amazed that she had come at all.

During their brief wait in the infirmary, while Alfred was smoking and Miss Eames was pacing up and down, Birdie had revealed to Jem (in an undertone) that there had been a raging argument at Mrs. Heppinstall's house. "Miss Eames said as how I wasn't to come," Birdie had whispered, "so I told her I'd come no matter what. And then she said she'd lock me in my room, and I said I'd get out. But it were Mr. Bunce as made her see reason. He told her it would be safer for *you* if I came, since there might be two bogles. And he asked her if she wanted to see such monsters roaming loose in a school."

Remembering this, Jem wasn't surprised when Alfred gravely informed Miss Eames, before entering the passage, that he would be using Jem as reserve bait in case more than one bogle came through the scullery door. "The first'll be heading straight for Birdie," Alfred said, "but if a second comes in afore its mate's bin dealt with, Jem'll lure it to the opposite end o' the room." Hearing Jem gasp, the bogler quickly tried to reassure him. "You'll be in a closed circle, lad. There won't be no gap for the bogle to break through. Understand?"

"Ye-e-es . . ."

"I'm reckoning it'll stand puzzled just long enough for me to kill the other," Alfred continued. "Providing you sing to it, Jem."

"And if you're wrong?" Miss Eames interrupted.

"If I'm wrong, the lad'll be safe enough. He'll have salt all round him, like a wall of iron."

"But what if salt don't work no more?" Jem's voice was a high-pitched squeak. "If they're hunting in packs now, mebbe other things have changed as well . . ."

Alfred dismissed Jem's fears with an impatient gesture. "If the salt should fail, you're as fast as a ferret. I've no fears for you." He glanced at Birdie. "And you're to join the lad in his circle if you cannot reach the door."

Birdie nodded in a businesslike manner.

"What must *I* do?" Miss Eames wanted to know. "Block the entrance?"

"You're to stay out here," Alfred replied. Then he began to address the whole group, his gaze moving solemnly from face to face. "After what happened in the viaduct, I ain't about to take no chances. Which is why you'll all stay mum while I'm in the scullery, laying down the salt. For we don't want no bogles popping up ahead o' time, do we?"

Jem shook his head. He couldn't have said a word even if he'd wanted to; his mouth was too dry. Something about the dark, echoing kitchen made him very nervous. So he stayed close to Miss Eames, sweaty and silent, as Alfred busied himself in the scullery. No one spoke for at least ten minutes. The only sound was the sighing of wind in the chimneys.

When at last Jem and Birdie were allowed into the passage, they had to scurry past Alfred—who stood, with his spear in his hand and his back to them both, on the threshold of the empty larder. It was a nasty moment. The passage was pitch-black and as narrow as a drainpipe. But it opened onto a room much bigger than any normal scullery: a long, damp, windowless space with a vaulted roof and strange niches everywhere. Jem realized at once that this room hadn't been built as a scullery. There weren't enough shelves, for one thing. The sink looked like an afterthought, and the light was very bad. As for the large iron rings embedded in the ceiling, Jem couldn't imagine what *they* were for. Hanging runaway boys, perhaps?

Luckily, the rings were placed within easy reach of each other, so Jem knew that he could always use them to swing along like a monkey if he had no other choice. But the closed circle of salt wasn't quite so comforting. It lay to his right as he walked through the door—and it looked much smaller than the unfinished circle to his left.

He found himself hoping that the bogle wouldn't have very long arms.

"Ssst!" Alfred had positioned himself beside the door to the passage. He hissed at Birdie, then waved her toward the larger ring of salt. Jem immediately went to stand inside the smaller ring. He kept his eyes on the door, which was the only way out. Alfred's glowing lantern had been left in a far corner. So had his hat and bogler's bag.

Jem took off his own cap just as Birdie burst into song.

"Oh! 'Twas on the deep Atlantic,
In the equinoctial gales,
That a young feller fell overboard,
Among the sharks and whales;
He fell right down so quickly—
So headlong down fell he—
That he went out o' sight like a streak o' light,
To the bottom o' the deep blue sea."

In such a confined space, Birdie's voice seemed incredibly loud. She looked too small to be producing a noise so clear and powerful as she stood with her back to Alfred, a little mirror flashing in her hand. Jem couldn't see her face from his side of the room. All he could see was a slim, dark silhouette, touched here and there with gold where her hair was spilling from beneath the brim of her bowler hat.

But he knew that he shouldn't be letting his eyes stray toward Birdie. His job was to watch the door. So he concentrated on the rectangular void beside Alfred, while Birdie filled the air with a cascade of silvery notes.

> *"The boats went out to look for him,*
> *And we thought to find his corpse;*
> *When he came to the top with a bang and sang*
> *In a voice sepulchrally hoarse,*
> *'Oh, my comrades and my messmates all,*
> *Pray, do not grieve for me,*
> *For I'm married to a mermaid*
> *At the bottom o' the deep blue sea.'"*

Jem wondered vaguely if Birdie had learned the song from her singing master. He didn't recognize the tune, though it had a jaunty, popular ring to it. No doubt Josiah Lubbock would have known its name; he was probably familiar with all the latest music-hall compositions . . .

Jem hadn't yet told Alfred that he'd had dealings with the showman. Though there'd been plenty of time to come clean while they were all in the infirmary, patiently waiting, somehow Jem had been unable to broach the subject — perhaps because he'd feared that Alfred wouldn't take it well. Jem was dreading the bogler's reaction. It would be harsh, he knew. There would be heated words. A beating, perhaps. Even dismissal . . . ?

Jem suddenly caught himself teetering on the very brink of despair — and realized that the bogle must be nearby. It had to be; nothing else could have made him feel like this. And Birdie, he noticed, had become slightly breathless.

"He told us how when he first went down,
The fishes all came round he,
And they seemed to think, as they stared at him,
That he made uncommon free;
But down he went, he didn't know how,
And he thought, 'It's all up with me!'
When he came to a lovely mermaid
At the bottom o' the deep, blue —"

The bogle moved fast. One moment everything was still; then a blurred shape burst over the threshold. Jem caught a glimpse of pulsing red bladders — peeled pink flesh — grinning layers of teeth. He saw giant claws lunge toward Birdie.

A split second later, Alfred moved. There was a flash of white salt. Birdie jumped. The bogle roared. Alfred hurled his spear.

The *BANG* was deafening. It was so loud that Jem blacked out.

When he came to his senses a moment later, he was flat on the floor, staring up at an iron ring in the ceiling. For a moment he lay there, stunned. Then he remembered the bogle and sat bolt upright, gasping for breath.

Across the room, Alfred was climbing to his feet. Miss Eames had suddenly appeared; she was bending over Birdie, who was on her knees, looking dazed. Though Miss Eames was moving her mouth, Jem couldn't hear her. Not through the ringing in his ears.

There was no sign of the bogle. It hadn't left a single stain, smell, or scratch. And no other bogle had emerged from the larder to take its place.

"Bzzzz-bzzz-bzzz-bzzz," Miss Eames was saying. But Birdie was shaking her head irritably, like a dog with ear canker.

Miss Eames turned to Alfred. *"Bzzz-bzzz*-wrong?" she asked, her voice hoarse with dismay. "What was that terrible noise?"

Alfred didn't reply. He was too busy grimacing as he thumped one side of his head with the heel of his hand. So Jem spoke for him.

"It were a bogle," said Jem. "It popped." Then, relieved that he hadn't gone deaf after all, he croaked, "We should get out afore another comes along."

"I don't expect there'll be another," Birdie croaked. "Ain't nothing like a dead friend to put you off yer food, and I don't believe there's a bogle in all London as didn't hear *that* one die."

"All the same, we shouldn't dawdle," said Alfred. And he glanced nervously over his shoulder.

22

Telling the Truth

Miss Eames insisted that they all take the same hackney cab. It wouldn't put her out, she said; Drury Lane was practically on the way to Bloomsbury. And a cab ride would be *much* more comfortable than a long, crowded trip on an omnibus.

But she was wrong. The cab wasn't comfortable. It was old and rickety, with broken springs and horsehair sprouting from its seats. The driver kept losing his way. And though everyone was shaken and speechless at the start of the trip, it wasn't long before squabbling broke out.

Jem was the first to break the silence. He baldly asked

for his cut of Alfred's twelve-shilling fee. Without a word of protest, Alfred handed over sixpence. But when he offered the same sum to Birdie, Miss Eames said, "This is the last time. Forgive me, Mr. Bunce, but I am fast losing patience. You promised that there would be no more bogling, yet here we are once again, shocked and bruised from another dreadful incident . . ."

Birdie turned bright red. Before she could say anything, however, Alfred frowned at her. For a moment their gazes locked. Then she swallowed whatever was on the tip of her tongue.

"Why, we haven't even solved the mystery of the New-gate Street plague!" Miss Eames went on. "I thought we agreed that you would cease work until we could account for this infestation—"

"It ain't just Newgate Street," Jem interrupted. As Miss Eames stared at him in the pale light of the carriage lamps, he said, "The viaduct's on High Holborn, remember? And Smithfield Market's up the end o' Giltspur—"

"Smithfield Market?" Miss Eames cut him off. She glanced from Jem to Alfred, both of whom were sitting opposite her. "Have you killed a bogle at the market recently?"

"No." Alfred took a deep breath. Then, looking her straight in the eye, he admitted, "I've a job there tomorrow morning."

Miss Eames flushed.

"But I'll not ask Birdie to help me," Alfred quickly added. "You can be sure o' that."

"She *cannot* help you!" Miss Eames exclaimed. "She has a singing lesson!"

"Which I could easily miss," said Birdie.

Alfred shook his head. "Nay, lass."

"I could!"

"You could not." His tone was harsh. "'Twould be ungrateful. And needless." Seeing Birdie open her mouth again, he lifted his hand to silence her. "I'll take Ned."

"Ned!" Birdie scoffed. Even Jem was startled.

"Ned's already in work," he reminded Alfred.

"Aye. But I've chink enough to recompense his master for a day's absence." Alfred paused as the cab hit a rut and threw its passengers to one side. Only after he'd righted himself did he proceed. "Ned's no stranger to bogles. And he ain't the type to lose his head."

It was true. Jem had to agree that Ned was a sensible fellow.

"I still don't see why you have to do this at all," Miss Eames protested. "Why not wait until we have more information?" She was speaking to Alfred, her unsteady voice pitched high above the rattle of the wheels. Alfred grimaced. He seemed to be looking for the right words.

It was Jem who finally answered.

"*I* have more information," he volunteered. "There's two bogles on Warwick Lane. One's in a beer cellar and one's in the vaults under Newgate Market. I ain't so sure about the market, but three kids was living in the beer cellar, and they disappeared one day without taking their dunnage with 'em."

There was a moment's shocked silence as everyone absorbed this news. Then Birdie demanded, "How do *you* know?"

"I went knocking on doors today, searching for bogles," Jem revealed. "But I didn't get no farther'n Warwick Lane."

"Warwick Lane?" said Miss Eames. "That runs beside Newgate Prison, surely?" When Jem nodded, surprised that she should be interested in the actual street (rather than what he'd found on it), she added, "I did wonder if the prison might attract bogles. It is, after all, a place of great misery and despair, full of evil and dissolute men. Could the traditional belief that bogles are demons have its roots in more than their fondness for dark holes? Perhaps they also prefer locations known for death and wickedness . . ."

She looked at Alfred, her eyebrows raised. All he did, however, was shrug.

"It could be the hangings they like," Birdie allowed.

"Or it could be the butchers. There's a good many butchers doing business around the markets, thereabouts, and for all *we* know, they're slaughtering their own beef . . ."

"I doubt that slaughterhouses are permitted within the city limits now that we have railway transport," Miss Eames objected. "It is a *most* unsanitary trade, which shouldn't be pursued in London's confined spaces."

"Whether it's done here or not don't matter to us." Alfred spoke gruffly. "For bogles don't eat cattle, neither living nor dead."

"But what if it's the *blood* they like?" Birdie exclaimed. She seemed to have forgotten all about Ned Roach. "I doubt there's a bloodier quarter in London, what with all them butchers doing business around Newgate and Smithfield. Mebbe we should try knocking on doors farther north, along Giltspur Street—"

"I have." Jem interrupted her almost without thinking. When the others gaped at him in confusion, he decided that he might as well come clean, since Alfred was less likely to lose his temper and lash out if Miss Eames was present. "That is to say, I asked Josiah Lubbock to do it," he confessed.

Miss Eames gasped.

"Josiah Lubbock?" said Alfred.

"He were sniffing around the Viaduct Tavern and heard me talking to Mabel," Jem went on. It was the truth—of course it was—but not the whole truth. "He said he'd have Mr. Watkins put up a bill, asking folk to report any missing kids."

Alfred narrowed his eyes.

"I told him he should search the streets north o' Newgate, while I went south," Jem revealed. "I told him to call in tomorrow, if he has any news." Conscious of the muscles twitching in Alfred's clenched jaw, Jem exclaimed, "He'd not be put off! And I made no promises!"

Miss Eames was shaking her head in grave disapproval. "Mr. Lubbock is a scoundrel, Jem. It is foolish to trust a man of his type."

"Yes, but the bill in the tavern is a good idea," Birdie piped up. Jem threw her a grateful glance, wondering when Alfred was going to comment. The bogler's silence struck him as ominous, to say the least. "If that whole quarter is stricken," Birdie continued, "then the folk living there should be told. So they can warn their kids about bogles—"

Suddenly the cab lurched to a halt. Up on his box, the driver intoned, "Drury Lane." Alfred immediately pushed open the door beside him.

"Thank'ee for all yer trouble, miss," he said, tipping his hat. "I'll bid you good night now—and Birdie, too."

"Please, Mr. Bunce." Miss Eames reached over to grab his cuff. "Consider what you're doing. For the sake of a few shillings, you're putting young lives at risk. Can this be justified when the circumstances are so very strange?" As Alfred opened his mouth, she continued urgently, "There can be no way of knowing how many bogles you might encounter at Smithfield. Yet you would parade two little boys like tethered goats in a jungle clearing—"

"Miss, I don't like this no more'n you do." Alfred's tone was very stern. He wrenched his sleeve from her grip, his face lengthening. "The last thing I want is to see children facing down bogles. But ain't it better to have trained kids do it, and come out alive? For them other poor creatures, as don't know a bogle from a beer keg . . . Miss Eames, they've no chance at all."

He gazed at her for a moment—and she stared back dumbly. Then he broke eye contact. "Get out," he told Jem. "I'll pass you the sack."

There was nothing in his voice to suggest that Jem was about to be punished. So Jem glanced at Birdie, who knew Alfred better than anyone. If there was a pitying look on her face, Jem would be running away as soon as his feet hit the cobbles.

But Birdie was fuming. She sat with her arms folded, glaring out the window.

"Jem!" Alfred snapped. With a start, Jem jumped to his feet. He pushed past Alfred and scrambled down onto the road, where he stood in a puddle, ready to receive the bogler's sack.

Soon he and Alfred were walking down Drury Lane. Though the evening had turned foggy, the street was crowded with theatergoers: gentlemen in top hats, ladies in fur-lined mantles. Jem saw the light of a shrouded gas lamp glinting on earrings and watch chains. He saw a pack of drunken clerks being followed by a pickpocket, but he didn't say anything. Nor did he peer too closely at the young crossing sweepers who were tumbling for tips on the corner of Princes Street. Though the thick, acrid fog caught in his throat, he tried not to cough.

He didn't want to draw attention to himself.

Alfred remained silent until they reached the lane where he lived. Then he paused in front of a lighted tavern window and turned to Jem.

"You'll tell me the truth, here and now, or I'll not let you in tonight," he said.

Jem swallowed. He glanced down Orange Court, which was a murky void lit by only one or two open doorways. Somewhere toward the rear of that narrow slot, high above street level, Ned was safely cuddled up in bed next to a blazing fire.

"I ain't a fool," Alfred continued. "I know you bin flamming and I want to know why."

"I never lied to you," Jem countered. "Not once."

"So what you bin keeping to yerself, then?" Alfred's voice was growing rougher by the second. "Out with it.

For I'll not stand about in a coal-black London Particular, coughing up bits o' lung, while I wait for you to fashion more lies—"

"I saw Eunice Pickles." Jem cut him off abruptly. "Two days ago, near the prison. She were heading for Warwick Lane."

Alfred absorbed this news in silence as an endless stream of swaddled pedestrians surged past him. At last he said, "Sal's daughter?"

Jem nodded.

"Have you seen her since?" was Alfred's next question.

"No." Jem lifted his chin defiantly. "But I'll keep looking till I find her again. Her *and* her ma."

Alfred didn't speak for a while. He simply stared at Jem, his eyes glittering in the dense shadow cast by his hat brim. At last he muttered, "Is that why you went searching for bogles? To see if you could catch a glimpse o' Sal?"

Again Jem nodded. "Josiah Lubbock promised to help," he mumbled.

"Aye, he'll do that. Then make you regret you ever asked." Alfred shook his head. "I thought you was a canny lad, but you ain't. First you bargain with a speeler like Lubbock, then you go putting yerself in the way o' Sal Pickles, who'd cut out yer throat sooner'n let you peach on her."

Still shaking his head, he turned on his heel and plunged into Orange Court. Jem stood staring after him, wondering what to do. Stay? Go? There was money in Jem's pocket, but it wouldn't last long. And he wasn't familiar with this part of London . . .

Then he saw Alfred's dim silhouette stop and turn. A pale hand beckoned. "You coming or not?" the bogler growled.

Jem hesitated. Was it an ambush? "You ain't going to beat me, once we get inside?" he squawked at last.

This time the silence dragged on and on. Finally Alfred murmured, "If that's what you think, then Sal's got more to answer for'n you'll ever know, lad."

He didn't sound angry—just very disheartened. Jem caught up with him again on the front doorstep.

Nothing more was said as they both trudged wearily upstairs, side by side.

23

An Unwelcome Addition

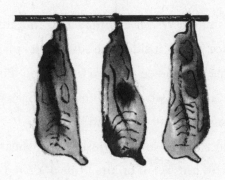

Josiah Lubbock didn't appear on Alfred's doorstep the next morning. But when Alfred, Jem, and Ned arrived at Smithfield Market — after a long and dreary walk in the rain — they discovered that Mr. Lubbock had preceded them.

"Yer friends are upstairs, in the office," Bob Ballard informed Alfred, after shaking him by the hand and greeting him in a deep, sepulchral voice. The butcher was tall and very thin, with a lantern jaw, hollow cheeks, and sunken eyes. He had almost no hair on his head, though his jutting eyebrows were thick and bushy. "I thought it best to leave 'em there, it being cleaner than the shop," he added.

Alfred blinked. "Friends?" he said. "What friends?"

"Mr. Gilfoyle and Mr. Lubbock." The butcher went on to explain that he would be unable to escort Alfred down to the goods depot, but that he had asked one of the market constables, Leonard Pike, to do it for him. "I'll fetch Constable Pike now, if you'd care to join yer friends," Mr. Ballard continued, pointing up at one of the endless galleries that flanked Smithfield Market's central avenue. Covered by a great, arched roof made of iron and glass, with dozens of cast-iron columns holding it up, the giant structure could have been mistaken for a cathedral if it hadn't been full of hanging beef. Even Mr. Ballard looked more like a clergyman than a butcher, despite his blood-smeared apron.

"If you take that staircase to the first floor," he instructed, "and stop at the second door to yer left, you'll find an office that lies directly above my shop. Look for the door marked 'Ballard and Sons.' Constable Pike will be there directly."

Alfred nodded but said nothing. His expression was grim. As he headed for the staircase, pushing past row upon row of dangling carcasses, he didn't even check to see if Jem and Ned were following him.

The two boys exchanged glances.

"Who is Mr. Gilfoyle?" Ned asked Jem in a low voice.

Jem shrugged. He was feeling guilty, and that made him cross. So did Ned's question, which seemed to suggest that Jem ought to know who Mr. Gilfoyle was. "If Josiah

Lubbock's here, it ain't down to *me*," Jem growled. "We never once talked o' the market, nor Mr. Ballard, nor this job."

Ned rubbed his nose pensively as Jem set off after Alfred. It wasn't easy dodging the porters, clerks, puddles of blood, and swinging sides of beef, but Jem was nimble enough to thread his way through all these obstacles without once missing a step.

He caught up with Alfred long before Ned did.

"I never told that slang cove *nothing* about Smithfield Market," Jem assured Alfred on his way up the stairs. "Whatever it is he knows, he must have heard it through yer door yesterday."

The bogler grunted. He had barely said a word all morning, perhaps because he'd been awake half the night. Jem had been vaguely conscious, as he tossed and turned, of Alfred's brooding silhouette hunched by the red embers in the fireplace. And the bogler's first stop, on their journey to Smithfield, had been the Cock and Magpie Tavern — where he had filled his flask with brandy.

It wasn't until he reached Mr. Ballard's office and saw Josiah Lubbock waiting inside that Alfred finally found his voice again.

"Damn yer eyes, Lubbock!" he snarled, advancing across the threshold. From behind him, Jem had a perfect view of Josiah Lubbock's servile grin—and the startled expression on the stranger hovering nearby.

Jem decided that this stranger had to be Mr. Gilfoyle, and that Mr. Gilfoyle had to be a gentleman. Everything about the man was either expensive or refined, from his shiny shoes to the crown of his glossy top hat. He was perhaps thirty years old, slight and fair, with large, gentle blue eyes and chiseled features. His hands looked delicate even through a layer of gray kid. He smelled good, his collar was snow white, and there was a diamond pin in his silk cravat.

I'll wager this toff has a fat pocketbook, thought Jem with a pang of regret for wasted opportunities. He'd never seen such a perfect mark; in days gone by, he would have thanked his lucky stars for a pigeon like Mr. Gilfoyle.

It made his mouth water to think how much the man's watch might be worth.

"I don't know what you told that butcher," Alfred was saying as he thrust his face into Josiah Lubbock's, "but I'm telling you now: *You ain't welcome here.*"

"Mr. Bunce," the showman replied calmly, standing his ground, "may I introduce Mr. Erasmus Gilfoyle? Mr. Gilfoyle is a Fellow of the Linnaean Society of London and has had his work published in half a dozen respected scientific journals. He is a naturalist, with an interest in sea monsters."

"In *alleged* sea monsters," Mr. Gilfoyle interrupted, looking pained. "That is to say, those unclassified marine reptilia described by Philip Henry Gosse as 'immense unrecognized creatures of elongate form' that may or may not roam the ocean." To Alfred he said, in a soft and very precise voice, "Forgive me, sir, but is there some sort of difficulty? I was given to understand that I might view your encounter with a species of carnivore presently unknown to zoological science. Am I mistaken? Or simply misinformed?"

Alfred opened his mouth, then shut it again. Jem wondered if he'd understood even half of what the naturalist had just said. Jem certainly hadn't. And Ned also looked confused.

"I would undertake not to interfere in *any way*," Mr. Gilfoyle went on, very quietly and earnestly. "My intention is to stand by in complete silence, taking notes. Would that disturb you at all?"

Still Alfred was speechless. Catching sight of Mr. Lubbock's smirk, Jem realized that the showman had cleverly decided to let Mr. Gilfoyle do all the talking. For it seemed that while Alfred didn't mind saying no to a seedy tout like Josiah Lubbock, turning down a polite request made by an educated gentleman was something that the bogler found hard to do.

"If you would care to review any paper I might write as

a consequence of this field research—" Mr. Gilfoyle began, but was cut off by the abrupt appearance of two new arrivals. One of them was a uniformed policeman who seemed to fill the whole office even though he wasn't very large. He was a stocky young man with a fresh complexion, red lips, and big gray eyes rimmed by a starry fringe of thick, dark lashes. If his expression hadn't been so blank, and his posture so stiff, he would have looked almost pretty.

The other new arrival was Birdie McAdam. She wasn't dressed in her bogling outfit but instead wore a blue velveteen jacket trimmed with black braid, a matching flounced skirt over two layers of silk petticoat, and a blue satin hat with a black feather in it. Surrounded by the dusty ledgers, smeared glass, and battered wooden wainscoting in Mr. Ballard's office, she seemed to sparkle like a diamond.

Ned's jaw dropped at the sight of her.

"Mr. Ballard told me to bring this girl up here," the police constable announced flatly. "She's bin asking for Mr. Alfred Bunce."

"I'm Alfred Bunce." Stepping forward, Alfred fixed Birdie with a wary look. "What is it?" he demanded. "Where's Miss Eames?"

"At home," Birdie replied. Jem guessed at once that she was a truant. Her defiant voice and elaborate outfit were all the proof he needed.

"Are you on the wag?" he asked her, with a sly grin.

Birdie flushed. "And what if I am?" she retorted. "Why should *you* be the only one to do as you like?"

By this time Alfred was scowling furiously. "You missed yer singing lesson?" he barked. "Is that what you're saying?"

"Ahem." Suddenly the policeman cleared his throat, putting an end to their conversation. "I beg your pardon, Mr. Bunce, but I don't have all day," he said, using the dull drone typical of London's police force. Jem had heard it dozens of times—and had come to the conclusion that bobbies were *trained* to behave like mechanical men.

"Forgive me, Constable—er . . ." the naturalist began, then hesitated.

"Pike, sir. Constable Pike," said the policeman. "And you are . . . ?"

"Erasmus Gilfoyle."

"And I'm Josiah Lubbock," the showman weighed in, with a smarmy kind of bow. Jem couldn't help wondering if he'd had trouble with the police before. "Is there a problem, Constable?"

"No, sir, there is not." Though the policeman spoke blandly, there was a glint in his eye as he turned from Mr. Lubbock to the bogler. "Mr. Ballard asked me to show Mr. Bunce the underground sidings. Am I to understand that you want these people to accompany us, Mr. Bunce?"

"Not him, I don't!" Alfred pointed at Josiah Lubbock. "*He* ain't invited!"

"Oh, come now," said the showman, appealing to Constable Pike. "Can a citizen legally be prohibited from entering the Metropolitan Meat Market?"

"I rather fancy he can, sir, if the railway sidings are his destination" was the constable's view. But as Mr. Gilfoyle started to protest, Josiah Lubbock suddenly — and unexpectedly — surrendered.

"It is of no consequence, Mr. Gilfoyle. As long as you yourself are present, I shan't insist on being there. Science must be served, after all."

Jem instantly deduced that Josiah Lubbock had already been paid. He was about to ask the showman how much Mr. Gilfoyle had actually stumped up when Mr. Lubbock continued, "Perhaps you'd like me to take Miss McAdam to her singing lesson, Mr. Bunce? Since she appears to be unwelcome here . . ."

"No!" cried Birdie. Wide-eyed with alarm, she turned to Alfred — who promptly rounded on the showman.

"You ain't to go *near* this girl," Alfred spat. "Nor the boys, neither! D'you hear me?"

Josiah Lubbock raised his hands in a gesture of injured innocence. "I was merely trying to help," he murmured as Birdie edged closer to Alfred.

"Aye — to help yerself," the bogler rejoined. Then

Constable Pike, who had been rocking impatiently from foot to foot, seized control of the debate.

"So who's to be in your party, then, Mr. Bunce? Aside from ourselves, that is." He jerked his chin at the naturalist, who was looking bewildered. "Will Mr. Gilfoyle be coming?"

Alfred glanced at Mr. Gilfoyle, before quickly looking away again. "Aye."

"And the two lads, of course?" said Constable Pike.

Jem awaited Alfred's answer with baited breath. He already knew that Birdie would be joining them, since she couldn't be sent home alone—not with Josiah Lubbock lurking in the wings, hoping to wheedle his way into her confidence. But with Birdie around, would Alfred even *need* two boys? And if he didn't, who would miss out?

Jem had a feeling that he himself would be the first to go. He wasn't entirely sorry about it either. Though he didn't want to relinquish his share of the fee, the prospect of facing an unknown number of bogles amidst the carcasses of a thousand slaughtered beasts made his blood run cold.

"I'll take all the children with me," Alfred announced. His hand dropped onto Birdie's shoulder. "And Mr. Gilfoyle—you're welcome to come along too, sir."

The naturalist smiled and nodded, though he still looked confused.

"As for this'un," Alfred went on, glaring at Josiah Lubbock, "he'd best stay clear, lest I lose me temper."

"Now then, gentlemen, let's keep it civil," the policeman intoned, before retreating back over the threshold. He planted himself in the gallery outside, like a theater footman. "This way, if you please. Mr. Bunce? Mr. Gilfoyle?"

As Jem shuffled out of the butcher's office, just ahead of Birdie and Alfred, he heard Josiah Lubbock calling after them, "I've some information for you, Mr. Bunce! Concerning the distribution of bogles in this neighborhood!"

"Ignore him," Alfred mumbled, giving Jem a quick prod.

"But that can wait until you've finished!" the showman added. "In the meantime, I shall continue my inquiries — *in accordance with your apprentice's instructions!*"

Jem winced. By that time, however, he was already clattering down the nearest staircase, toward a seething mass of men and meat.

Soon the roar of haggling butchers had swallowed up the sound of Mr. Lubbock's sharp, reedy, hectoring voice.

24

THE SIDINGS

Constable Pike headed straight for the very center of the market, where a flight of stairs led down to the goods depot. Alfred and the children followed him, while Mr. Gilfoyle brought up the rear. Soon they had left the noisy, crowded trading floor behind them—and found themselves on an equally noisy, equally crowded railway platform.

"Now, Mr. Bunce," the policeman said, raising his voice above the hiss of steam, the shrilling of whistles, and the shouts of meat porters, "Mr. Ballard tells me you're on the hunt for out-o'-the-way spots. Is that true?"

Alfred nodded. Beside him, Jem glanced around in dismay. The building upstairs had been bright and fresh, but this underground railway junction was dank and gloomy. Everywhere, wagons full of meat were being shunted around beneath arched vaults. Brakes squealed. Bells rang. Dozens of gleaming, silvery tracks converged into a kind of vast river, which was studded with platforms like sooty little islands. From each of these islands sprouted the pillars that held up the roof—endless rows of them, receding into the distance.

Jem wondered how large the depot actually was. From where he was standing, it looked as big as the market above.

"It so happens I know all the quiet corners hereabouts," Constable Pike went on, straining to be heard. "They're favored by those not wanting to be seen, so I make sure I pay 'em a regular visit. That's why Mr. Ballard enlisted my help, I daresay."

Alfred mumbled something, but Jem couldn't make out what it was. Then Birdie spoke up, her high-pitched voice cutting cleanly through all the rumbling and screeching and clanging. *"This is too noisy for a bogle!"* she announced, peering up at Alfred. *"Too noisy and too busy!"*

"Aye," the bogler agreed, before turning back to Constable Pike. "Where was them young'uns last seen? The 'prentice and the other boy?"

"That I cannot tell you, Mr. Bunce," said Constable

Pike. "I know nothing about either lad, save that one worked on a cartage gang, writing the slips and labels. There's many a youth employed down here in that capacity."

Alfred nodded. "And where can they be found, as a rule?" he asked.

"Why, with their checkers and truckers and callers, Mr. Bunce. Else they're up to no good." As Alfred frowned, puzzled, the policeman went on in a dry tone, "Some o' these lads can't be trusted. I've found more'n one little stash hidden about the place. Mostly meat, but sometimes coal."

"You just told us you don't know nothing about that boy," Birdie protested, "and now you're saying he were a prig!"

Constable Pike shot her a speculative look from under his thick, dark lashes, as if surprised by her use of a cant word like "prig." "No, miss, I'm not. I'm saying that if he strayed into a dark corner and met his doom there, it cannot have bin for any *good* reason — since there's proper plumbing supplied and rules about using it."

Jem realized that "plumbing" must mean "privies." Alfred said, "If the boy *were* hiding summat, or doing owt as would get him dismissed, where would he have gone?"

"I'll show you." Constable Pike promptly set off again, wending his way between pillars, sacks, trolleys, buckets, crates, coils of rope, and knots of laboring men. The place was stuffed with strange machinery — cranes and capstans and things that Jem couldn't even identify. But it all rushed past him in a blur because Constable Pike was in such a hurry.

Mr. Gilfoyle, who wasn't very nimble, began to lag farther and farther behind.

"Here," Birdie said at last, extending her hand to the naturalist after he had run up against yet another obstacle, "you'd best hold on to me."

"W-why, thank you," Mr. Gilfoyle stammered. "You're very kind, Miss — er . . ."

"McAdam. Birdie McAdam."

"Yes, of course."

"And this is Jem Barbary. And Ned Roach." Birdie waved her free hand at her two companions. "They're bogler's boys."

"I see. And that means — ?"

"We're bogle bait," Jem growled. He had mixed feelings about Birdie. On the one hand, he resented the fact that she would no doubt pocket a share of the fee, even though she didn't need it. On the other hand, he knew that he would need all the help he could get.

"Forgive me — you're what?" The naturalist almost had to shout over the squeal of rolling stock.

"Bogle bait!" Jem repeated. He caught a glimpse of Mr. Gilfoyle's shocked expression before they suddenly halted, having reached a very short, narrow, dead-end tunnel.

"This here siding is abandoned, since the turntable broke," Constable Pike explained. He indicated a kind of rotating bridge set into a shallow pit at the tunnel's mouth. Then he pointed into the tunnel, which was silting up with debris. "I've found more'n just rats in that rubbish, so it must be commonly visited."

Alfred frowned. Then he set down his sack, opened it up, and took out his dark lantern—which he proceeded to light. "You three, stay here," he told the children. To Constable Pike he said, "Would you mind if I walked on the rails?"

"They're not in use, Mr. Bunce," the policeman replied. "You may *lie* on 'em for all it matters to me." Watching Alfred jump down onto the tracks, he added, "Will you be needing my help, sir?"

Alfred shook his head. Then he moved toward the pile of shattered crates, unraveled baskets, torn tarpaulins, smashed glass, wheel spokes, crumpled paper, and dead rats that was piling up against the back wall of the tunnel

Jem pointed out, in a low voice, "It smells bad."

"Not bad enough," said Birdie. She sniffed the musty air as Mr. Gilfoyle cleared his throat behind her.

"Do—um—do bogles generally smell bad?" he meekly inquired.

Birdie shrugged. "Some do," she said. "But this . . . It don't *feel* like bogles."

Jem had to agree. There was no sense of foreboding—no creeping dread. He saw that Ned, too, was unaffected by any sudden mood changes; in fact, he looked calmer than anyone. Even the noise didn't seem to trouble Ned, perhaps because he spent so much of his time at Covent Garden Market.

Jem finally glanced up at Constable Pike—and the expression on the policeman's face made him blurt out, "You don't *believe* in bogles! *I* see what you're thinking!"

Constable Pike didn't so much as blink when everyone else turned to stare at him. "What *I* think is that some folk have jumped to conclusions," he drawled, keeping his own gaze fixed firmly on the bogler. "And what I *don't* think is that enough questions have bin asked, nor lines of inquiry followed. Kids disappear all the time, for any number o' reasons." Before Birdie could take issue with this, he raised his voice to address Alfred. "You done here, Mr. Bunce?"

"Aye." Alfred was already retracing his steps. "This ain't the place. There's nowt behind that pile o' scrap. Is there no likelier spot you can show me?"

There was. Constable Pike led his party straight to an even murkier corner, well away from all the hustle and bustle. Here, behind a low arch set into the wall, was a kind of shallow recess. And though the light wasn't good, Jem could just make out the tangle of pipes that filled this space, all slimy and bristling with valves.

"Those pipes supply the hydraulic accumulator, which is used to run the freight lifts," Constable Pike explained. He didn't have to shout anymore; it was much quieter away from the sidings. "And though it looks tight packed, you'd marvel at what can be squeezed in with a little effort. I once found a hoistman in here, sleeping off the grog. Not to mention a stolen fire hose."

Alfred grunted. Birdie said, "What's in the pipes? Water?" And when the policeman gave a nod, she remarked, "Bogles like water."

Mr. Gilfoyle immediately began to scribble something in his notebook. Alfred squatted down for a better look at the pipes, while Constable Pike observed, "They're wonderful things, them lifts. Must be a dozen, at least, excluding the ones that need repairs. I've seen 'em push half a carload of fat lambs straight up in the air, on a piston less than two foot wide."

But Alfred wasn't listening. "I don't like the look o' this . . ." he muttered, and Jem knew exactly what he meant. There was a cold, dead, airless quality about this particular patch of basement. Though it didn't feel exactly like a bogle's lair, it *did* feel like the kind of place a bogle might have passed through.

"You young'uns wait over there, by them boxes," said Alfred, straightening up. "Well away, now. Stay clear o' the walls and corners. And don't make no noise." He gave his sack to Ned, keeping only the dark lantern. To Constable Pike he growled, "Where does the water come from?"

As the policeman murmured something about artesian wells, Jem went to lean against a towering stack of crates. Birdie and Ned promptly joined him. They stood in silence for a moment, watching Constable Pike crouch down to show Alfred where the snoozing drunk had wedged himself. Mr. Gilfoyle hovered behind the other two men, still scribbling away.

"Why d'you keep doing this?" Jem finally asked Birdie, in a low voice.

Birdie frowned at him. "What?"

"You got everything you need—and more. Cake every day. Yer own room. Singing lessons. But you keep chasing bogles." Jem folded his arms, regarding Birdie from beneath the brim of his cap. "Miss Eames won't put up with it forever. Don't that trouble you none? There'll come a day when she'll not take you back."

"You don't know nothing about Miss Eames," Birdie hissed.

"I know she don't want you bogling," said Jem. "Neither does Alfred."

"He does!"

"He does not. I heard him say so. He can do without you, now he's got me."

"Tah!" Birdie made a scornful noise. Then Ned, who

had been listening carefully, said to her in his quiet voice, "If you're missing Mr. Bunce, you can allus visit him. He'll not turn you away, even if there ain't no bogle to kill."

Birdie shot him a startled look. "I know that," she muttered.

"Then why d'you want to keep bogling?" Jem was genuinely curious. "Are you bored?"

"I ain't bored." Birdie bit her lip before blurting out, "But I ain't useful! It's as if I don't matter no more! All I do is eat and sleep and go to lessons, and what good is that to anyone?" Her eyes filled with tears. "It used to be I took care o' Mr. Bunce," she quavered. "And I helped kill bogles, and minded little'uns, and now . . . now I'm just a burden!" Sniffing, she concluded miserably, "If I died tomorrow, I swear I'd not be missed."

"Why, that ain't true!" Ned cried. And then all hell broke loose.

It happened so quickly that Jem didn't have time to think. All at once his breath stuck in his throat, choking him. A chill ran down his spine. He caught a glimpse of something uncoiling above his head—and looked up to see a coal-black arm drop through a hole in the roof.

Birdie screamed. The arm had wrapped itself around her waist. For a split second Jem stood frozen with shock. But as she rose into the air, screaming and kicking, he darted forward to grab her. *"The spear!"* he screeched. *"In the sack!"*

The sack had already fallen from Ned's nerveless grip. While Ned pounced on it again, frantically raking through its contents, Jem wrapped his arms around Birdie's knees. He pulled with all his might, trying to use his own weight as an anchor. But he could feel his feet lifting off the ground.

Suddenly someone grabbed *him.* It was Constable Pike. Jem heard a shout. He felt a jerk that almost snapped his spine in two. Then, out of the corner of his eye, he glimpsed Ned hurling Alfred's spear.

KA-POW!

Next thing he knew, Jem was lying on the floor, face-up, covered in a thick layer of yellow goo.

25

THE PUNISHER

"Did you see that copper's face?" said Jem. "White as salt, even after three nips o' brandy."

"You ain't so rosy cheeked yerself," Ned muttered.

"At least I didn't faint."

"Neither did Mr. Gilfoyle," Alfred growled. "It were a dizzy spell is all."

"Will you *please* talk about something else?" Birdie exclaimed, her voice cracking. And the others immediately fell silent.

They were walking through West Smithfield, past a curving ramp that led down to the goods depot. It was still drizzling, but Birdie refused to wait for a cab or an omnibus within sight of Smithfield Market. She hadn't even wanted to linger in Mr. Ballard's office, where she'd been offered everything from smelling salts to a fainting couch. While Mr. Gilfoyle had sat with his head between his knees, and Constable Pike had knocked back glass after glass of "medicinal" brandy, Birdie had drunk one glass of water before announcing that she wanted to go. "I ain't staying here a minute longer" was how she'd put it as she limped out the door.

So Alfred had decided to head down Giltspur Street, toward Newgate.

Birdie was limping because the bogle had dropped her, injuring her foot. Her skin was peppered with red blotches like sunburn. These marks had been left by the yellow goo; they were itchy, but fading fast. Jem and Ned were also covered in them. As for Birdie's pretty blue dress, it was now streaked with pale patches where the yellow stuff had bleached it. Around her waist, the braided trim had shriveled up and turned brown, like scorched egg whites. The feather on her hat hung limp and sodden in the rain.

"Miss Eames is going to be so cross with me," she quavered as they trudged past Saint Bartholomew's Hospital.

"Nay, lass. She'll be cross with *me*," Alfred said. One of his hands was wrapped tightly around her arm; with the other he clutched his sack. The sack was also looking mottled, though Alfred's clothes were unscathed.

He had been wedged under a pipe during the bogle's attack.

"No more bogling," he continued. "Not in this neighborhood. It's too dangerous."

Birdie sniffed and wiped her nose. Jem muttered, "It wouldn't have bin so bad if that dozy bluebottle had remembered the trapdoor in the ceiling."

"But how can you blame him, when all o' them boxes was piled underneath it, on top o' the lift?" Ned spoke up in defense of Constable Pike. "Besides, it ain't bin used for a good three months. Mr. Ballard said so."

"The fault were mine," Alfred interrupted. "I should have checked. I should allus check."

"Upstairs? In a storage bay?" Birdie's voice was weak and husky. "How could *you* have known?"

"Seems to me there's so many bogles hereabouts, they've filled up the lairs they generally favor and have found less likely cribs as a consequence," Ned remarked.

"Aye," said Alfred. "Which is why we'll not be bogling here again."

Jem tried to conceal the relief he felt on hearing this. Behind his bold front, he hadn't yet recovered from the shock of the latest bogle attack. His hands were still trembling, and he was still gulping down great lungfuls of air. His beautiful new coat looked as if it had been splashed with lye. His arm hurt. What's more, he couldn't seem to shake off the sense of impending doom that the bogle had left in its wake.

Kicking a peach pit along the wet cobbles, he eyed every drain, alley, and doorway, half expecting to see a dark shape uncoiling in the shadows.

Then, all at once, he spotted a familiar façade. They had drawn level with the Viaduct Tavern, which no longer sported a notice in any of its windows.

"Where's that bill?" he asked. "The one Mr. Lubbock posted? I can't see it."

"That don't signify." Alfred didn't even pause. "Come along now, or we'll miss the bus."

"But why post it at all if it were up for only the one night?" Jem had stopped in his tracks, puzzled. He was scanning the tavern's façade, which looked damp and dismal despite its gilt trim, when all at once Mabel Lillimere emerged from the front door with a bucket of dirty water.

As she emptied the bucket into a drain, Jem called to her, "Hi! Miss Lillimere!"

The barmaid glanced up. When she saw Jem, however, she didn't smile. Instead, she flinched.

"W-why, Mr. Bunce," she stammered as her nervous gaze flicked toward Alfred. "Good morning, sir."

Then, to Jem's amazement, she scuttled back inside.

Jem's jaw dropped. He turned to Alfred and they stared at each other, astonished. Even Birdie looked perplexed.

Before she could say anything, however, Jem darted forward. "Miss Lillimere?" he cried. "Begging yer pardon, miss!" He reached the tavern door just as it swung shut but quickly pushed it open again. Alfred caught up with him a moment later.

"Wait—Jem—" said Alfred.

He was too late, though. Jem had already crossed the threshold.

Mabel was hovering just behind a wooden screen that separated the door from the nearest booth. Jem nearly bumped into her as his eyes adjusted to the dimness. Slowly her face became visible; he saw her pale cheeks, her furrowed brow, her trembling lips.

"I'm not to talk to you," she whispered. "I'm sorry."

"W-what?" Jem couldn't believe his ears. "Why?"

"Mr. Watkins said so." Mabel peered over her shoulder toward the bar. "I'll lose my place if I do."

"But—"

"I'm sorry," she hissed, then turned on her heel and whisked away. Jem would have followed her if Alfred hadn't grabbed him by the elbow.

"Leave her be," said Alfred. "Don't trouble the poor lass."

Jem didn't protest. He was too stunned. Speechlessly he allowed the bogler to drag him back outside, where Ned and Birdie were still waiting in the rain.

"What happened?" asked Birdie.

Jem shook his head. Alfred muttered, "Whatever happened, t'ain't nowt to do with us."

"Are you sure?" Jem couldn't understand it. "She's allus bin so friendly, and now . . ." He trailed off.

"Mebbe it's that slang cove. What's his name? Lubbock?" Ned hazarded.

"No." A loud voice broke into their conversation from several feet away. "No, I can assure you that *I* am not responsible."

They all jumped. Turning, they saw that Josiah Lubbock was approaching them from the direction of Saint Sepulchre's Church holding an open umbrella. As Alfred blanched and frowned, the showman raised his free hand in a defensive movement.

"Give me five seconds, Mr. Bunce, for you'll want to hear this."

"I thought I told you—"

"To keep clear. I know." Mr. Lubbock was looking far more lively and well groomed than Alfred's bedraggled little gang. The showman's voice was brisk as he soldiered on, ignoring all the glares and scowls confronting him. "I just had a word with Mr. Froome, the sexton of Saint Sepulchre's, about Miss Lillimere," he explained. "And though he was reluctant to talk, I finally coaxed a few interesting facts out of him. Would you care to hear them, Mr. Bunce?"

"No!" snapped Alfred, just as Birdie and Jem said, "Yes!"

"Then perhaps we should discuss it over there, in private." Mr. Lubbock flapped his hand toward the churchyard at the back of Saint Sepulchre's before promptly heading in that direction. Jem followed him — and was soon joined by Ned and Birdie.

Alfred brought up the rear. He dragged his feet and kept glancing over his shoulder, as if he expected an ambush. He didn't look happy.

"I stopped at the Viaduct Tavern earlier, to ask why my bill was no longer posted," Mr. Lubbock began, as he gathered his audience around him in the shadow of the empty watch house. He went on to describe how both Mabel and Mr. Watkins had refused to speak to him. The reason, according to Mr. Froome, was that someone called John Gammon had told them not to. "Mr. Gammon is a local butcher who took exception to my notice," Mr. Lubbock revealed. "And since he seems to exert a quite remarkable amount of influence on this little corner of London, Mr. Watkins had to obey — or pay the price."

It took Jem a few seconds to absorb this extraordinary piece of news. He was still turning it over in his head when

Alfred rasped, "You mean they was *threatened?* That poor girl and her master?"

"I believe Mr. Gammon is renowned for it in these parts," the showman replied.

"So he's a punisher," Jem said bluntly. He knew all about punishers—or "villains," as they were sometimes called. He'd even met a few of them in his time. "People stump up lest they lose an eye, is that it?"

Mr. Lubbock nodded.

"But that still don't make sense!" Birdie exclaimed. She was so absorbed in his story that she appeared to have forgotten her woes—at least for the present. "Even if Gammon runs the rackets in this neighborhood, why would he care about bogles?"

"Mebbe it ain't the bogles he cares about." Jem was thinking aloud, his mind working furiously. "Mebbe he don't want no one sniffing around asking questions about missing folk."

A sudden silence fell. Birdie shivered. Jem recalled the stories he'd heard about people who hadn't paid their dues to certain villains back in Bethnal Green.

Some had disappeared off the face of the earth.

"You know, if this gentleman *is* worried about investigations into missing people, he might need our help," Mr. Lubbock suddenly observed.

"Oh, no." Alfred's long face grew even longer. He took

a step backwards. "I ain't tangling with no butcher in the punisher business."

"But this plague of bogles is going to attract a great deal of unwanted attention if the death toll keeps rising," Mr. Lubbock pointed out. "And if that happens, any local ne'er-do-well is bound to come under official scrutiny. Don't you think Mr. Gammon might want to prevent this, no matter what the cost?"

Alfred gave a snort of disbelief. He was already retreating—and hustling Birdie along with him. "If you want to chase down a certified nobbler, that's your business. I'm getting out of here and taking these children with me. They'll not set foot in this quarter again."

"Not even with Mr. Gammon's cooperation?" Mr. Lubbock leaned toward Alfred in a coaxing manner. "Surely, if I were to convince Salty Jack of the danger he's in, and the wisdom of hiring a bogler to protect his own interests—"

"*Salty Jack?*" Jem interrupted. His voice was so shrill that everyone stared at him. But he had eyes only for the showman. "You mean this Gammon cove—the butcher—*he's* Salty Jack?"

"I believe that's his nickname." Mr. Lubbock eyed Jem curiously. "Why? Do you know him?"

"I know of him." Jem had heard the man mentioned, once or twice—by none other than Sarah Pickles. He grabbed the showman's arm. "Where's his shop? Does he have one?"

"Why, yes, but——"

"Where is it? Tell me!" Jem stared wildly at Mr. Lubbock. *"I've got to know!"*

26

RED LION COURT

Jem wouldn't listen to Alfred. He wouldn't listen to Ned. Even Birdie couldn't dissuade him from going in search of John Gammon. Jem was convinced that Salty Jack had to be harboring Eunice Pickles. Why else would she be loitering in the area? And if Eunice was living in Cock Lane, then her mother was almost certainly nearby.

"If I sneak into that butcher's shop," Jem announced, ignoring Ned's anxious frown and Alfred's furious glare, "I might spot Eunice—or someone else I know."

"If you sneak into that butcher's shop, you might end up minced!" snapped Birdie.

And Alfred growled, "You ain't going nowhere near that villain. D'you hear me? I'm a-taking you home."

Jem stubbornly shook his head. Home? He didn't have a home. And Sarah Pickles was to blame. "I'm doing this whether you help me or not," he announced, then turned on his heel and headed back up Giltspur Street, toward Cock Lane.

"*I'll* help you." Mr. Lubbock began to waddle after him. "You'll need to distract the butcher if you're to inspect his premises. And I'm very well versed in the arts of distraction."

"Jem! *Jem!* You come back here!" Alfred yelled. "This is yer last chance, boy! I'll not keep no 'prentice as won't follow orders!"

For a fleeting instant, Jem paused, thinking about the shilling tips, free clothes, and omnibus rides that he'd enjoyed under Alfred's protection. They would all disappear if he stopped bogling—as would his little corner of Alfred's garret room.

But then he told himself that Alfred was unlikely to keep bogling in any case. He'd already given it up once, and would probably do it again if Miss Eames kept nagging him to.

"You won't *need* no 'prentice if you ain't bogling no more," Jem drawled, comforting himself with the possibility that Mr. Lubbock might have a berth for a nimble lad. Especially if that nimble lad had done him a good turn . . .

Jem was half expecting to feel Alfred's hand on his collar. But when he reached Pye Corner unhindered, he realized that Alfred must have taken the other two children home. For one brief, stomach-churning instant, he felt abandoned. Then he reminded himself that he was on his own — that he had *always* been on his own. And if Alfred Bunce didn't want to help him, then it was time to form an alliance with Josiah Lubbock.

"May I ask what happened at the market?" Mr. Lubbock finally asked as they turned into Cock Lane. "I couldn't help but notice that the little girl wasn't looking her best . . ."

"We killed a bogle," Jem said shortly. He didn't want to discuss Birdie's narrow escape. He knew that he would have nightmares about it.

"I see." The showman nodded. "And my naturalist?"

Jem shrugged. He was assailed by a sudden memory of Mr. Gilfoyle's trembling hands and dazed expression, but pushed it to the back of his mind. He had more important things to think about — like John Gammon's shop, for instance. Where could it be? Cock Lane was much longer than he'd expected, and very narrow. The Fortune of War public house stood on one corner. Across the street, a little farther down, was the entrance to a court or alley, wedged between a druggist's and a wholesale provision merchant's. Then came an ironmonger's, then some scaffolding, and then . . .

"There it is," said Mr. Lubbock from beneath his umbrella. "I believe that might be Mr. Gammon's establishment."

Jem quickened his pace. But as he passed the mouth of the little side alley to his left, he happened to glance down it—and caught a glimpse of Eunice Pickles.

It took him a moment to realize what he'd just seen. By the time he did, he'd already taken a few more steps. "Damn me!" he exclaimed, then did a complete about-face and bolted back past Mr. Lubbock into the alley.

"Hi!" The showman halted and spun around. "Where are you going?"

Jem didn't answer. He had already lost Eunice. To his surprise, the alley was more than just a dead-end slot. Another narrow court branched off it before taking a sharp left-hand turn—and somewhere in this labyrinth Eunice had hidden herself. Turning corner after corner, she'd managed to duck out of sight.

Jem was confused by the court's eccentric layout. There were so many houses opening onto it that he couldn't tell where Eunice might be living. All the houses were old-fashioned, tall and skinny and half timbered, with protruding upper floors. Some bore curious carvings, black with dirt and damp. Many of the lead-light windows were boarded up. Jem spotted a privy in one corner of the inner yard, under a line hung with limp, wet washing. But he couldn't see another exit.

There were very few people about. An old man sat in a doorway, smoking his pipe. A young girl trudged across the muddy cobbles toward the privy, carrying a chamber pot. Somewhere an invalid was coughing and coughing . . .

Jem swiveled around smartly and retraced his steps. He was halfway back to Cock Lane when he ran into Josiah Lubbock, who had lumbered after him.

"What's amiss?" the showman demanded. "You look as if you've seen a ghost."

"Not a ghost," Jem replied. "Eunice Pickles."

"Aha!"

"We can't talk here. She might look out a window and recognize me."

Mr. Lubbock was quick on the uptake. He immediately turned and accompanied Jem, using his umbrella as a kind of shield. Only when they were once more in Cock Lane did he finally ask, "Which house is she in?"

"I don't know."

"But you saw her enter Red Lion Court?"

"Is that its name?" Jem glanced around, wondering distractedly which of the many painted inscriptions on the surrounding walls was actually a street sign. His heart was racing and his palms were damp. He felt almost feverish, despite his wet clothes. Then he spotted a dark, gaping entranceway just a little farther up the street, between two identical houses. "That there's a night-soil passage," he said. "I can watch Gammon's place *and* the court if I tuck meself away in there."

"And *I* could go knocking on doors," said Mr. Lubbock. Seeing Jem blink, he added, "Miss Pickles will not recognize *me*."

Jem couldn't argue with this. But he also couldn't understand why the showman was being so helpful. As he hesitated, wondering if there was something he had missed, Mr. Lubbock continued, "What was she dressed in? Can you recall?"

"Um . . ." Jem eyed the fat, red face hovering above him. It wore an expression of innocent goodwill that didn't fool him for one minute. But since he couldn't think of a reason *not* to answer, he sighed and mumbled, "A plaid shawl, black cloth boots, a straw hat, and a pale green gown, very dirty about the hem." He frowned as he cast his mind back. "I think it were figured muslin," he finished.

"You're a sharp-eyed lad." There was real appreciation in Mr. Lubbock's tone. "And Sarah? I believe you once told me she favors coal-scuttle bonnets?"

Jem nodded.

"Then I shall keep that in mind," said Mr. Lubbock. And away he went, leaving Jem to station himself in the night-soil passage down the street.

During his many years as a professional thief, Jem had always nursed a fondness for night-soil passages. Although these dark little alleys may have been designed as throughways for dustmen, they were even more useful as places where a lookout or pickpocket could loiter unnoticed. Since they usually led to dead-end yards full of stinking privies, they were never very crowded. Even courting couples were put off by the smell of urine and piles of rubbish.

From the night-soil passage on Cock Lane, Jem had a fine view of both the entrance to Red Lion Court and the entrance to John Gammon's shop. This shop was quite small. Its single display window was shaded by a dirty green awning and plastered with signs that Jem couldn't read. Sides of pork hung in full view of passersby. A basket of German sausages sat by the entrance.

Jem's gaze flicked nervously from one end of the street to the other. He told himself that he was willing to wait here all night if necessary. He saw people scurry past in the drizzle, their hats pulled down and their collars turned up. Some carried umbrellas. One or two lingered under awnings or in doorways. He identified a carpenter from his rule-pocket, a prison porter from his brass-buttoned uniform, a butcher from his blue smock.

Jem took special note of this butcher, discounting him only when the man passed Gammon's shop without a second glance. The old woman who shuffled into the shop some time later didn't look fat enough to be Sarah Pickles. Her hair was white instead of gray. But Jem was careful to monitor the shop door until she emerged again—this time carrying a brown-paper parcel.

One look at her sweet face told him all he needed to know. While Sarah might have shed weight, lost her teeth, and turned white haired from the stress of living as a fugitive, nothing could have replaced the hard calculation in her eyes with a kind and wistful timidity. Jem realized at once that this old woman was nothing like Sarah Pickles.

Suddenly he stiffened, catching his breath. He'd spotted Eunice. She was hurrying out of Red Lion Court, hatless and red faced. As she charged toward him, Jem retreated a little.

But she didn't even glance in his direction. Her anxious eyes were fixed on John Gammon's butcher shop. When Jem saw her vanish into its depths, he began to gnaw at his fingernails. What on earth was going on? Why were the butcher and the Pickles clan in cahoots like this? Did Sarah know where John Gammon had buried a body or two? Was that why he was helping her?

Perhaps she had entrusted the information to a third party and had threatened Salty Jack with exposure if she was arrested—or, indeed, if he tried to dispose of her. It was the only scenario that made sense. Certainly Sarah wasn't the type to make friends with a possible rival, even if he *was* from the other side of town.

Waiting nervously for Josiah Lubbock to return, Jem could only hope that Eunice had been flushed out by him. Could she be seeking advice, or refuge? Could she have excused herself to avoid answering questions? If that was so, however, the showman should have been close at her heels.

Unless he was busy talking to Sarah Pickles . . . ?

Then, all at once, something dawned on Jem. He gasped and bit down hard on his thumb. Sarah. Mr. Lubbock had used the name "Sarah." How had he known it? Jem had never once mentioned Sal's formal name—not in the showman's hearing. Neither had Alfred, nor Birdie, nor Ned. Yet Mr. Lubbock now seemed familiar with Sarah's identity. Somehow he had put two and two together. Perhaps he'd been reading last summer's newspaper stories. Perhaps one of the people working for him had jogged his memory.

He'll try to blackmail her, thought Jem, with mounting

despair. *He'll threaten to tell the police unless she stumps up.* It was obvious now why Josiah Lubbock had been so helpful. He'd been planning a caper. He was that kind of man. But he had no idea how dangerous Sarah Pickles could be when cornered.

He was a false, greedy, swindling fool.

Jem was about to slip out of the passage when Eunice suddenly reappeared in the doorway of Mr. Gammon's shop. With her was a burly man in a bloodstained butcher's smock and leather gaiters. He had a broad chest, massive shoulders, and huge hands. All the hair on top of his head seemed to have fled to his bushy sideburns and big, black handlebar mustache. His pale eyes flashed around the street before he advanced one step beyond his own threshold.

Jem decided that this hulking great butcher was probably Salty Jack. He watched the two of them walk away, Eunice scuttling and the butcher stomping. When they turned into Red Lion Court, Jem was drawn after them. He couldn't help himself. Though he knew in his gut that the butcher was dangerous—though he himself was very, very frightened—he pulled his cap brim down to his nose and sidled back into Cock Lane.

His thoughts were careening around in his head like panicky chickens. What should he do? Run away? Keep watch? Go knocking on doors, looking for Mr. Lubbock?

When he reached Red Lion Court, he stopped and peered into it. Eunice had already vanished. Her companion was entering the crooked side alley. There was no one else in sight.

"Jem?" somebody called.

Jem gave a start. Then he glanced up, his heart in his mouth.

Alfred Bunce was walking along the street toward him.

27

A View from the Top

I left the other young'uns at Bloomsbury," said Alfred. "Now I've come to fetch you."

Though not exactly threatening, his tone had an edge to it. His clothes were so sodden that they looked almost black. His wet mustache drooped. Water dripped from his hat brim. His shoulders were bent beneath the weight of his sack. All in all, he cut a gloomy, disheartening figure — yet the sight of him made Jem feel almost dizzy with relief.

"He's in there!" Jem gabbled. "Lubbock! With the butcher!"

"What?"

"He knows who Sarah is! He's bin scheming!"

"Whoa." Alfred placed a hand on Jem's shoulder, then leaned toward him and said, "Slow down. What's amiss? Tell me."

Jem explained what had happened. When he described the butcher's appearance, Alfred's face began to sag.

"This here ain't summat we can deal with," Alfred declared. "If Salty Jack's got ahold o' Lubbock, 'tis a police matter." As Jem opened his mouth to protest, Alfred continued, "Fetch Constable Pike."

"Constable *Pike?*"

"At the market. Off you go. I'll stay and keep watch."

"But—"

"If you cannot find Pike, bring another market constable. Or go to the police station at West Smithfield. We passed it earlier."

"But them traps won't listen to *me!*" Jem exclaimed. He stared at the bogler in disbelief. "They'll toss me out like a mangy dog soon as I ever set foot in the place!" Seeing Alfred frown, Jem knew that he'd struck a chord. "*You* go," Jem went on. "I'll stay. The crib I'm seeking must be at the rear o' the inner court, else I'd have spied one of 'em on a doorstep afore now."

Alfred hesitated. He glanced down the alley, then back at Jem. His grip tightened. "You'll keep watch?" he asked. "Nowt else?"

"I'll do nothing foolish," Jem promised.

"If anyone comes out, you're not to trail 'em," Alfred warned. "You're to stay where you are."

Jem nodded. Still Alfred seemed reluctant to move. At last Jem said, "We ain't doing no good standing here like a couple o' well pumps."

"You're right." The bogler abruptly released Jem before hurrying back toward Giltspur Street. Jem set off down the alley. He wanted to station himself at the entrance to the inner court. From there, he'd have a good view of every house opening onto the privy yard. He'd even have a sheltering doorway if the rain got too heavy.

The rain worried Jem. Though London was full of people leaning against walls and sitting on doorsteps, the number of folk taking the air always dropped dramatically in bad weather. No matter how cramped it might be indoors, a dry space was preferable to a damp one. For that reason, Jem couldn't help feeling that he would look suspicious, loitering in a persistent drizzle. Certainly there was no one else about—except the old man with the pipe, who was still eyeing the empty yard from his threshold as he puffed away. It was impossible to study any of the houses while *he* was there. Instead, Jem had to slouch listlessly, his head bent and his arms folded, trying very hard not to look like a cracksman's crow. Sometimes he would yawn, or shift his limbs, and then a sidelong glance would tell him that the yard was still deserted. But he couldn't inspect windows or check doors. Not beneath the old man's blank, rheumy gaze.

Suddenly the door behind Jem swung open.

"Hoi! Get out of it!" A blow to the shoulder sent him stumbling forward as someone small and shrill attacked him like a guard dog. She was a skinny, angular woman with a harsh voice and a sour face. Her apron was soiled, her hair greasy and unkempt. She carried a straw broom, which she jabbed at Jem as if he were a pile of kitchen scraps.

"I know yer game, you thieving little snipe!" she squawked. "You don't live here! Move! Go on!"

Startled, Jem began to edge away. But she chased him, still swinging her broom. "Hook it!" she screeched. "This is *private property!* We don't want no filthy housebreakers here!"

Jem didn't know what to do. Normally, he would have told her where she could stick her damned broom, but he didn't want to cause a ruckus. So he retreated toward Cock Lane with the angry fishwife snapping at his heels.

"Thief! Burglar! We're *respectable* folk in this neighborhood!" She kept swiping at his legs, pushing him out of Red Lion Court. Meanwhile, the nearby windows were filling up with spectators. Jem couldn't see a single familiar face among them, but he didn't want to take any chances.

Besides, he'd had an idea.

"You gammy old haybag!" he snarled, then took off toward Giltspur Street. By the time he reached Pye Corner, he'd shaken off the woman with the broom. Perhaps she'd turned back because she'd driven him into Cock Lane — or perhaps she was too old and breathless to pursue him any farther.

Whatever the reason, he was alone as he headed for Saint Sepulchre's. Here, he stopped by the watch house, to peer up at the houses backing onto the churchyard. Though screened by a few scrappy trees, these houses weren't hard to identify. Jem had last seen them from the front, in Red Lion Court. The privy yard lay just beyond them.

But he couldn't squeeze between them because they were rammed together like books on a shelf.

His gaze skipped up a cliff face of brick, wood, and peeling plaster. The walls of the houses were pierced here and there with small windows. They were also trimmed with rusty drainpipes. A couple of wooden boxes hung off the upper floors. From the chimneys all the way down to the coal sheds, there was a clear path for anyone with enough nerve, skill, and energy to use it. Jem's practiced eye picked out this path at once.

He glanced back at Giltspur Street. Thanks to the wet weather, it wasn't very crowded. Carriages were passing but not many pedestrians. The buildings opposite were veiled in rain. The churchyard was empty.

I can do it, he thought. *I can get onto that roof.* And from the roof he would have a commanding view of Red Lion Court.

Jem slipped through the churchyard fence and ducked behind a statue. Then he took off his boots and tied the laces together. He was about to sling them around his neck when the sight of his pale feet against the dirt made him stop and think. Peering up at the nearby houses, he saw that they were dark with soot. So he spent a couple of minutes rolling on the muddy ground, collecting grime.

Only when he was well camouflaged did he swarm up the nearest tree, pad swiftly over the roof of a coal shed, and attach himself to a crooked drainpipe that would (he hoped) carry him up the wall he'd chosen to climb. It didn't look like a difficult task, since the back of each terrace was studded with all kinds of flues, hooks, windowsills, gas pipes, stringcourses, planks of wood, missing bricks, and irregular patches. Jem's only concerns were the rain—which made everything slippery—and the people on the street. Though shielded by foliage during the first leg of his climb, he would be fully exposed upon reaching the third floor. It was his hope that any passersby at ground level would be keeping their gazes cast down, for fear of getting water in their eyes.

Jem decided to stay away from the windows. Instead, he used other footholds to inch his way, step by step, toward the roof. He found that the best way of doing this, as always, was to concentrate on the details directly in front of him and not think of what lay behind, or ahead. He tried not to listen to the sound of raised voices from within the building, or the clatter of hooves from without. He ignored the water dripping from his nose and the empty boots thudding against his chest. He simply kept going—hand over hand, breath after breath, stretching and heaving and pushing and straining.

At one point someone opened a window nearby. Jem froze. A pair of hands tossed a bucket of water into the churchyard, then slammed the window shut again. Only when a tuneful whistle had faded into silence did Jem once more start moving.

By the time he reached the eaves, he was gasping for breath. His muscles ached and his fingers were beginning to cramp. His face felt red hot. But he was able to haul himself up over the eaves and scramble across the slate roof until he reached a chimney. Here he rested for a moment, clinging to the chimney pots.

When his head cleared, he began to assess his surroundings. He was on the very apex of the roof. Behind him lay Saint Sepulchre's churchyard and spire. In front of him was Red Lion Court. He could see the uneven roofline of the houses enclosing it, but he couldn't see right down into the yard itself.

He would have to move forward if he wanted to watch people coming and going.

Unfortunately, the roof was quite steep. And wet. And full of holes. It had no fence or balustrade along its rim. But it *was* punctured by a couple of dormer windows, which reared up midway between the chimneys and the gutter. Jem decided that the closest of these windows would be a good place to start, so he carefully edged his way along the ridge until he was directly behind the little roof that covered the window. Then he slid toward this little roof until he was sitting right on top of it.

That was when he heard a familiar voice—and his heart missed a beat.

"If this cove were a young'un, I'd know what to do with him. But them creatures down there don't take their vittles full grown."

It was Sarah Pickles. Jem recognized her harsh drawl instantly. For one horrible moment he thought that she was on the roof with him. But then he realized that her voice was leaking through the open dormer window.

"Stop fussing," someone else growled. "There won't be no trouble with this here chest. The contents might take a week or so to perish, but no one'll hear it. And what's done with the remains is me own business."

"But he's fat as butter, Jack," Sarah objected. "What if he don't fit?"

"Oh, he'll fit," her companion said grimly. "Even if I have to take him apart with a boning knife, he'll fit."

By this time Jem had slipped down one side of the window. With his left arm clamped across its roof, he slowly positioned himself so that he could sneak a look inside. He wasn't particularly worried about being heard, because of the noise Sarah was making. And when he peeped into the garret, he saw what all the banging and crashing was about.

Sarah and the butcher were trying to stuff Josiah Lubbock into a large oak chest.

Jem pulled his head back quickly. He sat for a moment, sweating and staring at the sky. Sarah hadn't changed a bit. She was the same blowsy, shambling, sharp-eyed old crone she'd always been. But Mr. Lubbock wasn't looking as dapper as usual. His hat was missing; his suit was torn; his left ear was bloody. What's more, he was bound and gagged.

Jem decided, in a dazed fashion, that the showman probably wasn't dead yet — or why would Sarah have bothered gagging him? Then the noise in the garret abruptly stopped, and Jem began to wonder why. Had the job been done? Had Sarah left the room? He was about to take another peek when all at once a big, hairy arm lunged out of the window toward him.

Next thing he knew, he was caught by the ankle like a rabbit in a snare.

"No-o-o-o-o-o!"

Jem screamed. He kicked. He writhed and scratched and clawed at the slates, but it was no good; he was too weak, and his position was too perilous. One wrong move would have sent him plummeting to the ground.

Seconds later he found himself on the floor of the garret, with the butcher's hand around his throat.

"Well, I'll be blowed," Sarah Pickles remarked. "If it ain't Jem Barbary, come to pay us a call . . ."

28

CORNERED

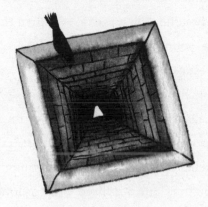

You know this kid?" said the butcher. Close up, he looked even more terrifying than he had from a distance. His neck was as wide as a bull's. His forearms were like giant hams. His eyes were even harder than Sarah's, though they resembled pale slivers of ice rather than dark chips of shale.

"He used to work for me," Sarah admitted. Then she gave Josiah Lubbock a prod with her foot. "I'm a-thinking he must work for this'un now."

"No! You're wrong!" Jem squawked. But he couldn't speak properly—not with all the pressure on his throat.

"Shut yer mouth." The butcher slapped him across the face. "No one's talking to you."

"It don't signify who sent him," Sarah pointed out. "He knows me and can swear to it in court. That's what should be worrying us, Jack."

"Seems to me you're more trouble'n you're worth, Sal," the butcher muttered. He was crouched over Jem, who could hardly breathe. "First the notice, then the slang cove, now this here young shaver. Seems to me I oughter throw *you* in the chest as well."

"And risk having our mutual friend in Whitechapel telling the beaks what he knows about yer business, Jack? I don't know as how *that* would be too smart." Sarah smirked when the butcher scowled. "I'll put this young'un out o' the way, don't you fret," she promised. "Just as long as you tend to his boss."

Suddenly Jack rose — and Jem found that he could gulp down air again. Coughing and gasping, he tried to stand up. But he was still on his knees when Sarah seized his earlobe, pinching it between her fingernails.

The pain was agonizing.

"*Ahh!* Ow-ow-ow-ow . . ."

"Get up," she ordered, yanking at the tiny flap of skin. "Come on!"

As Jem staggered to his feet, he saw through a film of tears that Jack had somehow maneuvered Mr. Lubbock into the huge oaken chest. *BANG* went the lid. *Click* went the lock. With the butcher's back to him, Jem saw his chance. He hurled himself *at* Sarah, instead of trying to pull away. She staggered beneath his weight as he barreled into her. "Ooof!" she said, releasing her grip.

But Jem wasn't halfway out the window before Jack caught him again.

"He-e-e-elp!" Jem screeched. *"Help! Murder!"*

WHOMP! This time the blow left his ears ringing. Lights danced before his eyes. His head swam and his stomach heaved and he must have blacked out for an instant, because the next thing he knew he was tucked under the butcher's arm like a side of pork, with the butcher's big, hairy hand clamped across his mouth.

"Lock the door behind us," Jack told Sarah. All at once the room around Jem began to bob and sway as he was carried out of it. He noticed dust, cobwebs, and joists riddled with dry rot. He caught a glimpse of an old wicker cradle. Then he was whisked into a stairwell lined with peeling wallpaper, where he felt so dizzy that he had to close his eyes for a moment.

"This ain't what I allowed for," the butcher was saying. "No questions asked, Sal—that's what you promised. No questions, no problems, no traps sniffing around—"

"Since when did the traps come into it?" Sarah interrupted sharply. "I ain't seen no coppers on our doorstep!"

Jem tried to announce that the police were on their way, but he couldn't. Not with Jack's hand over his mouth. All he could do was mumble and groan.

"Stow it," Jack warned. To Sarah he said, "You'd best clear out. Soon as you can. T'ain't safe here no more."

They were still hurrying downstairs, past landing after landing. The farther they went, the more obvious it became that the house was falling down. There were missing floorboards, smashed windows, broken banisters, holes in the walls. The plasterwork was crumbling away. Sparrows were nesting on architraves, and rats had chewed through joinery. Jem didn't see another stick of furniture until he reached ground level, where he spotted a second empty cradle through a half-open door. The room in which this cradle stood seemed to be in fairly good repair, though two of its windows were boarded up. Jem glimpsed a hearthrug, a coal bucket, and a bundle of clean, white muslin stacked on a rocking chair. He even spied a line of wet washing: a baby's chemise, a flannel wrapper, a bib, a bonnet, a petticoat. Squirming with fear in the butcher's grasp, Jem wondered fleetingly if Eunice had become a mother since her removal from the East End. Surely she was too old?

Then they plunged into a basement, where a fire was burning and lamps were lit. Jem saw at once that Sarah must have been living in this dingy cellar for some time. A large bed stood behind a ragged curtain. More damp laundry hung in the old-fashioned chimney corner. The floor was littered with soiled plates and food scraps.

The cradle by the bed was empty.

Eunice sat on a chair by the fire, staring blankly into space. But she looked up to see who was coming downstairs — and when Jem appeared, her mouth dropped open. "What's *he* doing here?" she demanded. "We don't take 'em that old, do we?"

"Hush!" her mother snapped. It was too late, though. Jem's eyes widened as he realized what was going on.

Sarah Pickles was a baby farmer. She *had* to be. The cradles, the clothes — they all made sense now. Sarah and Eunice were being paid to raise the children of poor working girls who couldn't (or wouldn't) do it themselves. No doubt Sarah had promised to "adopt" the babies for a lump sum, then had sold them, or dumped them, or perhaps even . . .

"This way," Sarah instructed. She jerked her chin at Jack before shuffling toward the far end of the basement, away from the fire. When Jem saw that she was heading straight for what looked like a murky, tumbledown, subterranean burrow, he began to kick wildly, panic-stricken.

"Damn me!" the butcher swore. "He's a blooming eel, is this'un!"

"It's just through here." Sarah ducked under a low stone archway, jingling a handful of keys. Meanwhile, her daughter was squinting vacantly at Jem.

"Will the bogle take a big'un?" she asked. "Ain't babies what it likes to eat?"

Jem squealed. Sarah laughed.

"He's tender enough," she assured Eunice. Then she turned to Jem with a sinister smile on her face. "You should have bin bogle meat six months ago," she crooned. "But better late than never, I allus say."

"*Nnnnnnnnnn!*"

"If you call for help," she added, "it'll bring the bogle up faster." There was a painful creak of rusty hinges as she pulled open an iron hatch that looked like an oven door. "In there," she told Jack. "Hurry, now."

By this time Jem was frantic with terror. He couldn't think straight. He couldn't believe what was happening. As Jack tried to bundle him through the hatch, there was a mighty battle; Jem wedged his foot against one side of the hole and braced his back against the other. He snatched at everything he could reach — including the butcher's mustache — to give himself a fighting chance. He yelled loudly enough to burst eardrums, then gave Jack a sharp kick and a bloody nose.

But the butcher was far too strong for Jem. After a flurry of blows and curses, Jem realized that he was falling. He hit the ground and lay on his back for a moment, winded and confused. The fall hadn't been long — a few feet, at the most. The floor beneath him was very uneven, spongy in some places and hard in others. And there was light. Jem stared up at it. Far away, overhead, was a small square of light . . .

The hatch clanged shut. Hearing this, Jem snapped out of his stupor. He sat up and saw that he was in a large pit. Once, perhaps, it had contained a chamber of some sort (a bread oven?), but the roof had collapsed long ago, leaving a litter of rubble that had since been covered by leaves and twigs and other windborne refuse. When Jem spotted a dead pigeon, he looked up again. Of course! He was in a chimney. He was at the bottom of a huge, ruined chimney that must have been six stories high.

And if there was one thing he knew about chimneys, it was that sweeps' boys were climbing them all over London.

He tried not to think of bogles as he jumped to his feet, scanning the walls that encircled him. There were no drainpipes or windowsills inside the chimney. He couldn't even see any fireplace openings; either they had been bricked up or they'd never existed. But that didn't matter. It would be easy enough to use all the cracks and fissures and missing bricks as footholds. There was even a narrow ledge running all around the chimney about four feet above his head.

Jem decided that if he climbed onto the pile of broken masonry opposite the hatch, he would be able to reach up and grab this ledge. From there he would have a clear shot at the crest of the chimney. So he moved across the floor, wincing every time something clinked or crackled beneath the soles of his bare feet. It occurred to him that he must have lost his boots in the fight with Salty Jack, because they weren't hanging around his neck anymore. But he didn't have time to mourn their loss. He had to focus on the task ahead.

Broken bricks slid from beneath him as he staggered to the top of the rubbish pile. Their crunching and clattering seemed to echo around the hollow space, making Jem lick his lips nervously. He couldn't tell exactly where these noises were coming from. He didn't like to think that something might be crawling through the rubble nearby. There was so much debris everywhere that it was impossible to see any lurking drains or trapdoors.

He clamped his fingers around the ledge and heaved himself up until he found a foothold. Though very narrow, the ledge gave him enough purchase to pause and reflect on his next move. There were several options, none of them good. Though the hand-size hollow to his left was reassuringly deep, the fissure above it was quite a stretch for somebody his size. And the uneven patch to his right might have been a comfortable distance from the next one, but it wouldn't give him much to hold on to . . .

Suddenly Jem recognized the feeling of despair that was beginning to overwhelm him. For an instant he froze. Then the despair was swamped by a wave of terror as he thrust himself up the wall, grabbing at whatever he could reach. Already he could smell something very bad. A scraping, sliding noise from the pit announced that he wasn't alone—not any longer. But he couldn't look down. He *wouldn't* look down. He had to concentrate on the wall directly in front of him, not on what lay behind, or ahead.

Could this bogle actually *climb*?

He whimpered as the creature below him hissed like a steam engine. Blinking back tears, he fixed his eyes on an iron bolt, seized it, then reached for his next handhold—a crack where the mortar had crumbled away. Good. Excellent. He hauled himself up another few feet.

All at once he felt a puff of air against his ankle, as if something had just missed his leg. This time he couldn't suppress a sob. But he knew that he mustn't look down. If he paused for even an instant, it might prove fatal. If he tried to rush, it might be even more dangerous. So he kept moving, carefully, doggedly, up and up and up. He tried not to listen to the noises below him: the patter of loose rubble, the click of teeth, the hissing, the slurping, the mysterious rattling. And the higher he went, the easier it became.

Hollow. Hole. Protruding brick. Hollow. Crack. Missing brick. Jem channeled all his thoughts toward these little details, until he unexpectedly found himself in a pale patch of sunlight. When he put his hand on a bird's nest, he realized that he must be close to the top of the chimney. He was nearly there! Only a few feet to go! It wasn't raining any longer; for some reason, he hadn't noticed this before. But it was an encouraging sign, and he threw himself at the wall with renewed energy, oblivious to his scraped knuckles, aching head, and sore lip.

The end came without warning. He pushed himself up, and there, before him, was empty space. Not a wall. Not even a hole in a wall. Just a vista of rooftops, with the gray sky beyond. Jem didn't hesitate for a second. He threw one leg over the chimney's crumbling rim and hoisted himself onto it, clinging desperately to the brickwork.

Then, at last, he looked down.

29

THE CHIMNEY

Jem couldn't see the bogle. He couldn't see anything down the chimney because it was much too dark inside. But he knew that he wasn't safe — not yet. So he looked around for an escape route.

The flue beneath him was in bad repair. It towered above the surrounding rooftops, separating Sarah's house from the one next door, which was only about three stories high. Jem quickly grasped that if he wanted to get away, he would either have to cross Sarah's roof (and risk being caught again), or climb a very long way down the other side of the chimney. After a moment's thought, he decided to risk the first option—since Sarah couldn't possibly know where he was.

Besides, he'd had enough climbing for one day.

From the top of the chimney to Sarah's roof was a ten-foot drop. Jem tried to reduce this distance by lowering himself down until he was hanging by his fingernails. When he finally let go, a few loose bricks came with him. He hit the slates with a crash, then began to slide toward the gutter.

Luckily, there was a hole in the roof. Before tumbling off its edge, Jem was able to grab an exposed beam. He suddenly found himself on his stomach with his head dangling over the eaves, staring straight down into Red Lion Court.

For a moment he thought he was dreaming. There, directly below him, were Alfred Bunce and Constable Pike. The two men were peering around, as if unsure of which house to approach first. Constable Pike stood with his hands on his hips. Alfred was scratching his cheek.

"Hi! HI! MR. BUNCE!" Jem bellowed.

Alfred glanced up. So did the policeman.

"SARAH PICKLES!" Jem continued. "SARAH PICKLES IS IN HERE!" He gestured at the house beneath him, hoping that Alfred would understand. Constable Pike certainly didn't. He turned to Alfred and seemed to ask a question.

"HURRY!" Jem roared. "OR SHE'LL GET AWAY!"

Then something occurred to him. He scrambled back

up to the roof ridge but found that he couldn't see the churchyard from there. So he began to inch down the south slope of the roof, until he reached another patch of missing slates that gave him something to hold on to. With one hand wrapped around a joist, he lowered himself toward the rear gutter—and suddenly spotted Sarah Pickles.

She was scurrying past the coal shed at the back of the house, heading for the churchyard.

"STOP! THIEF! MURDER!" bawled Jem, intent on keeping Sarah in his sights. Instinctively he sprang to his feet. Then he tried to keep pace with her, hopping along the gutter like a sparrow. But she was already squeezing through the churchyard fence, into Giltspur Street.

"STOP! POLICE!" he howled, waving his arms. No one seemed to hear him. Though the street was much busier now that the rain had stopped, not a single soul paused or even glanced up.

So he turned and retraced his steps, still yelling at the top of his voice. "SARAH'S ESCAPING! SHE'S HEADING FOR NEWGATE!" he cried, hoping that Alfred was in earshot. He almost *ran* back up to the roof ridge, then sat down and began to slide toward the front of the house. His plan was to warn Constable Pike about Sarah. But when he peered into Red Lion Court, he couldn't see Alfred or the policeman.

Had they gone inside already?

Swearing like a sailor, Jem made for the closest dormer window. This wasn't the one he'd used before. It didn't lead to the locked room. But it was open and easy to reach, and since it was identical to the other window, Jem could only assume that it would give him access to the internal staircase.

He scrambled up the north face of the roof, knowing that he had to be quick. Unfortunately, he was too quick. Too impatient. A slate cracked under his foot. As it slipped from beneath him, he made a grab for the window.

The window, however, wasn't close enough. And his own lunge threw him off balance. Suddenly he was rolling, rolling, rolling . . .

The gutter saved him. He caught it and hung on tightly, his legs flailing around in the air. "HE-E-E-ELP!" he screamed, as something went *crack.* The gutter shifted. *Ping!* A nail popped, then another. *Ping! Ping!* And the gutter started slowly peeling off the edge of the roof.

When Jem tried to scream again, his voice stuck in his throat. Every time another slate cracked or nail popped, there was a jolt. He would fall sharply, just a foot or two, as the rusty strip of metal to which he clung pulled away from the roof a little more.

He couldn't believe it. He was dangling like bait on a hook. "Help . . ." he whimpered. "Help . . . please . . ." By now he was level with the fourth-floor windows, but not one of them was directly beside him. And he knew that if he were to swing on the rusty gutter, it might fall off . . .

"Jem!" A voice suddenly hailed him from somewhere close by. He heard a squeak and a thump. Looking around, he spotted Alfred leaning out of a fourth-floor window about ten feet away.

"I'm coming," Alfred said calmly. "Don't you move."

"Help . . ." Jem croaked.

"Shhh! You'll be all right. Just listen to me."

Jem hardly dared breathe as he watched Alfred climb onto the windowsill. It was a wooden windowsill embedded in dirty gray stucco, because the top two floors of the house were half timbered. Slowly Alfred straightened up, grasping the edge of the lintel for balance. Then he leaned toward Jem with his free hand outstretched.

But they were too far away from each other.

"Can you reach me?" asked Alfred, his voice tight with strain.

Jem shook his head.

"Jem. Look here." Alfred locked gazes with Jem, who felt a tiny flutter of hope at the sight of the bogler's worn, pouchy, familiar face. Alfred's dark eyes were as calm as his low, gruff voice, though his skin was flushed and sweaty. "Keep looking. That's it. Straight at me," he instructed, then began to edge along the horizontal piece of timber that ran beneath the windowsill.

Jem nodded. Slowly Alfred's extended hand drew closer and closer. Slowly his other arm straightened, until he'd gone as far as he could without releasing his hold on the lintel. Soon he was pressed flat against the wall, as if crucified.

All the while, his eyes never left Jem's.

"Can you reach me now?" he asked hoarsely. "Try, lad. I know you're stouthearted. I'll not let go, I promise."

Jem was breathing in short little gasps. He couldn't utter a word. All he could do was nod again, before carefully unclamping his right hand from the gutter and stretching it toward Alfred's. They were so close! Only about six inches separated their two hands. Jem began to lean forward, just a little . . .

Crack! The beam beneath Alfred snapped suddenly. He nearly lost his balance but swung back toward the window just in time. There was a horrible moment as he hung off the windowsill, bracing himself against the wall with his feet. But he managed to heave himself up again while people screamed and shouted in the yard below.

Jem realized that they had attracted an audience.

"Stay there," said Alfred, gasping for breath. He was crawling inside. "Don't move a muscle."

"Come back!" Jem wailed. "Please!"

"I ain't going nowhere, lad. Just give me a minute."

The bogler vanished. Jem began to cry. Silent tears ran down his cheeks; he felt bereft, and so alone. But soon he heard a sharp, "Jem? *Jem!*" and saw that Alfred had moved downstairs, to a third-floor window.

The bogler was already scrambling onto its sill. This time, however, he had company. Watching him rise shakily to his feet, Jem saw that a sturdy arm in dark blue serge was fastened around the bogler's waist.

It was Constable Pike's arm.

"Jem?" Alfred exclaimed. "You need to come down a little, lad! You need to bounce yer weight about!"

"N-no . . ."

"You'll not fall. You'll only drop a portion—nowt else. And I'll catch you." As Jem hesitated, Alfred went on quietly, "You're a brave boy. The bravest I know, if pigheaded. How am I to box yer ears if you don't let me catch you?"

Jem licked his lips. His gaze drifted past Alfred, toward the little circle of spectators on the ground. They seemed so far away.

He shut his eyes.

"Jem? *Jem!* Can you hear me?" When Jem gave a nod, Alfred continued, "Try to climb up that there gutter, lad. It's sure to pull loose and bring you down level with us."

Jem had opened his eyes again. He fixed them on the twisted piece of metal hanging in front of his nose. *One step at a time,* he told himself. *Don't think about nothing else.* He moved his right hand up the gutter. Then his left. Then he unclamped his knees . . .

Ping! There was a screech of metal. The drop sent him swinging like a pendulum. Suddenly he was jerked sideways, so abruptly that he collided with something. *"Let go!"* a voice yelled in his ear. He felt a band of pressure across his chest and hands hauling at his clothes. Alfred said, "Hold on to me, Jem. You don't need that gutter no more."

For a moment Jem couldn't unlock his grip. His fingers seemed fused to the metal. But he finally managed to unpeel them, and was dragged across the windowsill with Alfred's arms laced around him from behind. They sat on the floor together. *Whoomp!* Then Jem found himself staring straight at Constable Pike's knees.

"Are you hurt?" asked the policeman. "No? By God, you're a lucky lad!"

Jem coughed. "L-Lubbock," he stammered.

"What?" Constable Pike leaned down. "What did you say?"

"Mr. Lubbock." Jem's voice cracked. He cleared his throat and tried again. "Mr. Lubbock's upstairs, locked in a chest. They tried to kill him. They tried to kill *me* . . ." This time Jem broke down altogether, and Alfred's arms tightened around him.

"Who did?" Alfred demanded. "Eunice?"

"Sarah," Jem sobbed.

"Sarah Pickles?"

"She escaped down Giltspur Street. I saw her go." Jem twisted around to address Alfred. "She's got a bogle in here! It's bin eating babies! I don't know how many was fed to it . . ." When Alfred's eyes widened in shock, Jem exclaimed, "Didn't you see? Didn't you look in the cellar?"

"No." Alfred shook his head. "We came straight up."

"We saw no one but you," Constable Pike added.

"Then they must have escaped. They must have run out the back while you was coming in the front." Jem wiped his face with a trembling hand. "We'll never get her now," he said brokenly. "She's gone. They're all gone . . ."

"Mr. Bunce?" A faint call suddenly reached their ears from somewhere down below. *"Mr. Bunce! Are you in here?"*

Jem blinked. The policeman frowned. Alfred said, "Is that Birdie McAdam?"

"We did it, Mr. Bunce! We caught her!" The voice was definitely Birdie's. Jem would have known it anywhere. But he could hardly believe what it was saying. *"Did you hear me, Mr. Bunce?"* she cried. *"Me and Ned—we did it together! We saw her and we stopped her and we fetched the police! It's true, I swear! We caught her ourselves! WE CAUGHT SARAH PICKLES!"*

30

SAFETY

Red Lion Court had become quite crowded. The old man with the pipe had been joined by at least a dozen more curious spectators. There was also a large, sandy-haired policeman, who greeted Constable Pike with the casual familiarity of an old friend. And Birdie was present, of course, as was Ned Roach.

Birdie didn't look bedraggled anymore. She had changed into a pearl-gray alpaca dress, trimmed with white satin. She seemed to glow against the grim background of muddy cobbles, sooty bricks, and damp stucco.

"What happened?" she exclaimed as Alfred and Jem emerged into the watery afternoon light. Behind them came

Constable Pike, who was supporting Josiah Lubbock. After being locked in a sea chest for so long, Mr. Lubbock could barely walk. He was also dazed with shock, and practically speechless. The only phrase he'd managed to utter since being released was a hoarse "Thank you!" after being informed that Jem had picked a lock to get him out. ("I'll pretend I didn't see this," Constable Pike had murmured as Jem fiddled about with a bent wire.)

"We was heading for the butcher's shop on Cock Lane but spied people running in here," Birdie declared, after receiving no answer to her first question. "So Constable Knowles decided to investigate, and me and Ned had to go with him—and who should we see but Jem Barbary, hanging from a window like wet washing!" Before Jem could even begin to explain, she repeated, "What happened? Why ain't you in the butcher shop? Where *is* the butcher?"

"Where's Sal Pickles?" Alfred rejoined harshly, still clasping Jem's arm. "You claim you caught her, but I don't see her about."

"Why, she's on her way to West Smithfield." The sandy-haired policeman spoke before Birdie could, taking charge in an understated way. "My question to you, sir, is this: Can you help us with our inquiries? For there's been talk of housebreaking and kidnapping, but I've yet to hear the full facts."

"Perhaps we'd best step inside first." Constable Pike

glanced at all the surrounding eavesdroppers. "I don't fancy discussing this here matter in public."

His friend agreed. So they all moved back into Sarah's house, where they stood at the bottom of the staircase. Then Alfred told the policemen about Sarah Pickles, and Birdie explained how she and Ned had escaped from Miss Eames's custody (by climbing through a bedroom window), after Birdie had decided that she *must* speak to Alfred. Knowing that the bogler was returning to help Jem, she and Ned had caught a bus to Newgate, then started walking up Giltspur Street—only to spot Sarah Pickles heading straight for them.

"I yelled, '*Stop, thief!*'" Birdie revealed, pink cheeked with excitement. "And when Sarah tried to run, Ned brought her down. And Constable Knowles heard me—"

"And Sarah tried to escape," Ned broke in.

"She did!" Birdie agreed. "And the police didn't like *that!*"

"Ahem." Constable Knowles cleared his throat. He was so large and barrel chested, with such rough-hewn features, that everyone respectfully waited for him to speak. Even Birdie fell silent as he turned to Constable Pike and said in a slightly ponderous tone, "I saw two respectable-looking children involved in a disturbance with a woman whose general appearance suggested low origins. Then

Constable Maybrick, who was with me, said he recalled the name Sarah Pickles and thought it might belong to a fugitive from justice, though he wasn't sure. The children being clean and well dressed, I thought it wise to investigate their allegations." As Constable Pike nodded, his friend finished, "Constable Maybrick took Mrs. Pickles directly to the lockup, but Miss McAdam suggested that I seek out a certain Mr. Alfred Bunce, who might be able to clarify matters."

"This here is Mr. Bunce," said Constable Pike, pointing. Everyone promptly turned to look at Alfred.

Alfred, however, was looking at Birdie. "What's so important as couldn't wait a few hours?" he rasped. "What's so important as to make you flout the wishes of yer elders, insulting Miss Eames and putting Ned in harm's way?"

Birdie flushed, then lifted her chin. "I wanted to warn you about a notion I had," she said. "If the butcher's bin threatening folk hereabouts, then mebbe all the bogles in this neighborhood is down to him. For if he's bin luring 'em in, somehow, to scare those as don't want to pay up—"

"It ain't him," Jem interrupted. "It ain't the butcher. It's Sarah Pickles." This possibility had occurred to him almost as soon as he'd had time to think—and the longer he thought about it, the more likely it seemed. As every eye swiveled toward him, he explained dully, "Sarah's bin earning her keep as a baby farmer. She'd take the chink, but instead o' raising the children, she'd feed every one of 'em to a bogle."

Ned gasped. Birdie blanched. Constable Knowles raised a puzzled eyebrow at Constable Pike, who kept his gaze locked on Jem.

"I don't expect she paid no heed to the consequences," Jem continued. "I don't expect she *planned* to draw bogles from every corner o' London, by giving 'em a feast o' flesh. But if you ask me, that's why they're here. It's like feeding pigeons. They come and they come and soon they're nesting in yer eaves." With a sidelong glance at Alfred, he finished, "And if there's drains and sewers running beneath us, then Sarah might easily have fed more'n one bogle. Don't you think?"

Alfred nodded slowly. But Constable Knowles didn't seem convinced.

"You ain't talking about *boggarts,* surely?" He turned to Constable Pike. "In *London?*"

Constable Pike grimaced. "I seen one o' them things, Bert. And whatever you call 'em — bogles or boggarts or fachan — you'd not want to fall foul o' one, believe me."

"Especially if you're a child," said Alfred. Ever since hearing about the babies in the basement, his face had looked drawn and bruised. Turning to Mr. Lubbock, he asked, "Did *you* hear Sal talk o' feeding babies to bogles?"

Mr. Lubbock shook his head. He had propped himself against the lowest banisters and was rubbing the angry red marks on his wrists. "I no sooner mentioned Sarah's name to her daughter than I was knocked out," he croaked. "I assume that someone was hiding behind the door, then attacked me when I came in."

"Was that after you threatened to blackmail 'em?" Jem muttered. But he fell silent as Alfred's grip tightened on his shoulder.

"So Jem's the only witness," Alfred rumbled. "Pity."

"There's baby clothes in that room over there." Ned pointed across the hallway to a half-open door. "I don't expect Sarah paid good money for *them*."

"No," Jem agreed. "She'd sell 'em, though."

"Mebbe the clothes came with the babies!" cried Birdie. "Mebbe there's mothers as could identify the clothes—"

"I'll search this place for evidence," Constable Pike interrupted. "In the meantime, you should all go to the station with Constable Knowles and report to the sergeant there. Else Mrs. Pickles won't be charged."

Jem wanted to ask if anyone had seen Eunice or Salty Jack leave the building. But he realized that no one around him knew what Eunice looked like. As for John Gammon . . .

"Salty Jack?" said Constable Pike when asked. He gave a snort of derision. "If Salty Jack was ever here, he's gone now."

"My word, if we could lay our hands on *that* gentleman . . ." Constable Knowles trailed off, looking wistful.

Constable Pike pulled a sardonic face. "Salty Jack's an eel," he told Alfred. "You'll never prove a thing against him."

"But he were the one as threw me into the bogle pit!" Jem exclaimed.

Constable Pike sniffed. "We've had witnesses stand by while Jack put an ax through a man's gut," he countered. "We've had ten men watch him set fire to a cellar full o' gin. He's bin charged with affray, assault, and passing bad coin. And do you think any of it could ever be proved in a court o' law?" He shook his head, gazing at Alfred. "If you take my advice, you'll not tangle with Salty Jack. Not head-on. Bigger men than you have tried and failed, though I shouldn't be the one to say it." Seeing Alfred narrow his eyes suspiciously, the policeman quickly added, "Don't think I'm in that villain's pocket, neither, for I'd as soon cut off my own arm! I'm telling you this, Mr. Bunce, for the sake o' your lad, who's as brave a young'un as I ever saw and doesn't deserve to be put in the way o' John Gammon."

Jem winced. He found himself edging closer to Alfred.

"Concentrate your efforts on Sarah Pickles," Constable Pike finished. "That's where you'll get a result—and may see something further come of it too. For who's to say she'll not give up her cronies? Stranger things have happened."

Before Alfred could reply, the policeman saluted Constable Knowles, turned on his heel, and clattered downstairs to inspect the basement. There was a moment's pause. Then Mr. Lubbock whined, "I'm not feeling well. I don't think I should go to the police station. After all, what can I possibly add? I saw nothing—I was in a box."

"You're coming," Alfred said flatly. And Constable Knowles backed him up.

"We'll be needing a statement from you, sir. Once it's given, you'll be free to leave." The policeman began to shepherd everyone out the door, batting the air gently with his big, red, meaty hands. "We shan't keep you long, for it's not far. Left into Giltspur Street, then a step or two past Hosier Lane . . ."

They all did as they were told, leaving Red Lion Court under a barrage of questions from the crowd. Constable Knowles answered these questions using a standard set of replies ("Move aside, please!" "Police business!" "There's nothing to see here!"). It wasn't until they reached Cock Lane that Birdie finally hissed at Jem, "Did you say Sarah's bogle was in the chimney?"

Jem nodded. He didn't want to talk about the bogle.

"It needs to be killed," Birdie went on. "I wonder if Mr. Bunce will come back and kill it?"

"I ain't convinced Mr. Bunce'll ever bogle again," Ned muttered, with a nervous glance at Alfred's back. "Not after that job in Smithfield."

Birdie frowned. Jem swallowed. "If there ain't no more bogling, you'll not see much more o' *me*," he said hoarsely. "Mr. Bunce won't want no crossing sweeper cluttering up his place, bringing in half o' what's needed." Seeing Birdie's confounded expression, he whispered, "What're you staring at? It's the truth, ain't it?"

"Is *that* what you think?" She shook her head in amazement. "Seems to me you don't know Mr. Bunce at *all*."

"He'll not cut you loose." Ned spoke to Jem in an earnest undertone. "He may seem hard on occasion, but he ain't. He's as good a friend as you'll ever find. I'm proof of it, for I had no claim on Mr. Bunce, yet he took me in like a Samaritan."

"He'd as soon feed a baby to a bogle as throw you onto the street," Birdie insisted. She seemed almost offended on Alfred's behalf. "You believe that, don't you, Jem? You *must* know you're safe with Mr. Bunce."

Glancing at the bogler, Jem suddenly realized that she was right. Alfred had come back to Cock Lane for Jem's sake. He had risked his own life to save Jem's. And though Jem had defied him, lied to him, and run away from him, Alfred hadn't abandoned his half-trained apprentice.

To Jem, masters had always been enemies. They'd squeezed him dry then thrown him away like orange peel. But perhaps Alfred wasn't a master. Perhaps he was something else.

"Er — Mr. Bunce?" A gentle voice suddenly hailed Alfred from across Giltspur Street. Looking around, Jem saw that Mr. Gilfoyle was standing near the hospital. As they all paused to gape at him, the naturalist tipped his hat. Then he tentatively approached them, ignoring Mr. Lubbock in his eagerness to address the bogler.

"What a mercy I found you again, Mr. Bunce! For I should very much like a word." Seeing Alfred grimace, Mr. Gilfoyle quickly added, "This is not a commercial transaction. This is official business. I understand your reluctance to commit yourself, but I am appealing to your sense of civic duty."

Alfred frowned. "Civic duty . . . ?" he echoed.

"I am asking for your help, sir, not on my own behalf, but on behalf of the Lord Mayor of London. For I know a man on the Metropolitan Board of Works, and he is *extremely* anxious to consult you." Taking a deep breath, Mr. Gilfoyle concluded, "The fact is, Mr. Bunce, that news of your prowess has reached the upper levels of our city's municipal government, where help is desperately needed . . ."

31

THE COMMITTEE

"Ah. Mr. Bunce, is it not? And you must be Miss Eames."
The gentleman opened his door a little wider. He seemed
to shine like a billiard ball, thanks to his gold-rimmed spectacles, glossy silk waistcoat, gleaming bald head, and bur-
nished, patent-leather shoes. "Come in, please," he said,
waving his visitors toward the room behind him, where
a line of high-backed chairs faced a large mahogany desk.
"Are these your assistants? They're much younger than I
anticipated . . ."

Jem and Birdie exchanged a quick, nervous glance.
Birdie looked like a china doll in her prettiest pink dress.

Jem was wearing an outfit bought by Miss Eames especially for the occasion: a three-piece suit of speckled brown tweed, brown boots, and a bow tie. ("For I don't want it thought that we are not *respectable* folk," Miss Eames had declared.) Even Ned had received new trousers and a new shirt, though Miss Eames claimed that he didn't deserve them. She was still angry about Birdie's behavior the previous week — and Jem suspected that she blamed Ned for it. This was quite unfair, of course, but it allowed Miss Eames to give Birdie "one more chance."

After all the plain food and lectures that Birdie had endured since her escape through the bedroom window, Jem was surprised that she hadn't run away for good.

He stood now with his hat in his hands, gazing awestruck at the richly furnished office into which they had been invited. The coffered ceiling was made of carved oak. The stained-glass windows were hung with velvet curtains. The walls were covered in huge, gilt-framed paintings, while the desk in the middle of the room was almost as big as a hansom cab.

"Welcome to the City of London Sewers Office," said the bald man, sliding behind this desk. "My name is Mr. Joseph Daw, and I am the Principal Clerk. Please do sit down."

Alfred waited until Miss Eames and Birdie had seated

themselves, then followed their example. Jem and Ned did the same. Jem was feeling very uncomfortable; his new suit made his legs itch, and his starched collar cut into his neck. He was also unnerved by all the dark wood in the room, which made him think of a magistrate's court.

"I have invited you here today at the behest of the Chief Engineer of Sewers," Mr. Daw went on. "He has heard about you, Mr. Bunce, from two sources: namely an Inspector of Sewers named Wardle, and a Clerk of Works named Harewood. Are you acquainted with either of these gentlemen?"

Alfred shook his head, looking almost as uncomfortable as Jem felt. Though he wasn't wearing any fancy new clothes, he had washed his face and put on a clean shirt. Even so, he didn't cut a very stylish figure.

"Well," said Mr. Daw, "I gather that Mr. Wardle was approached by another man named Calthrop—"

"We know *him!*" Birdie announced. She didn't seem the least bit intimidated by Mr. Daw, or his luxurious office—and Jem had to admire her for that. Miss Eames, however, flashed her a warning look. And Mr. Daw raised his eyebrows.

"I see," he murmured, peering at Birdie through his spectacles, which were sitting at the very end of his long, thin nose. "Then you are undoubtedly aware that Mr. Calthrop is the foreman of a sewer gang in the Holborn

Viaduct. Mr. Harewood, on the other hand, is friendly with a highly regarded naturalist called Gilfoyle . . ."

He paused for a moment, as if wondering how to proceed. So Miss Eames helped him.

"Forgive me, Mr. Daw," she said, "but Mr. Bunce knows Mr. Gilfoyle. In fact, Mr. Gilfoyle recently told Mr. Bunce that an engineer of his acquaintance had been describing recent building work around London. During this conversation, which touched on the topic of horse-drawn railway vans, the subject of missing van boys had come up. So when Mr. Gilfoyle later became aware of certain . . . um . . . unusual creatures infesting the city's drains, he naturally raised the matter with his friend, the engineer—"

"Who referred it back to his superior, the Chief Engineer of Sewers." Mr. Daw finished the sentence for her, as if he were growing slightly impatient. "The Chief Engineer has also been hearing complaints from various flushers regarding a plague of very large and dangerous vermin in the area around Holborn."

"Bogles," said Birdie.

"Bogles. Yes," Mr. Daw replied.

Jem felt suddenly convinced that the Principal Clerk didn't like children, didn't trust women, didn't know what to make of Mr. Bunce, and didn't believe in bogles. Somehow this was obvious from the way he looked at Birdie, pokerfaced, from beneath his heavy eyelids. But it was also clear that whatever his own views might be, Mr. Daw was a very good civil servant who would follow to the letter any instructions he might receive.

"After consulting Mr. Gilfoyle and your friend Mr. Calthrop, the Chief Engineer decided that these ... er ... 'bogles' might very well constitute a threat to the health of the city," Mr. Daw explained. "Naturally, he was concerned that very little seemed to be known about them. And he was *extremely* anxious not to ... um ..." Again the Principal Clerk paused, as if weighing up various words in his head. When at last he spoke, he did it very slowly and precisely. "The Chief Engineer was anxious not to arouse public interest in what might well prove to be a false alarm," he concluded. "That is why no record of our meeting today will be kept, and why the committee being proposed will be an unofficial one."

Jem pulled a wry face. He understood exactly what the Principal Clerk was getting at. Mr. Daw didn't believe in bogles, and neither did many of his colleagues. So while they were allowing the Chief Engineer to pursue his little project, he had to do it secretly, in case the newspapers found out.

I know yer game, Jem thought, folding his arms as he eyed the man across the desk. Alfred, meanwhile, was frowning.

"Committee?" he said. "What committee?"

"The Committee for the Regulation of Subterranean Anomalies," Mr. Daw smoothly replied. "Such a committee would not be utterly unprecedented, since the city's more ancient records do mention a 'Guild of Bogglers and Feend-Seekers.'" Suddenly he allowed himself a little smirk. "Nowadays, I suppose, an exact equivalent might be the 'Worshipful Company of Bogle Hunters.' However, I think that a less *showy* title would better suit our purposes."

He went on to explain that the Town Clerk and the Chief Engineer had agreed to form a committee that would address London's bogle problem. Mr. Erasmus Gilfoyle would be on the committee, as would his friend Mr. Mark Harewood. Inspector of Sewers Mr. Eugene Wardle would also be included.

"Mr. Gilfoyle has requested that you yourself should sit on the committee, Mr. Bunce," Mr. Daw remarked, "along with anyone else you might care to nominate."

"Miss Eames," said Alfred.

Miss Eames couldn't suppress a pleased smile when she heard this. She even colored a little. Glancing at Mr. Daw, Jem saw him purse his lips in disapproval.

"It would be very unusual to invite a lady onto a committee of this sort," the Principal Clerk observed. "However, since it is an *unofficial* committee, I suppose some advisory role could be arranged—"

"What about me?" Birdie broke in. "And Jem? And Ned?"

Mr. Daw looked as if he had sucked a lemon. "This is a serious matter, my dear," he said with strained civility. "It will require a degree of knowledge and responsibility that no mere child could supply."

"But *we* know more about bogles'n Mr. Gilfoyle does," Jem pointed out. He regarded Mr. Daw coolly, his arms still folded. For a brief instant their gazes locked.

Then Mr. Daw gave a sniff. "Of course the choice of participants will be your own, Mr. Bunce," he said at last, addressing Alfred. "It is important to realize, however, that you and your fellow members will be charged with a solemn duty, incompatible with the kind of frivolous conduct normally found in a schoolroom."

"We don't none of us go to school," Jem growled. He was waiting to hear what Mr. Daw would say to that when Miss Eames silenced him. She placed a firm hand on his shoulder, turned to Mr. Daw, and asked, "What precisely is this committee expected to do, Mr. Daw?"

"Why, everything required of it, Miss Eames. If creatures need to be studied, then you will arrange it. If they need to be killed, you will arrange *that*."

"It takes money to kill bogles," Birdie interposed.

"Six shillings for each bogle, and a penny for the salt," Jem added.

"Funds will be supplied for any purpose pertaining to the committee's frame of reference," Mr. Daw announced drily. "I believe the Town Clerk's Department has the matter in hand. My advice is that the committee hire Mr. Bunce for an agreed sum over a stipulated period of time. But that will be for the committee to arrange." He glanced at his fob watch, then explained in a bored voice, "It has been proposed that the first meeting be convened next Monday, in the Metropolitan Board of Works building, at ten o'clock. If this isn't agreeable to you, Mr. Bunce, you must address your objections to Mr. Harewood, whose office can be found there." Raising his eyebrows, he concluded, "Have you any questions you'd care to ask?"

No one did. So Mr. Daw stood up and ushered them out of his office, pointing them toward the nearest exit while imploring them not to lose their way. It was easy to get lost in Guildhall, he said, since it wrapped around a large courtyard.

"I'm sure we'll manage," Miss Eames replied crisply. Sure enough, she remembered exactly where to go, leading the others back to the main entrance through a maze of corridors and stairwells. They passed the Chamberlain's Office, the Common Council Room, and the almost completed library. They dodged an endless parade of clerks, who scuttled around like cockroaches in their dark suits.

After a while Jem whispered to Birdie, "If this here committee hires Mr. Bunce, he'll need a 'prentice or two."

Instead of smiling, Birdie frowned. When she saw Jem's puzzled expression, she lowered her voice to say, "I don't think I can bogle no more."

Jem gaped at her.

"I'm too slow," she continued glumly. "You saw me at the market."

"But that were an ambush!" Jem hissed. "You can't blame yerself!"

"I ain't so sure o' that. Seems to me *you'd* have bin quick enough to get away." As Jem wondered if she was right, Birdie heaved a sigh and said, "I've lost the skill of it. Coming so close to a bogle's teeth . . . ain't that proof enough?" Sadly she concluded, "It's bin giving me nightmares. If Mr. Bunce needs two 'prentices, he'll have to hire Ned."

"I doubt he'll need two of us" was Ned's contribution. "Not now Sarah Pickles is banged up. For the bogles under Newgate is sure to disperse without a regular feed, and that means they'll not be found close together no more."

"True enough." Jem was impressed by Ned's reasoning. "But what about Salty Jack? *He's* still out and about. Suppose he keeps feeding 'em?"

"He won't," Ned murmured. "He's got nothing to feed

'em *with*. I doubt he's got a single debtor less than sixteen years old; why would he?" After a brief pause, Ned concluded, "Besides, he may end up in the jug alongside Sal Pickles."

"Not he," said Birdie as Jem shook his head. He knew that Miss Eames had consulted a lawyer friend, who had dismissed the possibility of gaoling John Gammon as long as Jem was the only witness against him. It would be Jem's word against Salty Jack's, unless Sarah decided to speak out—and at present she wasn't saying anything. ("The proof against Mrs. Pickles has been provided by several bereft mothers," the lawyer had remarked after briefly reviewing the case, "whereas the proof against Mr. Gammon is confined to the recollections of one boy whose character does not appear to be stainless. A good barrister could argue that Mr. Gammon thought Jem a thief, and confined him in the hope that the lady would call a policeman. If such a defense was presented, it would be very hard to refute.")

"Mr. Bunce ain't about to take on Salty Jack Gammon," mumbled Jem. "Nor will Miss Eames if she can't find no lawyer to back her."

"Then someone should make sure John Gammon knows he ain't pursued," Ned advised Birdie. "For if *he* thinks he's safe, we can all of *us* feel safer."

"You think so?" Jem didn't. Not entirely. He'd known other men like John Gammon, and understood that they were always a threat, no matter what their mood. On the other hand, if Jem was hired by the London Sewers Office, his official status would offer some protection against Salty Jack. Why, the very sturdiness of Guildhall itself made him feel secure and important . . .

By this time they were outside the Great Hall, heading for the main entrance. Jem couldn't see any other people about. But suddenly a voice said, "Pardon me, sir—are you Mr. Alfred Bunce?" And a porter emerged from a booth near the front door.

He was an imposing figure, very large and blond and arrayed in a splendid uniform trimmed with gold. At the sight of him, Alfred stopped short. "Aye. Bunce is me name," he said.

"I'm sorry to trouble you, sir, but I've been asked to convey a request." The porter flicked a rapid look around the lofty vestibule, with its vaulted roof and stained-glass windows. Apparently satisfied that he wasn't in danger of being overheard, he lowered his voice and said, "Informal, like. From the kitchen staff."

"The kitchen staff?" Miss Eames echoed.

"Yes'm. They heard as how you were expected here today, and would be very grateful if you'd pay 'em a call."

"Why?" asked Jem, hoping that this "call" might involve gifts of food. But the porter glanced at him nervously, as if reluctant to answer. There was a brief pause.

Then the big man stooped and muttered into Alfred's ear, "They think they've a bogle, Mr. Bunce. In the west crypt, where the wine's kept. And they want you to kill it before the Lord Mayor's dinner next week . . ."

Glossary

BAISD BHEULACH: a Scottish shape-shifting demon

BASILISK: a legendary reptile reputed to be the king of serpents

BAUCHLING: shuffling

BEADLE: a minor official who carries out civil, educational, or ceremonial duties

BEAK: a magistrate

BITE: nonsense

BLOWEN: a girlfriend

BLUEBOTTLE: a policeman

BLUE RUIN: gin

BLUFFER: an innkeeper

BOB: a shilling

BOGGART: a bogle

BOGLE: a monster, goblin, bogeyman

BOOZING KEN: a public house

BROLLACHAN: Scottish shape-shifting demons that take the form of whatever one most fears

CANT: slang

CAPER: a criminal scheme

CHINK: money

COPPER: a policeman

COSTER: a street seller

COVE: a man

CRACKSMAN: a burglar, lock picker

CRACKSMAN'S CROW: a housebreaker's lookout

CRIB: a house or lodging

DAVY LAMP: fire-burning safety lamp for flammable atmospheres

DIDDLE: gin

DOG SOUP: water

DOWNY: cunning

DRUGGET: a coarse woolen fabric used as a floor covering

DUDS: clothes

DUN: to demand payment

DUNNAGE: clothes and possessions

DUNTERS: monsters that infest Scottish castles

DUSTMAN: garbage man

DUW: God

EACHY: a species of slimy lake monster

ERLKING: a malevolent creature that haunts forests

FACHAN: a Celtic monster so frightening that it induces heart attacks

FLAM: a lie

FLAMMING: lying

FLASH: showy

GAMMON: to deceive or lie

GAMMONING: lying

GAMMY: false, hostile

GANGER: a foreman or supervisor

GAOL: jail

GRIDDLE: to beg, scrounge

GRIDDLING: begging

GRIFFIN: a legendary creature with the body of a lion and the head and wings of an eagle

GRINDYLOW: a bogeyman from Lancashire or Yorkshire, typically found in bogs or lakes

HACKNEY CAB: a two-wheeled carriage for hire

HEAVY WET: a porter

HOG: a shilling

HOISTMAN: a shoplifter or thief

HOOK IT: move it

HUMMING: deceiving

JACULUS: a small mythical dragon

KINCHIN CRACK: a fine girl

KNOCKER: a small Welsh bogle that lives underground

LAP: tea

LONDON PARTICULAR: a thick London fog

LURK: a trick, scam

LUSH: drink

MAUN: must

MUDLARK: a child who scavenges on riverbanks

MUG I FOG: pipe I smoke

MUN: must

NAVVY: an unskilled laborer, especially one who does heavy digging

NECKCLOTH: a noose

NIMM'D: stole

NOBBLER: a thug

OMNIBUS: a very large horse-drawn vehicle for moving large numbers of people

ON THE WAG: truanting

PEACH: to inform

PENNY GAFF: a cheap, lower-class theater or show

PIGEON: a vulnerable target

PRIG: a thief; or to steal

PRIVY: a toilet

RACKET: a shady or illegal pursuit

RED CAPS: monsters that infest Scottish castles

SCRAGGED: hanged

SELKIE: a mythical creature that lives as a seal in water but sheds its skin to become human on land

SLANG COVE: a showman

SLAP: theatrical makeup

SLAVVY: a maid of all work

SLUAGH: evil Scottish spirits of the dead that wander the earth

SLUMMING: cheating

SNECKDRAW: a sly, crafty person

SNEEZER: a drink

SPEEL: to cheat

SPEELER: a cheater

SPRING-HEELED JACK: a legendary character of the Victorian era known for his startling leaps

SQUEEZER: gallows

STRETCHED: hanged

STUMP UP: pay

SWEATED: pawned

TOFF: a well-to-do person

TOGS: clothes

TRAPS: police

WATER HORSE: a Celtic monster that's half horse, half fish, and lives in bodies of water; otherwise known as a kelpie

WORKHOUSE: an institution that houses and feeds paupers

Turn the page for a preview of

The Last Bogler

the sequel to A PLAGUE OF BOGLES

UNDERGROUND

Newgate Market was an empty, echoing shell. Doors hung askew. Windows were smashed. Iron hooks were rusting away. The market clock was no longer ticking, and the stalls were silting up with rubbish.

All of the butchers had long ago moved to Smithfield, taking their sides of beef and saddles of mutton with them.

"I don't know why this place ain't bin torn down long since," Alfred Bunce remarked. He stood hunched in the rain with his bag on his back, gazing across an expanse of muddy cobbles toward the central pavilion. Water dripped off his wide-brimmed hat and trickled down his long, beaky nose. Even his drooping mustache was sodden. "Ruined buildings breed every kind o' strife, from coining to murder," he added. "Bogles would be the least o' yer problems round here."

Beside him, a brown-eyed boy was scanning the shops that fronted the square. Some of them were boarded up, and those that remained in business were for the most part seedy-looking taverns or coffeehouses.

"I don't see Mr. Wardle," said the boy, whose name was Ned Roach. He was dressed in a navy-blue coat with brass buttons, very worn about the elbows, and a pair of buff-colored trousers, damp and soiled. A flat cap sat on his springy brown hair. Despite his missing tooth and scarred hands, he looked respectable enough. "Which o' these here establishments would be Mother Okey's?"

"Ask Jem," Alfred replied. "He knows the neighborhood better'n I do."

"Jem!" Ned turned to address another boy, who was lagging behind them. "You bin here once. Which pub is Mother Okey's?"

Jem Barbary didn't answer. He was too busy peering at the dark silhouette of someone who was skulking on a nearby doorstep. Ned didn't blame Jem for being nervous. This was John Gammon's territory, and Gammon was a dangerous man.

"What's that feller doing there, lurking like a cracksman's crow?" Jem hissed. He was smaller and thinner than

Ned, with so much thick, black hair that his head looked too big for his body. He wore a bedraggled suit of speckled brown tweed. "D'you think he works for Salty Jack?"

"Mebbe he's sheltering from the rain," Ned offered.

But Jem scowled. "I don't trust him. I don't trust *no one* hereabouts."

"Which is why we should pick up our pace." Alfred spoke in a gruff, impatient voice. "Wardle said to meet at Mother Okey's. Any notion where that might be?"

Jem considered the half-dozen public houses scattered around the market square. "'Tain't that'un," he announced, pointing. "That there is the Old Coffeepot. I spoke to the barmaid last time I passed through."

"And that?" Alfred nodded at the nearest tavern. Although it had a sign suspended above its front door, none of them could read the lettering.

"There's a cat on that sign," Ned observed, "so it's more likely to be the Cat and Fiddle. Or the Cat and Salutation . . ."

"Here!" Jem suddenly clutched Alfred's sleeve. "Ain't that Mr. Wardle?"

It was. Ned recognized the man who had emerged from the old-fashioned alehouse to their right. He was large and middle-aged, with fuzzy side-whiskers and a slight paunch. Though respectably dressed, he had an untidy look about him — almost as if his clothes were buttoned askew. Wisps of wiry gray hair escaped from beneath his bowler hat. His necktie was crooked. There was a crusty stain on his waistcoat lapel, and an unshaven patch on his chin.

Even when he spotted Alfred, his worried expression didn't change. The anxious lines seemed permanently engraved across his brow.

"Mr. Bunce!" he exclaimed. "You found me!"

"Aye," said Alfred, touching his hat.

"I was afeared you might have taken a wrong turn." Mr. Wardle's small blue eyes swung toward the two boys. "I see you brought your apprentices with you."

Alfred gave a brusque nod. "Can't kill a bogle without bait," he growled.

"Yes, of course." Mr. Wardle blinked uneasily at Ned, who wondered if the Inspector of Sewers could even remember his name. They had first been introduced to each other only a week before, at the Metropolitan Board of Works, where they had all sat down at a very large, round table to launch the Committee for the Regulation of Subterranean Anomalies.

But more than half a dozen people had been present at that meeting, and a lot of business had been discussed. And since neither Ned nor Jem had made much of a contribution, it seemed likely that Mr. Wardle had forgotten who they were.

"This neighborhood ain't safe for Jem," Alfred continued. "There's a butcher as runs all the rackets hereabouts, and he's got a grudge against the lad. We ain't bin troubled thus far, since the butcher don't know where I live. But the longer we stay, the more likely it is we'll be spotted by one of his cronies. And I don't want that."

Mr. Wardle looked alarmed. "No, indeed," he said.

"So you'd best tell me about this here job, and then we can set to it," Alfred finished. "Back at the Board o' Works, you mentioned there's three young'uns vanished, and one sighting in a sewer. Which sewer, and where was the kids last seen?"

Mr. Wardle hesitated for a moment. "Perhaps it's best I show you what was shown to me," he finally suggested, before heading across the cobbled square toward the central pavilion. Alfred hurried after him, with the two boys in tow. As they approached the dilapidated structure that had once sheltered row upon row of hanging carcasses, Ned felt uneasy. There was no telling what might lurk in that labyrinth of dark, rotting wood. As Alfred had so truly said, bogles might be the least of their problems.

"You don't think this is an ambush, do you?" Jem whispered, as if he were reading Ned's mind. "You don't think Mr. Wardle is in John Gammon's pocket?"

"No." Ned was sure of that. John Gammon was a "punisher"—he liked to threaten local shopkeepers with bodily harm if they didn't pay over a portion of their earnings to him. But Eugene Wardle wasn't a local shopkeeper; he was a municipal officer who hailed from Holloway. "Ain't no reason why Mr. Wardle should know Salty Jack Gammon. *I'm* just concerned them missing boys is all a hum. Mebbe Jack's bin spreading tales, to lure us into a dark, quiet corner—"

"It ain't no tale." Jem cut him off. "There's at least one kid gone, for I heard it from the barmaid at the Old Coffeepot when I were here last." After a moment's pause, he added, "She said the lad passed a bad coin at the inn, then legged it into the market cellars. No one's seen him since."

". . . chased a printer's devil into the cellars, after he passed a counterfeit coin," Mr. Wardle was saying as he led Alfred through the gloomy depths of the central pavilion. There was a rank smell of old blood and manure. Water was pooling under leaks in the roof. Here and there a rat would skitter out of the way, frightened by the crunch of broken glass underfoot. "The second child was a young thief who went down to look for scrap metal," Mr. Wardle continued, "and never returned to the sister he'd left waiting above. The third was a coal merchant's son who used to play in these stalls, though no one can be certain if he found his way beneath them."

"And the sighting?" asked Alfred.

"Ah," said Mr. Wardle. "Well, that didn't happen up here." He stopped suddenly, having reached a kind of wooden booth, behind which lay the entrance to a wide room with an opening in its stone floor. "You see, the heads of four sewers meet under Newgate Market. They used to be flushed out regular from a big cistern fitted with iron doors, though it's not much used these days. I had a team of flushers down there last week, oiling the screws and checking the penstocks. They caught a glimpse of something that scared the life out of 'em. And when they alerted me, Mr. Bunce, I thought about you." The Inspector stamped his foot, as if marking a spot. "That cistern's close by, and one of the sewers runs beneath the cellar—which used to be a slaughterhouse, or so I'm told. They had to wash down the floors—"

"And the dirty water had to go somewhere," Alfred concluded with a nod. "There'll be drains, then."

"I believe so."

Alfred dropped his sack and began to rifle through it, pulling out a box of matches, a small leather bag, and a dark lantern with a hinged metal cover. "You boys stay up here till I call you," he told Jem and Ned as he struck a match to light his lantern. "I need to look downstairs and don't want no bogles lured out ahead o' time."

Jem grimaced. Ned couldn't help asking, "You think there's more'n one of 'em, Mr. Bunce?"

Alfred shrugged and said, "Ain't no telling, in this part o' the world. That's why I had to risk bringing Jem."